ISLAND OF IGNORANCE

IAN C. DOZIER

ISLAND OF IGNORANCE

iUniverse books may be ordered through booksellers or by contacting:

iUniverse
1663 Liberty Drive
Bloomington, IN 47403
www.iuniverse.com
1-800-Authors (1-800-288-4677)

Because of the dynamic nature of the Internet, any web addresses or links contained in this book may have changed since publication and may no longer be valid. The views expressed in this work are solely those of the author and do not necessarily reflect the views of the publisher, and the publisher hereby disclaims any responsibility for them.

Any people depicted in stock imagery provided by Getty Images are models, and such images are being used for illustrative purposes only.
Certain stock imagery © Getty Images.

ISBN: 978-1-5320-8970-1 (sc)
ISBN: 978-1-5320-8971-8 (e)

Print information available on the last page.

iUniverse rev. date: 12/05/2019

CHAPTER 1

The woods were alive on the island that night. Crickets were playing their songs, and the wind was blowing through the trees, making them sway and touch as if they were bending to whisper secrets. Distantly the sound of waves could be heard crashing on the shore.

As Lucid crept, slowly inching his way forward under the canopy of the woods, he could just barely navigate with what little moonlight pierced the thick trees. He paused to wipe the sweat from his face and ran his fingers through his long black hair that hung wildly to his shoulders. He felt strong—was strong, in fact, from years of training and climbing. He turned and just barely made out the shadow of Jon, his best friend. It had taken great convincing and more than a little bartering to get Jon to accompany him.

Lucid knew he was the opposite of Jon in terms of looks and personality, but that meant nothing to him as he loved Jon like a brother. Still, Lucid was far too busy loving life to share his friend's taciturn nature and sometimes downright morose outlook on the world. Jon was good-looking enough with his short, sandy hair, stocky build, and green eyes to catch the attention of any girl, yet it seemed to Lucid that the only thing he lived for was being the best fighter.

Lucid saw the alert, irritated look on Jon's face through a tiny sliver of starlight breaching the canopy as his friend crept to his side. Lucid turned back to his path, smiling.

Up ahead he spotted what he was looking for: a small village clearing in the thick woods, clearly visible at this distance with the dull firelight glowing all around. As he crept closer, Lucid realized his heart was pounding. He never dared sneak so close to the village of the others on his two previous trips. To his knowledge no one ever had. He had stumbled upon the village while exploring the woods several months back and since then frequently wondered about its origins. But for him the curiosity outweighed the fear, so interested was he in a people living so close yet in another world, another time.

As they approached, closer than Lucid had previously dared, he could smell cook fires, curing fish, and the unmistakable hint of excrement. He could also hear faint voices in low-toned grunts and growls. Apparently the people of the village spoke some sort of different language. *Interesting,* he thought.

He turned to Jon, who was shaking his head slowly and pointing back toward the direction from which they'd come. Lucid shook his head, pointing to a large rock just a few feet ahead of them with some brush around it for cover. He crept silently up to it and lay down flat on his stomach. He smiled as he felt Jon lie next to him. From this vantage point they had a good view of the strange little village.

This was the first time Lucid had seen these people from this distance, and they were huge. He was not short by average standards and most likely had more growth in him yet, but these men were built on a different scale, the smallest of them seven feet or more of thick, pale muscle. All of them had bald heads as if they shaved them clean each day. Their skin was so white it was almost translucent. Muscles on a ridiculous scale rippled all over their bodies, even in the most unnatural places. They were for the most part uneducated, filthy giants with ragged, odd attire that was tight against their bodies in mostly browns and grays. They had an ancient way of life. They had no stone structures, they used ancient-looking homemade tools, and there was not a book in sight. However, they appeared, at least from a distance, totally physically superior to Lucid's people. They had quick, agile movements and used sharp gestures while communicating.

Lucid and Jon lay for a while, watching until Jon nudged his friend, pointing to the sky. Lucid inhaled a long breath and nodded, knowing his friend was right. If they were to make it back by sunrise, now was the time to leave. Jon got up to slowly creep back toward home, Lucid reluctantly following. Lucid took one last look at the village, quietly got to his feet, turned, and froze.

There, a few dozen feet away, was a girl holding a basket, and she was looking right at him. She was not a brutish, ragged-looking girl with the unhealthy white color of skin or grotesquely large muscles either. She was standing just outside the firelight, but still the tiny slivers of orange and red danced across her perfectly symmetrical face and her golden hair, which fell free in waves down her back. She looked to be the same age as Lucid, not quite a woman but definitely not a child.

Lucid's heart was pounding so hard that he was sure she could hear it. He glanced sharply toward the village then back at her. She raised an eyebrow curiously at him, which struck Lucid as an unexpected yet familiar gesture, then gave a slight nod toward the way Jon was walking. Then the beautiful girl disappeared into the trees.

The walk home always seemed shorter than the trip there. Before Lucid knew it, the end of the woods came into sight. However, just as he and Jon entered the main courtyard, the morning bells began to ring from the top of the cathedral. Lucid glanced at Jon miserably, and they sighed, changing directions to head for school instead of their respective beds.

The lack of sleep made it difficult to retain any of the knowledge that spewed forth from Lucid's teachers that day. Thankfully he at least hadn't fallen asleep, he thought as he sat at the desk behind Jon in his final class.

Lucid leaned forward and whispered, "How did you not see her?"

Jon shook his head, yawning, and turned slightly. "It was late, and you were tired. It is not hard to believe you were just seeing things."

Lucid pressed his lips together. "She was there," he said again.

"Lucid?" the instructor asked. "Is there some bit of information you wish to share with the class?"

He shook his head. "Sorry, Mr. Bates, just a little tired is all."

"Hopefully not too tired to answer my question?" Bates pressed.

Lucid thought, trying to remember the question he'd been asked. "People are inherently ruled by emotion, love, anger, and loyalty," he answered. Mr. Bates's stern gaze never left Lucid's face, but there was a hint of a smile at the corner of his lips.

"Yes, and the moment we relinquish these traits will be the moment we give up what makes us human. The key is to learn to read these emotions through body language and facial expressions," Bates continued as he began pacing around the room.

Lucid leaned forward and said quietly, "I'm not crazy. I know what I saw."

Jon shook his head, frowning, and said, "You're full of shit, and you still owe me ten gold and two smokes."

Lucid took a quick jab at his friend's kidney, causing Jon to grunt as quietly as possible. Lucid chuckled, which earned him a reproachful look from their teacher.

The gold was nothing, common currency on the island, easily accessible because Lucid was royalty and rich. The smokes, however, required a little finesse, as he had to steal them from his father.

When the class ended, Lucid walked with Jon to the training yard. He felt as if all his energy had been depleted, so even walking seemed to make him light-headed. As he shuffled through the corridor toward the exit, he spotted his little sister, Brynn, walking with a group of girls and shot her a wave and the biggest smile he could muster. It clearly wasn't convincing enough, because when their eyes met, she had a huge grin and she was shaking her head. He chuckled despite himself. *She is too smart for her own good,* he thought. He and Jon exited through two huge, wooden doors that were standing wide open to allow for foot traffic. Down a stone stairway large enough to fit ten people shoulder to shoulder, the training yard lay at the base of the steps.

The school was one of the three largest structures in the valley, built right into the mild slope of Jacques Ravine. Adjacent to the school on one side was the royal wing, where all the highest-ranking members of the city lived. The other side was the cathedral, where Minister Tiller tended to the needs of the citizens. The front of the school jutted out from a massive hill of rock with beautiful four-story archways and columns supporting the high granite awning. The rest of the high city of Altheia was built into the ravine, extending both north and south. Royalty, as well as some of the most prominent families, had elegant homes carved into the rock of the ravine. The rest, and least-impressive, of the homes, also called "the lower dwellings" or LD, were simply scattered groups of huts along winding dirt roads that led down to the shore of the Gulf of Winds, although the name "lower dwellings" was misleading because all the smaller buildings were well crafted, still strong, and in neat rows. Instead, the name referred to the buildings' physical location, as the city rose in elevation slightly, starting at the beach and ending at Jacques Ravine.

Lucid stopped short upon reaching the training yard after realizing he and Jon were the last to arrive. Lieutenant Jake Trigo was there already, taking the class through their stretches, glaring at them. He was tall and stout with a strong jaw, cropped sandy hair, and intense eyes. When he glared, Lucid knew it would not be good for him. Jake was the leader of the king's men and was said to be not only a master of all three disciplines of martial arts but also deadly with any weapon known to humankind—and he was Jon's father as well.

Lucid wasted no time and quickly retrieved his blunted training blade from the small armory, Jon right behind him.

When the warm-up stretches were completed, Trigo looked to the class. "Everyone pair up. Spar training. Let's go."

Lucid and Jon took their regular positions, albeit a little slower than usual. It seemed Jake could smell the exhaustion. He was never one to give breaks. Usually this was Lucid's favorite class as he lived and breathed weapons and martial arts training, but today all he could think about was collapsing into his bed.

After what felt to Lucid like an eternity of half-empty thrusts and blocks, all mostly a blur of sleep deprivation, Trigo finally dismissed the class. Lucid gave Jon one more fist bump, both boys sweating profusely but excited to finally get some rest.

As he replaced his blade in the armory and walked to the palace, Lucid began to question himself. The trips to the unknown village were fun and exciting, but he was beginning to think they were not worth it. If not for her, the excruciatingly beautiful girl whose face was now seared into his brain, he would consider giving up his little expeditions. Who was she? What was she doing there? Why did she not look like them? What were they all doing there?

Lucid arrived at his chambers and opened the door, and there sat his father. King Normin was the lord of the island, master of its people. He stood as Lucid entered, and Lucid noticed, not for the first time, how very fit his father still was for a man who had seen almost fifty years. Normin smiled often, stressed about little, and had a certain wisdom about the world, much like Lucid. The king's hair was dark yet streaked with gray, and his head sported no crown. He wore a traditional white shirt with sleeves rolled up, dark pants as was common on the island, and stained and worn leather boots. His skin was dark from the sun and his hair tousled from the wind. Normin looked much like any other citizen of the city.

On any other day, Lucid would truly enjoy sitting and hearing stories of his father's childhood and of their people's past. But not today.

"Hello, son," Normin said as Lucid closed the door behind him. "You look exhausted."

Lucid may have been worried about that statement were it not for the tiny smile that tugged at his father's lips. If that wasn't enough of a sign that his father would look the other way from a little mischief, his continuing the conversation without asking any more questions hammered the point home. Besides, reprimand would have been unnecessary as Lucid and Jon actually made it all the way through their daily classes ... miraculously.

"As you know, two days from now is your seventeenth

birthday and the schooling graduation ceremony, so I have a little something special planned for this year's celebration."

Lucid stepped around his father and sat on his bed, glancing at the feathery softness longingly.

Normin continued, "With that, however, you will officially be your own man—and not just a common man, but a prince of the people. One day you will be king." He paused, stood, and strolled around the room, refusing to look into his son's eyes. "And so it is time for you to know the truth, er, certain truths." Normin stopped pacing and looked at Lucid for a long moment before finishing, as if he were battling himself internally. "Tomorrow evening you will meet with me and Trigo in the royal council chambers at evening bell."

At that, Lucid's heart sank. The only time he ever needed to attend a council meeting was when the old men wanted to scold him about responsibility or finding a wife. He had no desire to sit and hear politics, so he avoided the meetings with tenacity. Normin put a hand on Lucid's shoulder as he looked into his eyes. He gave a shallow smile and a reassuring squeeze. "Do not be late." He turned on his heel and walked out, leaving Lucid with plenty of unanswered questions.

At this point Lucid was too exhausted to give it much thought. He pulled his clothes off and collapsed into his bed, drifting off to sleep quickly.

Lucid awoke early the next morning, despite his exhaustion from the previous evening. His thoughts were filled with questions, and his mind wandered throughout the day, making it impossible to focus on his studies.

After what seemed to be the longest day of his short life, the evening bell finally rang from the island's cathedral as Lucid made his way up the winding stairs to the royal council chambers. The large room was on the second-highest floor of the palace. Its tall windows, interspersed around the chamber, let in the natural light of the fading sun. Normin stood at one such window, looking out at the ocean. "Son" was all he said in greeting when he heard Lucid enter. Either his father was not nearly as upset as he thought or Lucid had clearly overthought the reason for this meeting.

Lucid sat at the large dining table in the center of the room and tried to look relaxed. On the table sat the largest and possibly oldest book Lucid had ever seen.

After what felt an eternity, his father sat and spoke. "The world is not as it seems," he began. After a pause and a slight shake of his head, he turned and sat down at the head of the table. He continued, "We are not alone on this island. A very long time ago, a race of people landed here and attempted to completely destroy our people and take over the world our family had built here. There was a war and a final battle, which our ancestors won. An agreement was made to end the bloodshed. It is a testament to the mercy of our ancestors, a fact I take great pride in. Instead of genocide, our people chose peace and friendship. Since that time we have lived together in harmony for hundreds of years. They are a strong, brutish race with ancient customs thousands of years old. Their life span is much longer than our own."

Normin trailed off as the doors to the chamber opened. He rose, as did Lucid. Lieutenant Trigo entered. Lucid almost fainted as he saw what entered behind him, although as his father spoke he knew what the man was getting to. Now that Normin had revealed some of their story, Lucid began to realize just how dangerous his trips to the village were.

Yep, the boy thought. *I'm fucked.*

Trigo was trailed into the royal council chambers by one of the villagers, ducking his head to pass through the doorway. He was huge, massive. Lucid had seen their size, but never in the same room. He was increasingly terrified at what the outcome of this meeting might be. His face began to sweat, and he felt light-headed. He glanced to his father, but Normin only smiled, walking up to the giant man to shake his hand. After a few short, indistinguishable words between the two men, Lucid's father gestured to him, who was sweating and pale. Lucid was unsure what shocked him more, that his father knew the villagers' language or that he himself had never noticed the green fire that burned in the giant's eyes.

When the towering man came to shake his hand, Lucid finally got a good look at him. At least eight feet tall and four feet wide, he had muscles that rippled all over his body under the thin rags they called clothes. Lucid could not hold the man's gaze long; those intense eyes threatened to burn through his own. It seemed he could use the man's head as a mirror as it was so large and bereft of hair. Lucid thought his face looked very odd without eyebrows. He didn't realize he was shaking until he reached out to clasp hands with the giant.

"Prince Lucid Altheia, Lucid, this is D'matrius 9, leader of his people," King Normin introduced the pair. The big man gave a slight squeeze and a small nod.

"No worry." The sound of the giant surprised Lucid, like a bear's growl in a tiny cave, accompanied by the strangest accent he had ever heard. "You take things better than"—D'matrius glanced toward the king—"other ancestors," he said.

Both men laughed, killing some of the tension in Lucid's gut. Lucid smiled when he caught the joke and laughed awkwardly and entirely too loud, he thought. He slowly made his way to his seat as his father showed D'matrius to his. The monster's frame would not fit into a chair, so he simply took a knee at the table, even then still towering above them. Trigo was all but invisible as he took his post, standing by the door.

"I am sure you will have questions, Son, so you may ask, but wait until I am finished," the king said. Lucid nodded. "D'matrius's ancestors and ours agreed to make peace and share our world. Now we coexist solely based on secrecy, privacy, and the Treaty of 4281. D'matrius and I go to great lengths to make sure our people know nothing of each other. And it *must* stay that way. Every new king meets the leader of the gvorlocks when he comes of age, and swears an oath to uphold the treaty. Stand up, Son." Lucid did as he was bade and approached his father.

"Raise your right hand," Normin said, and again Lucid followed directions. Normin drew his sword and raised it vertically toward Lucid. The prince grasped the blade just above the hilt with his left hand as was customary.

"Repeat after me: I, Lucid Altheia, swear to uphold the treaty peacefully by my honor and the honor of our family. I will do nothing to disturb these people or allow this secret to become public knowledge from now until the day I die," the king said.

Lucid repeated his father verbatim. Then Normin sheathed the blade and gestured for him to sit. After a brief conversation in the giant's language, the giant and Normin rose and shook hands with Lucid following suit. Then the huge man exited, escorted by Lieutenant Trigo.

"What the fuck is that thing?" Lucid asked of his father after the two were gone.

Normin sighed and sat in his customary chair at the head of the large rectangular table. "I told you, they are called gvorlocks. And I would appreciate if you did not let D'matrius hear you call him a 'thing.'"

Lucid frowned as he sat next to his father. "You know what I mean. They do not look human at all. Where did they come from?"

"I am not exactly sure as the history on the subject is vague. Secrecy, even from future generations, was a must, and steps were taken so that descendants like us would only know what we needed to know," Normin replied. Lucid did not like that answer. He stayed silent, waiting for his father to speak again, a trick he'd learned from Normin that he found worked well. Finally his father threw up his hands. "I swear I do not exactly know where they came from. One account says they came from below the earth, and another says the sky. I myself have done extensive research on the subject using the oldest texts of the library and can honestly only tell you what I know. It does not matter now. What does matter is that you keep peace with these people and instill the same behavior into your children. The treaty is all that keeps them from attempting to take what is ours." He smiled and raised his mug after a small pause. "I am proud of the man you have become, and I have no doubt you will be one hell of a king someday," Normin told his son as he took a sip of his beer. Lucid nodded and gave a half smile. *Too much responsibility,* he thought.

"There is one more small matter we must discuss," Lucid's father told him as he set his mug back on the table and leaned forward. "It's more of a personal family goal that your grandfather and Inder's father started when I was a boy, and I am proud to say we are very close to completing it." He paused for emphasis and gave Lucid a genuine smile, his eyes taking on a fierce pride. "We've built a ship," he said simply, and sat back, waiting on his son's reaction.

Lucid blanched, narrowing his eyes at his father after a moment's thought. "Okay, if I was paying attention in history class, and I'd like to think I was, a ship is a very large, different style of canoe, capable of fitting hundreds of people and crossing the seas. Vessels like that are how our ancestors got to Blysse."

Lucid's heart started beating fast as he recited that last part. Did his father mean to attempt to find other islands? He always joked about such things, but with Lucid looking into his father's eyes now, there was no joke there. The histories told of great wars in the distant past with advanced war machines beyond comprehension that wiped out most, if not all, the continents. And the lands that did survive were said to be toxic, uninhabited wastelands.

Normin sat up and said, "There are other islands, I know it in my heart. If the ancient histories are to be believed, there were a great many continents in this world. And I intend to find them."

As Lucid left the royal council chamber after the meeting with his father was done, he headed for his bed with his mind in a whirl. All this new information—treaties, new languages, strange people from another world. And of course there was the ship. Did his father really intend to attempt to travel the world? Looking for ancient islands and settlements was beyond comprehension. At least that meeting answered some of his questions, but he still had so much to ponder. As he entered his chambers and collapsed into his bed, all he could think about was the one question they had not answered: who was the girl?

Lucid and Jon sat on the beach together, drying in the sun and watching the waves build, crash, and retreat. It was the first day of the week's end, and Lucid was free of school and any other responsibilities. Swimming was one of the city's favorite activities in the hot summer months, so there were children splashing in the shallows and parents hovering close by. Lucid could hear their laughter coming in with the wind. He couldn't blame them. The prince always felt revitalized after any time spent in the ocean. He supposed there was something magical about salt water and the steady sea breeze.

"So, what was this meeting about last night?" Jon asked. "Didn't get busted, did we?"

Lucid smiled and shook his head. "No, but I was sure that was what it was about. I was so nervous, I almost pissed myself. Wait, how did you know about it?" Lucid asked. Jon chuckled slightly. A laugh from Jon was rare. Perhaps he was in such a happy mood because he was relieved that no one knew of their little trek.

"So?" Jon asked again, ignoring his prince's question.

Lucid looked over at Jon and shrugged. "Not supposed to talk about it," he said.

Jon's only rebuttal was a mischievous half grin. "Yeah, me either," he finally replied. Lucid narrowed his eyes, and Jon's smile got larger. "What?" Jon inquired. "You think you are the only one with an important father around here?"

Lucid laughed. He should have known his friend would have the same access to information as he did. Hell, Trigo's having been at the meeting should have given it away. Lucid's mind was just reeling at that moment.

"So I suppose you are also the proud owner of a ridiculously thick book?" Lucid smiled, and Jon scowled. "Don't be like that. This is a huge opportunity for me," the prince continued. "Learn as much of their tongue as you can as fast as possible." Jon was already shaking his head. *Damn, he knows me too well.*

"You want to talk to the girl, fine, but I will have nothing to do with it," Jon said as Lucid got up and dusted the sand off himself, gathering his things to leave.

"It blows my mind that you are not even a little curious.

Plus, you forget yourself, Mr. Trigo, as it is your duty to protect the king at all times," Lucid told Jon as the latter stood with his friend and began grabbing his own things as well.

"I'm not a king's man yet, and you are not the king yet. But I cannot let you go get yourself caught, or mauled by a jaguar so fine, Your Highness," Jon said as he made an exaggerated bow. "If it please Your Grace, I'll accompany His Lordship and keep his royal ass out of trouble."

Lucid almost died laughing at his friend as during that entire exchange, Jon's face remained serious. Lucid's laughter went on for a minute, Jon soon joining in. They both laughed as they climbed the sand dune that marked the end of the beach and the beginning of the grass surrounding the city.

Lucid stopped walking. His smile died as his face turned dark. "But after that …" Lucid put a hand on his friend's shoulder, stopping him with a fierce expression. "After that will be a much more serious and dangerous mission. We will get Russell." Lucid could tell the heart of his friend just dropped by the look in his eyes. "Tomorrow night after supper, meet me in my chambers, and we will plan every detail."

Jon hesitated so long that Lucid began to think he would refuse. Then, stone-faced and determined, he looked into his friend's eyes and silently nodded his consent.

CHAPTER 2

Daryl took a few deep breaths, prepared himself for the worst, and opened the chamber door. As usual, the overwhelming smell was absolutely nauseating as Lord Hinson's portal opened and he stepped in. Daryl was at the end of healers' apprentice schooling, and unfortunately part of his duties included dealing with the waste of the sick and dying. Entering, he could see the room was still in shambles, half-eaten plates of unrecognizable food strewn all over the place, flies buzzing around the plates. It was as if he'd stepped up a single stair as he walked in the door and onto the very thick layer of soiled clothes that acted as the room's flooring. Breathing through his mouth only, he hurried to the bed and reached under to remove the overflow of filthy excrement that served as Lord Hinson's chamber pot. As careful as Daryl was, a little of the gunk spilled out away from him, and he looked up to thank God he had not spilled any of the toxic waste on himself. Taking a quick peek to see if Lord Hinson had seen his slip, he exited the room as slowly as possible, the snoring signaling that he was in the clear.

Daryl hated his duties at this exact moment almost every morning. Hinson was ancient and had been slowly getting worse over the last year. the state of his room told Daryl that his family checked on him very little, if at all. After a small shudder and the emptying of Hinson's disgusting chamber pot into his rolling waste barrel, Daryl was quick to move to the next room.

Not sick or old, Alisha Blake, his next stop, was gorgeous,

absolutely irresistible to Daryl. He relished the small respite each morning from the disgusting monotony to spend precious few moments with the love of his life. Just as he was about to knock and enter her chambers, however, he felt a slight touch on his shoulder and spun quickly, perhaps guiltily thinking that his relationship with Alisha might be compromised. His father was the master healer, so consequences of sexual relations before marriage might be more than Daryl cared to endure. But of course it was only the prince and Jon standing there, attempting not to laugh at the startled look on Daryl's face.

They knew all about Daryl and Alisha's relationship as they had all grown up together. Their parents were all close friends and peers, members of the council. Alisha's father approved very much of her choice in companion, but Daryl did not want to push it. He should have known it was Lucid and Jon, however, by their uncanny ability to move with absolutely no sound.

"What in two shits are you guys doing here?" he asked.

Lucid glanced down at the cart. Covered in filth, it stank horribly. A fly was buzzing around it. Lucid swatted at it absently and asked, "Do you say things like that because you are forced to work with shit all day?"

Lucid and Jon were, hands down, the reason Daryl had not gone insane over the last few years. The constant, and sometimes stomach-turning, workload of the healers was exhausting both physically and mentally. However, the prince was never shy about including Daryl in some much-needed respite from his studies. Just two weeks ago, Lucid and Jon had taken him to a spot on the cliffs near the edge of the city where they liked to jump off into the water. The height of that cliff was insane to Daryl. To peer over the edge and into the blue of the sea was like looking into the maw of a huge beast. Daryl had feared that jump since he was a child, yet with a little trickery

Lucid and Jon had him tumbling over the edge, praying to God to have mercy on his doomed soul. After his fifth jump, Daryl decided that this was one of the best days of his life. He loved Lucid and Jon and their crazy antics dearly and liked nothing more than hanging out with the two of them.

Lucid stepped forward and put both hands on Daryl's shoulders. The look in his eyes was pained yet determined as he said, "I need your help, Daryl. I can trust no one else with this."

Daryl looked down for a moment in thought. When he looked up to answer his friend, he asked, "Russell?"

Lucid nodded solemnly.

Honestly, he was surprised it had taken this long. Daryl already knew what his friends were planning. He'd grown up with Russell just as they had and knew that the boys had all been a little less of themselves since Russell's father, Percy, had deserted Altheia, taking a part of them with him. Lucid's possible success in this crazy venture would change their friend's life for the better forever. Still, he had known this was coming. The day Russell had left he knew. Yet if they were caught sneaking around Drondos, they could be imprisoned— or worse.

Daryl nodded his consent, wondering how in hell he would be able to perform for his love waiting behind the door. In the end, he decided he would slip in and do his duties silently, not waking her, and then move on to finish his work. She would be wroth with him, and he might be the proud owner of a new bruise or two, but he did not mind.

As he worked, he thought he was doing well so far, making very little noise as he stole glances at her while she slept. *Damn, she's gorgeous.*

He had no official duties pertaining to Alisha, but he liked doing things for her, so he straightened up her chambers as quietly as possible. She would get so angry when Daryl would empty her chamber pot, but he knew that secretly she appreciated it. Still, there was a bowel boycott after the first few attempts, and now he found it empty most mornings. *Mission accomplished,* he thought. Yet as he was walking out, he felt an arm slide around his neck. The empty chamber pot rang as it hit the stone floor. He could think of nothing else when he felt her naked heat pressing against his back. "Daryl Wilkins! Thought you were sneaky, huh? What the fuck?" Alisha said.

She soon released him, and he turned to look at her. He knew when she threw out his last name that she was actually upset. Alisha was just a few inches shorter than he with dark hair flowing down to her lower back. She wore it up most days to prevent it from interfering with her work, so anytime Daryl saw her with those thick locks hanging free, he melted. Her brown eyes were lit with anger, and although she was naked, she looked ready to throttle him.

He just shook his head and moved toward her, embracing her and looking into her eyes with such a contented expression that she softened and kissed him hungrily. Blood pounded in his ears, and instinct took over him. Alisha was not the type of young woman to spew forth all her feelings and problems and expect someone to take care of them. Nor did she expect such things from him. She was unlike any girl Daryl had known in his nineteen years.

The daughter of the master craftsman, she was smart, strong, and hard as granite. She was only a year older than he at twenty, yet already she had revolutionized the art of the bow in ways no one could have imagined.

After Alisha pulled Daryl down to her bed, they wrestled for dominance and ecstasy until they were both exhausted and panting with exertion.

"Why does it always feel like I have gotten my ass kicked?" Daryl asked as they lay together afterward. Alisha laughed and rolled over to bite his chest. Daryl grunted. She smiled.

"Don't be a baby. What's wrong? You have never attempted to avoid me before," she said. Daryl sighed. He saw no need to hide anything from her; she would take his secrets to the grave.

"Lucid wants me to help him get Russell," he told her.

"You mean steal him from Drondos?" she asked in reply.

God, I love her, he thought. "It's not stealing. He is not a goat or a loaf of bread." She just stared. "He will come willingly," he said in the awkward silence of her stare and she just blinked. "I am sure Lucid has it all planned out. And I'm pretty sure he has the king's permission to bring him here. It will be fine."

Alisha mounted him quickly, kissed him, and pulled back sharply. Then she slapped him square in the face. Daryl saw stars as she said, "Don't fucking die."

She rose and began to dress, leaving Daryl's cheek stinging and his mind racing. Lucid may be the prince, and he had total confidence of success on this mission … but the consequences. Daryl loved his prince and would do anything for him. They had been friends since they were still at the teat. But Daryl knew well Lucid's inability to foresee what the consequences of his actions might turn out to be. Russell's father, Percy, was a volatile sort and not one to forget. That man could hold a grudge against the sun. And if Drondos were anything like Altheia, then Percy would be revered there for his drink-making skills and probably had the ear of the king, or at least knew someone who did. *This may start a wheel of actions leading straight to war,* Daryl thought.

CHAPTER 3

The party was a lavish event. The royal dining hall was decorated with streamers and banners, music echoed through the palace, and the citizens of the city were crammed shoulder to shoulder, eating and dancing. Everyone was celebrating because the prince was officially finished with Altheia schooling and was now a man. Altheia loved their royal family, and that love definitely extended to the prince and princess.

Vincent stood in the darkest corner he could find, right near a cask of ale that was perched on a large table laden with cups. He did not partake; he would need a clear head. Dressed in his finest clothes, he easily blended into the large crowd with few looks of suspicion.

No one had recognized him so far; that was good. He was but a child when last these people had seen his face, yet he had seen many of them. His work kept him in both Altheia and Drondos regularly, so he had taken steps over the years to make sure no one from this city would recognize him. Plus, he kept his home in Drondos, so it would not be good if anyone knew who he was here.

Vincent spotted his target, Bruce Mathis, over near the banquet table, making his way down the line and stacking up his plate with food. Bruce was the head of the farmers, responsible for all the city's grain, and it shocked Vincent that the man kept the key to the food stores on him at all times. He supposed it made sense—a lot of food locked up in that tower.

Vincent did not particularly care about the grain—he ate well enough—but Ivan had offered him such a large amount of money that he could not pass it up. Such currency was useless in Drondos as the fat bastard had stolen all the craftsmen for himself, yet Vincent could buy whatever he needed from Altheia.

"I just want to thank everyone for coming," he heard the king's voice say when the music stopped abruptly. The crowd quieted quickly, and Vincent saw King Normin standing on a slightly raised platform against the north wall of the dining hall.

"It's been a very fun evening. I'm sure my son, Lucid, man of the hour, would agree. Come here, Son." He gestured for the prince to join him on stage, and soon Lucid was standing next to his father, the crowd cheering.

After listening to the king drone on about his son, Vincent glanced over to Bruce and noticed he was almost finished eating. He prepared to make his move, reaching into the pocket sewn into his coat to check his clay.

Still moist, he thought as he slouched, drooled a little on himself, and stumbled over to Mathis. His timing was perfect. As soon as the head farmer slid his chair back to stand, Vincent was there to connect with it. He hooked the leg of Bruce's chair with his ankle, and they both went down in a tumble of fine clothes and limbs. Quick as a rabbit, he snatched the keys and stuffed them in his pocket. With his left hand he pressed the clay around the key while fumbling on the ground with his right.

"Oh, so sorry, sir," he slurred. Vincent pretended to have trouble getting up while slowly pulling the clay in half to release the key. As he finally climbed to his feet, he used Bruce's cloak to pull himself upright, and as he did so, he dropped the keys carefully back in the man's pocket.

A few nights later, as Vincent moved through the tight, dirty alleys of Drondos, he could not help but rethink his purpose in life. It might have been the muddy shit he was walking through, its stench overwhelming in the summer heat. *Might be age,* he thought. It wasn't his job, as he did not really dislike his work.

As he approached the end of the alley, he crouched low, hugging the side of Jameson's dilapidated shoe store. The tandem guards passed him, mere inches away. They noticed nothing.

He continued his stealthy trek toward the third house on Maple Street. His timing would have to be perfect as his client insisted on receiving the item at once, claiming his next, time-sensitive mission would continue from there. Vincent shook his head at the thought.

Maybe that was why he was rethinking everything he did. It consumed his spare time. Not to say he wasn't good at it; he was the best.

Soon he approached his goal, a large two-story house made of wood with a strong, clean look. Following his previously laid-out plan, he crept up to the south side of the house. As usual, the window on the upper floor was open to allow for breeze. He climbed the framing of the lower window and grabbed the lip of the open one. He pulled his head up just enough to see the sleeping child under the window. With a silent sigh, he swung up and perched on the edge of window, fingers just able to grasp the top edge to hold himself in place. He had accounted for the child, but seriously, right under the window? His only options were to try to climb down the frame of the bed or to jump and risk someone awaking because of the noise. He chose the former option and was surprised when the climb down the frame was easy and silent.

Nice bed, kid, he thought.

Vincent took his time creeping silently out of that room, down the hall, and into the room next door. It definitely was not the work. He enjoyed it; it was challenging and extremely rewarding. He had been thinking over the last few years that he lacked companionship, even feeling a bit lonely. His work allowed no room for friends or female companions, although he thought frequently about settling down and spawning his own little thief-assassin babies.

Vincent entered the study, removed the fancy painting, and opened the safe quickly, removing its only contents: a small locked box made of wood and metal. He replaced it with his replica and then put everything back to normal and quietly checked the hall before retracing his steps to the room next door.

As he entered the room, he could immediately tell something was wrong. He did not have to wait long to find out what as he heard a low growl erupt from the darkness.

How the hell did I miss that?

Before he even thought about it, he had his dagger out and in the dog's throat, silencing the beast. He gathered up the dead dog and tossed it out the open window quickly before too much blood escaped. Then he bent down to wipe up the few droplets and stuffed the rag back in his satchel. As he looked up to exit the window, his heart sank. He couldn't help but think that had it not been for the bully he'd had to cow earlier, he might have made better time and been able to plan ahead for the complication of the child and his protective little friend.

Vincent had been delayed by a man in an alley just past the salt store viciously beating a much younger man. He could not help himself. Bullying a bully was always a pleasure to him. He had flashed his dagger and his teeth, and that was all the convincing the man needed to leave his charge alone, storming off to Salty's tavern.

The little boy's eyes were open now and, just like the bruised and puffy face of the young man during his earlier encounter, brimming with tears. The poor kid's mouth was frozen open in shock. He feared to even move, to breathe. Vincent took a steadying breath and, without a word or sound, crept out the window, pretending to have never seen the child was awake. He thought it a clean escape as most likely not one person would believe the young child's story about a ghost in a mask killing his dog and throwing it out the window. A disappearing dog and a fake box in the safe might be enough evidence to back the child's story, but there was nothing to be done about it.

Am I losing my edge? Vincent thought.

His mind and body were just like a well-used blade. No matter how much you take care of it, eventually its life comes to an end.

Once he was back on the ground, he gathered up the dead dog and headed for the west side of town. He had a perfect spot in mind to dump the corpse where the poor animal could rot in peace and where it was unlikely someone would find it. On his third turn down the alley behind Dutch Street, however, he stopped abruptly and found himself looking at three young men dressed in black, standing frozen once they had turned the corner and spotted him. The youth in the back of the group was dragging a dead guard.

Dressed in mostly black himself, blood all over him and a with dead dog that he had yet to discard slung over his shoulder, Vincent simply said just above a whisper, "I will forget this unfortunate meeting if you will swear to do the same."

The lead youth smiled and nodded. He turned his back to the wall to allow Vincent to move past, and his fellows followed suit. As he passed and saw their faces, he realized with amusement that this was none other than the prince of Altheia, Trigo's son, and the head healer's boy, all three faces fresh in his mind, his having seen them at that royal event.

Vincent would never admit to anyone that he'd been born in Altheia, so he kept a special eye on the comings and goings of the royals in their sister city. Plus, the market in Altheia was wonderful and had everything, so that was where he did most of his shopping.

He had to stifle a laugh and was positive the prince noticed his delight. *Smart kid,* he thought.

Vincent said nothing and continued his slow trek, finally dropping his bloody failure in the woods on the west side of town before turning toward the small shack just outside the city that his client had agreed upon. Two jobs in a week would set him up well. With this coin plus the money he had saved, he finally had enough to stop working. Maybe he would abandon both cities and build himself a small house on the other side of Blysse.

I could just disappear. He had thought about it many times, the only real doubt in his mind being the seclusion. Maybe when he stopped working he could finally spend some time finding a nice woman, and possibly he could convince her to go with him.

All of this was going through Vincent's mind as he approached his meeting spot at the small hut. It was just a tiny shack made by sticking large limbs in the ground and bending them over to make a sort of woven dome. Vincent had put it together himself for meetings just like this one. Something felt wrong, however, as the suspicious absence of the droning of insects and the noises of small animals was more obvious than shouting. As he was just about to enter the hut, two swordsmen dressed in black, almost invisible the moment before, struck at him simultaneously from the left and the right. They were easily dispatched, but the third, unseen before, managed to sneak up behind Vincent. Pain exploded across his lower back. He vaguely felt the killer slip the box from his pocket as his head swam and the world began to darken. The pain was absolutely crippling. His knees buckled, and try as he might to stay upright, he saw the ground come at him—and he knew no more.

CHAPTER 4

L yasareoss awoke that evening drenched in sweat, having had one of the strangest and most vivid dreams of her life. She sat up abruptly, breathing hard with her heart pounding, yet she could not remember why, only a vague sense of urgency that faded quickly. The familiar darkened thatch of the hut's roof served as a reminder that dreams were her only real escape.

She wiped the sweat from her face, swung her feet out of bed, and threw on her simple brown dress. At first she thought the dreams were nothing, a misconception of her wandering brain as she slept. But lately they had become more, as if the voices in her dreams were attempting to keep her attention or even teach her things. Her mother had told her when she was younger that it was their gods speaking to her, but that was so long ago that it seemed a child's fantasy. It was starting to get easier to remember faces and phrases, but no matter how hard Lyasareoss tried, the memory of what was said always faded when she awoke.

The ritual bang on the door of the communal hut that all the slaves shared came as usual. The gvorlocks were nocturnal, so work for Lyasareoss began at sundown. She was exhausted, both mentally and physically, to the extreme. The hard labor the gvorlocks demanded was taking its toll. Still, she was one of the youngest of the current slaves, and her body was strong. She did have nourishment once a night and she was still alive at least.

The face that appeared at the door was none other than

Tr'vastious, the second-in-command and a brutal beast. "Get to work." He turned and abruptly left, leaving Lya to wonder if she had imagined it in her sleep-fogged brain.

She went over to Astelle and nudged her awake. Astelle was pregnant. Lya worried over her friend regularly. "How are you feeling this morning?" Lya asked quietly.

Astelle yawned, rubbed her eyes, and stood to wiggle her swollen toes. She grimaced. "Ready to get this baby out of me."

Lya frowned. Astelle was young, younger than Lya, and unfamiliar with the ways. Lya had seen two other pregnant slaves before, and when the time came, a gvorlock healer would come get the birthing mother and enter the woods, the young woman never to be seen again.

"It will be here before you know it," Lya told her friend, helping her get her swollen belly in her own brown dress.

The father of the unborn child, Doirion, Tr'vastious had killed quickly. He'd said, "You breed when we say you breed."

The hut was a simple structure made mostly of small braches woven together and covered in thatch. It looked to Lya like a large, round bush that was dead. It was always too hot in summer and too cold in winter, and it did not repel all the water during strong rains.

The slaves exited the hut into the gloom of the communal fire, where D'matrius, Tr'vastious, and Kinetrius were speaking together with two new faces that Lya recognized only vaguely. The entirety of the village only consisted of six other huts; however, these were aligned in a perfect circle surrounding a large stone pit. The gvorlocks' huts were much better constructed of strong limbs and interwoven palm leaves that they had to replace regularly.

The slaves strode past the small gathering, beginning the night's labor. They harvested water, firewood, and vegetables;

skinned and cleaned the animals the gvorlocks hunted; cleared trees; and made and mended clothing, basically everything except hunt. Lya and the other slaves could just barely keep up with the laborious responsibilities.

The fruit trees lay just a small distance away from the village. The firelight still visible, illuminating Lya's work. Just as she was finishing picking the night's fruit, she heard the faintest scuffle. Perhaps a boot grazed a large rock. She looked carefully out of her peripheral vision, spotting a shadow of a person slowly getting up about twenty yards from her. She quickly scooped up her basket and purposely made herself seen on the way back. She suspected it was Tr'vastious spying on her in the woods, and if that were true, she had to know.

Lya was surprised, though, at what she saw: not Tr'vastious but a very handsome young man dressed in dark leathers and staring at her wide-eyed. She had to bite back a smile because the look on his face was a mask of shock and fear. She had never seen anyone like him. He had dark shoulder-length hair, slightly mangled, no doubt from his journey here. His dark eyes flickered in the dim firelight.

There are others in this place? Lya thought.

She raised an eyebrow curiously, then pointed her head away from the village. The man looked so relieved that Lya thought he might cry. As he very silently, to his credit, crept away, he looked back to take one more glance. When he was out of sight, she allowed herself a smile.

That was interesting, she thought.

She returned to her work as quickly as possible so no one would notice her small delay. As the night wore on, she could think of nothing else but the mysterious man from the woods.

That day, Lya's dreams were haunted by the dark-eyed stranger. She had visions of him old and successful, looking peaceful and happy, and then other visions where he died very young, not yet in his full prime, battling against unimaginable odds. So vivid was his face, she had no trouble remembering this time. It hit her somewhere in her dream-fogged mind that the fragility of the events that occur is shocking, the slightest decision sending ripples infinitely into future choices. Why that particular thought was so prominent, she could not begin to comprehend.

Lya awoke suddenly and violently, drenched in sweat. She had to take a minute calm herself.

That was intense, she thought.

By the time she caught her breath, there was not much left of the dream she could remember except the young man's face. Whoever he was, one thing was for sure: there was something special about this man, something that stood out in a way she was unfamiliar with. Lya had to believe that their meeting was no accident. She could see it in his eyes, feel it even. She had to find out more, but how? All she could do was pray to the gods that he would return.

And so the gods provided. Less than a week later, he showed. She had to stifle her excitement as he and his associate were almost spotted by Kinetrius, the sentry. When she caught those crazy, intense eyes, she made a small wave and gestured for the man to come closer, in an area well hidden by trees. As he approached, she finally got a good look at him.

He was beautiful. He stood straight before her and bent over at the waist, possibly some sort of primitive greeting. She smiled when he straightened and was incredibly surprised when he spoke to her in Lockian.

"Hello, pretty female," he said at length.

He smiled at her, and she laughed.

"You speak our tongue?" she asked, incredulous.

His brows knit together as he said, "Yes, small amount. I been spooning. Not easy to speak. I am Lucid Altheia, and this my ... fiend Jon Trigo. Very pleased to meet."

She laughed and corrected, "I *have* been *learning*, not *spooning*. And I think you mean *friend*, not *fiend*." His Lockian was barely adequate, yet she was pleased to see him, broken communication or no.

"My name is Lyasareoss. You can call me Lya," she told him.

His smile grew, showing perfect white teeth. Lya felt it was contagious as she herself grinned widely.

"You don't look like them," Lya noted, tilting her head toward the village.

"No, my people are not same. We live ... other end of ... land," Lucid said, gesturing toward the way by which he'd appeared through the thick woods.

Lya smiled again. Had she ever smiled this much? Her happiness upon speaking with him, however, melted a moment later as they heard a twig snap from not far off. Tr'vastious was undoubtedly wondering what was taking her so long. Her gaze had shifted that way for just an instant to see if anyone was coming, and when she looked back, the boys were gone. Her eyes bulged, her mouth agape.

Amazing, she thought; they had disappeared incredibly fast without the slightest noise. After a moment they reappeared, melting out of the woods silent as death. As Lucid walked back up, Lya studied him.

He moved with agile grace, clearly practiced and mastered, like a hunter, a predator even. Only when he stopped in front of her did she realize she was staring, her heart racing.

"I must be going," Lya said, breaking the silence. "It was nice to meet you. Maybe we will meet again?" She made the last part a hopeful question.

Lucid smiled again. He bent over at the waist once more, bowing longer this time, and when he rose, he said, "I would be very pleased."

She gave a small wave as she stepped out of sight and back toward the village. Lya was so excited to have seen and spoken with him, she almost missed Tr'vastious at the edge of the clearing, staring in the direction where Lucid and Jon were retreating through the woods. Lya watched him stare for a few breaths, and when he looked up, she met his gaze. Startled as he began walking her way, she stumbled to get back to her duties, tripped, and dropped her basket of fruit. As he approached, he showed no sign that he noticed her on her knees frantically picking up the remains of her basket.

"What are you doing in the woods?" His tone was more demanding than asking.

"Am I not allowed to relieve myself anymore without being subject to a beating?" Lya replied, standing to look in his face.

Tr'vastious stared at her for a full minute, those glowing green eyes looking fierce with suspicion and anger.

"I heard you speaking," he said with less volume yet much more vehemence.

Lya swallowed and tried not to show any outward sign. When she hesitated, he slapped her with the back of his hand, knocking her to the ground. It was such a violent blow, Lya saw stars and her head swam. As she brought her hand up to cover her stinging cheek, her ears began to ring. She almost missed Tr'vastious saying quietly, "I'll be watching you."

Just for good measure, he placed a solid front kick with his heel right between her eyes, and the world went dark.

Lucid was so excited to have spoken with her and even to have learned her name that he was frozen in place for a moment.

He watched as she walked back toward the little village, smiling like a child with a birthday cake. After a few moments Jon touched his shoulder, and Lucid turned to head home, but as he did so, he heard a smack and a shout—a female shout.

Lucid began creeping toward the commotion very slowly. Jon attempted to grab his arm and stop him, but Lucid knew something was wrong, so he yanked his arm free and continued moving. He reached a spot hidden by trees, and he could see Lya on the ground, blood streaming from the side of her mouth and a gvorlock standing over her. Lucid stared for a minute before the huge creature planted a kick right in the center of her forehead. He watched in horror as Lya crumpled unconscious.

Lucid immediately began to move toward her, but this time Jon's grip was iron and the look in his eyes was so intense, it gave him pause. They had a silent battle of wills while Lucid contemplated the consequences. In the end, there simply was nothing he could do without breaking the treaty his father had been so adamant about. His face burned with anger and he could hear his teeth grinding, but he began walking away, taking one last glance back to see another, older-looking woman gather up Lya and helping her to their hut.

After what felt an eternity of walking in silence, Lucid decided it was clear to speak. "What the fuck!" he yelled to no one in particular.

The anger after seeing such a beautiful young woman brutalized by someone thrice her size had not faded as they walked. "We have to help her," he told Jon.

"Lucid," Jon said carefully, "we already have a plan in motion. Timelines are extremely important. You love to say that. The ink is not even dry from planning the Russell mission, and now you want to steal the gvorlocks' women?"

Lucid stopped walking and fixed his friend with a scowl.

"It's not … stealing, and it's not women. It's *woman*—just her. Besides, what do you think my father would do if he found out there are people here and the gvorlocks are treating them like that? Where do you think they came from? They have to be our people, either lost or stolen by these beasts." He hooked a thumb behind him.

"I'm sure your father knows. He's known about these gvorlocks since before we were born."

"But has he been here to see for himself as we have? The meeting took place in Altheia. Who's to say my father or any of my grandfathers have been here?" Lucid replied.

Jon was silent for a long while. "Maybe we should have a chat with your father."

CHAPTER 5

King Normin Altheia rose before sunrise as usual but with an uncharacteristically ominous feeling. The early morning before the sun broke over the sea was usually Normin's favorite time of the day. This was the reason he never drank much beer at night; the hangover feeling absolutely ruined his morning. His servants knew well not to bother him at that hour, and the stresses of the kingdom never seemed to cross his mind in those tranquil moments of gray and brightening blue.

He moved through his normal routine of coffee, a smoke, and small talk with his wife, Alice. The only thing he could think of was the unpleasant information he was about to drop on his son. The history of their people and the gvorlocks was, to put it plainly, insane.

"What if he doesn't take it well? It is a lot to drop on him in one day. I may not tell him all," he told the queen.

He was unsure how his son would take it. Lucid was such a happy kid without a care in the world. Normin loathed having to tell him the brutal truth of the war all those years ago. Plus, who knew how accurate the histories passed down from father to son actually were. As Normin contemplated, a thought struck him. How many of his ancestors had left out pieces and parts of the story? How much information had been lost? He would not further contribute to this and decided he would tell his boy everything, lightly.

Alice had flipped in the bed, lying on her stomach with her feet at the headboard. She lay that way most mornings as

Normin got ready, mostly so they could speak intimately but also so she could share his morning smoke.

"Lucid is perfectly capable of handling things. Also, it will be years before he has to actually do anything. It's just information, love," she told him.

Normin nodded, but still he was not sure. He looked into his love's brown eyes, which were looking back into his with such a calmness that it stilled his heart. Alice was still beautiful after two children and more than forty years. She had the darkest of black hair with not a touch of gray, and although her skin did not see the sun as much as it had in her youth, it was still well tanned and smooth. He planted a kiss on her forehead.

"I'll see you this evening," he told her as he headed for the door.

He stopped on the stairs at his favorite window. The placement of this particular spot afforded him the perfect view of his kingdom. Looking down the west side of the palace of Altheia, he was at the center of a bustling city, spreading out along Jacques Ravine, just a mile inland from the Gulf of Winds. Normin looked across from the castle at the main square of Altheia. A huge statue of his distant ancestor King Jerald stood in the center, carved of stone. Jerald silently guarded the peaceful streets and added to Altheia's plentiful shade. Small vendor shacks lined the edge of the smoothed-rock courtyard displaying wares of all sorts where a person might buy anything he needed at fair prices. Beyond the main square, small dirt roads leading in all directions snaked through large swaths of even more shops and homes. Normin took pride in the fact that his city was a well-oiled machine, each citizen working perfectly in sync with the next. They were farmers, craftsmen, scholars, and healers, and they all loved their king. It was not a particularly large community, especially when compared to cities of old from the history books, but as his forefathers had predicted, it was growing exponentially with each generation.

Normin finished his descent to the small dining room on the fourth floor of the palace reserved for council meetings and, although it was early, poured himself a beer. His daughter, Brynn, was already there at her writing desk in the corner, bent over and studying her tallies intently. The king smiled. "Good morning, dear."

She looked up then and smiled back. "Morning, Daddy," she replied, and immediately went back to her stack of papers. She was tall for her age, was thin as a twig, and looked just like her mother. Her long black hair was tied up neatly, and her light brown eyes sparkled with delight at simply being there and somewhat involved. Normin determined that his decision to saddle her with the census responsibility was a good one. Brynn seemed to really enjoy it, and for being only eleven years old, she handled it very well.

The morning council meeting, and similarly the rest of the afternoon, went by in a flash. Then the meeting Normin dreaded came. It went slightly better than expected, and a new pride for his son settled into his mind. Lucid was brilliant and always able to adapt no matter what the situation, and D'matrius, or so Normin thought, was a giant teddy bear.

However, the inquisition by D'matrius was troublesome. That Drondos was sending scouts to Altheia made him uncomfortable. To the best of Normin's recollection, that would be a first, at least as long as he had been alive.

Still the meeting with his son nagged at him. *What does he truly think of all this? Is he mature enough to put real thought into it?* The next thing he knew, as he was lost in thought, his feet led him out of the palace and to the edge of the LD, where vendors shouting wares could be heard, among the general din of work tools and dozens of conversations. After explaining to Lucid what he and his friend had accomplished, Normin felt the need to visit Shadow Cove, so dubbed because it was his secret spot where he was building the culmination of a lifetime's work. The *Hope* was anchored there, an enormous wooden ship capable of accommodating all the original families of the resettlement as he liked to call it.

Normin exited the city through the LD and entered the woods on the west end. He found the small game trail made larger by the sailors and followed the ascending path to the cove. Once he was clear of the trees, all he could see from this elevated position on the rocky cliff was the ocean. He took a moment to rest and to breathe the fresh sea air. The sun was almost touching the water. It made for beautiful colors as he found the hidden trail leading down toward the *Hope*. Soon the crow's nest on the top of the cog's single mast came into view, and Normin could hear shouts and the clacking of metal tools on wood. As he exited the trail at the bottom of the cove, he paused to take in the scene.

The *Hope* was built entirely of the finest oak on the island. Normin looked at the freshly finished wood and inhaled the glorious scent of sawdust. Eighty-one feet from its lengthened stern to the aft castle, the ship shone in the late evening sun. He could see the craftsmen entering and exiting the hold and the cabin as they hurried to complete the final touches of the interior.

When Normin arrived at the *Hope* and started up the gangway, he could hear the shouts of Captain Inder drilling his men, running them back and forth across the deck in the fading light of early evening. Some men worked ropes, others cleaned decks, and still more walked by with various tools or materials. After walking across the main deck, Normin headed for the ladder on the starboard side of the aft castle that led to the helm. Captain James Inder was the man Normin had chosen to learn about and lead this sailing dream of his, and he could not have chosen better. Inder's family were engineers, so he was intelligent, and his father, Bob, had begun the design, so the captain had a strong grasp of the ins and outs of working the ship. He had already taken the *Hope* in a circle around the island and declared her sound.

"Come on, Aimes, you can move faster than that, you lazy fuck," Inder was shouting.

The man smiled and embraced his king when Normin approached the railing in front of the helm where James stood shouting. Normin was no stickler for formalities and knew his friend well; he was a hugger. Just as wide as he was tall, James was a bear of a man with huge hands and a thick beard that met his combed hair perfectly. For whatever reason, Inder had the foulest mouth of anyone the king knew, yet he would embrace everyone as a brother, even people he did not know.

"Good to see you, Captain. How goes the training?" the king asked.

"These sorry goat swallowers have a long way to go yet, but the officers and I know our fucking duties well enough. We've already sailed around the island smoothly a few times with no fuck-ups. I'd say she's ready for a longer goddamn journey."

Normin asked, "Did you say 'around the island'?"

Inder nodded. "Only way to really stretch her legs," he replied defensively.

"Do not sail by Drondos. A scout has been snooping around the north side of town. I don't want Ivan to know what we have. I don't have any plans in the near future to let this ship become public knowledge. For now it's merely a fail-safe," Normin told his captain.

Inder spit a dark liquid over the side of the ship. "Forgive my boldness, sir, but fuck that. She is much more than that. I will avoid Drondos the best I can, but this ship is capable of fully supporting and holding the entire fucking contents of our grain silo with room to spare. Fail-safe?"

Normin ignored the insolence because the look in James's eyes when speaking of the *Hope* was so insanely proud, he could not fault him for speaking his mind.

"Is there something I and all these sorry shits should be worried about? Something we need to be prepared for? I have never heard of Drondos sending spies. I don't fucking like it," James said.

Normin simply put a hand on the big man's shoulder and gave him a reassuring smile. "I promise, my old friend, when I know, you will know. For now, just keep up the good work." He hesitated as they both looked around at the nicely stained deck and polished side rails. "She's beautiful."

Inder smiled, and Normin clapped him on the shoulder one more time before turning and heading down the ladder and across the main deck toward the gangway. His next stop would definitely be George's shop in the LD, he decided.

George was the head of the craftsmen and incredibly good at building. He did regular work for Normin and did maintenance on the royal wing, so his main shop was below the palace. However, he was also responsible for most all the work required of the craftsmen in the LD, which he let his daughter, Alisha, handle most days.

It was getting late in the day, the sun beginning to dip below the waves, but Normin knew Alisha would be there working after regular customer hours were over. It was not for her incredibly detailed chairs or her excellent other wares he visited this day. Alisha had been working on a form of bow and arrow that would launch itself at the pull of a trigger, an elegant weapon that Normin knew for sure could turn the tide of any battle, making him obsessed with the invention. He checked on her progress regularly, and so far she had the main elements of the design figured out, but she still struggled to build a mechanism that could withstand multiple fires without failing.

When Normin arrived at the little shop, he heard the clank of a tiny hammer in the back. He stepped around the vendors' counter and into the workshop, where Alisha sat at a table, bent over a small metal assembly. When she spotted him, she set down her hammer, stood, and curtsied.

"Your Majesty," she said, unsurprised to see him.

"Hello, Alisha. How are you progressing today?" the king asked.

She smiled a huge, triumphant grin, and there was a pride in her eyes such that Normin had not seen up until this moment. She said, "I think I have it. I just need to attach the mechanism and test it a few hundred times, but I'm almost positive this one won't fail."

Normin smiled back at her and stepped toward the small table, looking over her work. He knew she was close, and he had come prepared. He untied a small sack from his belt and dropped it on the table with a thud. She opened it and gaped.

"Money for materials. I want a hundred of them. Every one of my king's men will have one," he said, glancing at her as he smiled. "And of course I have to have one for myself."

She laughed and curtsied once more. "It will be as you command, Your Majesty. As soon as I finish building and testing this one, I will get started."

On Normin's way back to the palace, Jake Trigo found him and fell in beside him as he walked. The head king's man had such a knack for this no matter where Normin went. Trigo was silent for a few steps, then said, "There was a scout spotted in the woods last night."

Normin stopped walking and looked into his friend's eyes. "So I suppose you heard D'matrius at the meeting? Glad to know we have another source of confirmation. Not very good, is he, this scout?" Jake gave him a half smile, and Normin continued: "Is he here now? Maybe we should send him some soup or something."

Other than Percy and his son, Russell, no one had ever crossed between cities because there was no need. Both cities were perfectly capable of supporting themselves and their own people. It was sort of an unspoken agreement that they left each other alone. If Drondos was sending someone to watch Normin's city, that could mean a dozen things—and none of them good.

"Who?" was all Normin said, but Jake caught his meaning.

"I believe it was Barret, old Hugh Jones's boy. He was making a delivery last night to the palace, and when he was leaving, he spotted the man on the north side of the woods. Said he was just standing there. He watched as long as he dared," Jake told his king.

Normin began walking again, thinking. After a time he turned and told Jake, "Put someone on it, your best man. And the next time someone from Drondos wants to spy on my city, bring him straight to me."

CHAPTER 6

errence Williams, the first commander of Drondos, stood by King Ivan's personal bed chamber watching him stuff his face with a meal that could potentially feed an entire family. Terrence could smell a hint of mold and the overwhelming stench of his king's body odor. He looked around at the faded wood their ancestors had used to build the rickety palace. Even with its being close to falling down from disrepair, it was still the nicest and sturdiest building in Drondos with breathtaking views of the ocean from the cliff on which it sat.

Drondos was a cheap, barbaric version of Altheia that Terrence found lacked any sort of structure or substance. A few generations back, a group of men thought they could build a better life for themselves on the other side of the island, and so a sister city sprang up, slapped together quickly with mostly wood and thatch. The result was abhorrent.

As his king chewed in silence, Terrence looked out the window to the tight, muddy alleys that led to small choked streets laden with the excrement of livestock. The late evening sun beat down mercilessly on Drondos as the founders had thought it a good idea to strip the surrounding land of all its trees to build the palace and outer wall. The first commander could see a few citizens sweating miserably as they went about their business.

"So, how did the scouting go last night? Everything seems to be in order?" the king asked.

The meeting between the two men was taking place in the

king's personal chambers, Terrence supposed, because Ivan trusted no one except for his personal bodyguard, Luke Bristol, who stood behind the king and glared at Terrence. Luke was tall and lanky, said little, and had no qualms about killing people. In fact he did so regularly, and he did not care who it was. Men, women, and even children died on his blade upon Ivan's orders. Terrence hated the heartless prick.

"It went well, Your Grace," Terrence replied. "All is in order, and the mission will commence three days from now as planned."

King Ivan nodded. He was a short man, balding at the top of his large head with plenty of gray creeping in at the sides. Ivan had a large hooked nose and a pronounced brow and somehow always smelled of sour milk. He tossed the turkey leg he was eating down on his plate, wiped his oversized greasy fingers on his fine tunic, and stood.

"That is good news. I cannot stress to you enough how much we need that grain. Without it, our people will starve this winter," the king told Terrence.

If you would put a fork down every now and then, Terrence thought, *our people would have plenty to eat.*

"Of course, sire, it will be done," he replied instead.

As Terrence looked at his king, he suppressed a wave of revulsion. He had been the king's first commander for many long years. Hell, they'd grown up together. Ivan was a few years Terrence's senior and Terrence had watched the slow progression of his king's weight over the years. In their younger days, they were fit men, two of the best fighters in the city, prone to weekly climbing expeditions around the island's cliffs, as was custom in both cities. Now it was a wonder how the man found his own cock under all the fat protruding from his midsection. Terrence did not think that stealing Altheia's grain stores was a particularly good idea and had argued against the raid. But in the end, it was all wasted breath. Subsequently, he had planned the most lucrative mission possible. And it all went according to plan, unnoticed as well.

Terrence shifted his footing to relieve the pain in his left knee. After forty years of wear and tear, thirteen of those years in the barracks, his knees and back ached daily.

"Are you not worried that Normin will find out?" the commander asked.

Terrence had been wondering that himself. It was not as if they could put the blame on another. The city of Altheia and its sister town, Drondos, were the only settled communities on the island. That much grain going missing would surely draw the other king's attention, and Normin was smart enough to know that his own people would not be so bold or so stupid. Plus, the order to burn the tower was troublesome and unnecessary.

"I don't care what that pussy thinks," Ivan snarled. "Let him come after me. I will burn his perfect little city to the ground!"

It was an empty threat, Terrence knew, as Altheia was much older and more established, its people adored their king, and every one of them would fight for Normin. Most likely Drondos would pay a heavy price for this raid, no matter what his idiotic king spewed forth from his fat, grease-soaked lips. Terrence had to suppress the urge to pull the long, giant sword strapped to his back and end this sorry excuse for a king.

"There was one more thing reported by the scouts. The prince was seen reentering Altheia from the woods on the west side of the city. They say it was just an hour or so before sunrise, and it was only him and Trigo's son," Terrence said.

The king looked perplexed as he thought for a moment, then he told his commander, "That seems significant. Not sure how yet. But keep your scouts on it. I would like to know what he is up to."

Terrence bowed slightly. "As you say, Your Grace. Now if you will excuse me, I have to brief the men."

At the king's nod, Terrence left his master's chambers in the royal manse and headed for the soldiers' barracks. The large building shared by all Drondos's soldiers was adjacent to Ivan's manse, so it was a short walk. The men had already been briefed; Terrence simply could not stand being in Ivan's presence. The group of men he'd selected were not happy about the mission, but the need to feed their families outweighed the fear of any consequences of their actions.

When Terrence reached the meeting chamber in the barracks, all his top men were gathered, awaiting final word from King Ivan. Immediately upon his walking in the door, before he had even closed it behind him, General Grant said, "So, the old fool intends to proceed?"—more a statement than a question.

Grant was a grizzled old veteran with his white hair and his square jaw. The man had massive shoulders and was easily the strongest soldier in Drondos despite his age, probably sixty years or better; he never would admit the exact number. Terrence loved the true old man and all his wisdom.

"Yes," Terrence replied simply.

There was nothing more to say. The mission had previously been planned meticulously with no room for error, although the shared feeling in the room was simple to puzzle out. Even if they succeeded, which they definitely would, the aftermath would be bloody and there would be a reckoning.

"Smith, I need you to continue your reconnaissance on Altheia and the prince," he said to his scout.

Stanley Smith was gangly but fit and incredibly adept at

living quietly in the thick-wooded areas of the island. The scout always had strong information.

"If Normin takes a shit that seems odd, I want to know. That goes double for after the raid: I want to know immediately if he intends to mobilize troops. And this Lucid business, him sneaking around alone at night, is worth checking into. Try to get closer. I'd like to know what he's up to," Terrence finished.

Smith nodded, looked down at his hands clasped together on the table, and took a deep breath.

"Is everyone clear on the mission?" Terrence asked of his men. There were nods of agreement accompanied by grim faces, as if Terrence were asking these men to attack their ancestors themselves—and he was.

CHAPTER 7

L ucid paced in his chambers as he waited on Jon. He was getting older now and considered himself to be somewhat of an adult making his own decisions. Yet lately it seemed the choices he made had a much larger effect, not just on him and Jon but also on the entire city—and beyond. The future seemed to spiral out of control on his watch when he thought too many steps ahead. One thing was clear: change was coming.

He could feel it, sense it, and even smell it. Most likely it was the stink of his infectious decisions. What he and Jon had planned for that evening could very well start a war, never mind what would happen if the gvorlocks found him in their village. He could not help himself; he was profoundly curious about the girl and these gvorlocks, as they called themselves.

Lucid had learned much about their language and customs from his father's tome yet oddly had learned nothing about their normal-looking guests wandering about their village.

Jon's knock at the door startled Lucid out of his reverie. He immediately opened the door to admit his friends.

"You know I love you guys for this. I would never ask you to do something for which the repercussions might get you hurt or killed. But you know what is at stake: one of our brothers, a missing piece of our lives that I, for one, am sick of hurting over. Each time I have gone to see him in the last several months, he has looked worse," Lucid told them, looking into their eyes with an expression so fierce that he could see their fear and nervousness melt away, replaced by determination and focus.

"Let's bring him home," Lucid said.

It was all he needed to say. The three of them stepped out into the night. The run to Drondos was a long one as Lucid knew very well, but the sun had descended below the waves and the day's heat faded quickly. Their feet ate up mile after mile of soft sand as they headed north toward their goal. Lucid had to take a break after an hour or so and walk for several minutes before they all caught their breaths enough to continue the run down the beach to the other side of the island.

Lucid ran hard, feeling the sweat soak into his clothes. The prince looked around and noticed his friends were feeling much the same. After what felt an eternity, he spotted the dark rooftops and spotty lights of Drondos. Lucid stopped a safe distance away and allowed them all to rest and begin to breathe normally.

"I assume you know where his house is?" Daryl asked as they began to walk up the hill just off the beach that overlooked the main courtyard.

"Of course. Percy's drunk ass should be at Salty's, so no problem." Lucid crouched and told them, "We will run straight to the beach on the way out, so stay with me. No more talking."

Daryl and Jon both nodded. Lucid rose. They all headed toward the outer wall of the city. Long trees stacked horizontally ten feet high and lashed together formed the barrier, so the climb over it was easy. As soon as their feet touched down, they all froze.

"Hey! What are you doing?" shouted a guard.

He was tall and stout, armored with worked leather and carrying a long sword, which he drew as he advanced. Lucid and Daryl froze for reasons of their own.

The first thing that came to Lucid's mind, his being the prince, was *We cannot kill anyone here.* He really did not want to start a war or endanger his people. The prince cared deeply for the citizens of Altheia and had come to love many of them as his own family.

Daryl was not a fighter. He'd received the same training as all the boys in Altheia, plus a special style taught only to healers, but fighting was never his true focus. He was meant to heal people, not hurt them. He looked sick as Lucid glanced toward him.

Jon, however, did not hesitate for even an instant. He must have known what was at stake. Whether Jon acted in defense of his prince, or to avoid being imprisoned, or simply because he would stop at nothing to see Russell back in Altheia mattered not. His form was beautiful, amazing actually, so much so that it puzzled Lucid. Before Lucid had enough time to draw a breath, Jon drew and punched two feet of long sword right through the guard's heart. The poor fool did not even have time to raise his blade in defense. The man looked down at the metal and gasped, his eyes going wide in shock. Jon withdrew his blade quickly, and the man dropped.

"Whoa," Lucid and Daryl breathed out simultaneously.

Jon wiped his sword on the dead man's tunic and sheathed it, bending to grab the corpse. "Help me with this," he said.

Daryl and Lucid moved to help drag the man away from the small clearing along the inside of the outer wall and into a dark alley. After rounding one corner, they found themselves face-to-face with a man dressed in dark colors with what looked like a dead dog slung over his shoulder.

He said he had seen nothing if the same was true for them, and he crept right past with only the slightest glance at each of them. Lucid swore he spotted the faintest half smile on the man's face and thought it odd, but he had other concerns at the moment.

Lucid had Jon drop their dead man in a pile of trash in the alley, and then they all continued their journey. They crossed a hard-packed dirt road lined with small huts and finally approached Percy's house. Lucid, spotting the trail of blood leading to the medium-sized hut with sturdy beams and a thatched roof, glanced to Daryl and Jon, who looked just as worried as he.

"Nice for Drondos standards and much nicer than any of the other shacks on the street. Percy must have gotten a good deal to abandon his town and turn his back on his people," Jon mentioned quietly, referring to the sturdy home, as Lucid tried to get a look into the tiny window that sat at the top of the front door.

Only a single candle burned, and the house was silent. Lucid gestured for Daryl and Jon to stay quiet as they entered. When Lucid opened the door and saw the face of his friend sitting at the table with an empty bottle, cup still in his hands, it was all he could do not to burst into tears, go into a rage, break everything, and burn Percy's piece of shit house to the ground.

Easily down fifty pounds, Russell looked so thin that it hurt. Both his eyes were almost completely swollen shut. One leaked blood down his cheek. Lucid could also see dried blood on the side of Russell's face from some wound on the top of his head, the source hidden by his long, dark hair. The little that could be seen of Russell's eyes was glassy as he stared at the empty cup in front of him. When Russell saw his friends, he smiled a bloody smile and slurred, "Hey, boys!" waving his arms drunkenly.

"What the fuck happened? Your face. Russell, are you okay?" Lucid said, approaching Russell like a cornered deer.

"Fine, fine," he said, looking down at his cup, blood spraying from his lips as he spoke. "Got a little out of hand ..." He paused and tried to take a sip from his cup. When he realized it was empty, he rose to his feet so quickly that Lucid tensed as Russell screamed, "*He would have killed me!*" He sank back down in his chair and said much more quietly, slurring every word, "I saw it in his eyes. He would rather be rid of me than bloody his knuckles every night."

Lucid, continuing to approach slowly, said, "That's why we are all here right now. I have gotten permission from my father to take you back to Altheia, to get you away from Percy so you can live a normal life."

Russell stared at him for a long time, his jaw clenching and unclenching. "You realize," Russell slurred, "what that … Percy … Ivan …" He paused and took a breath. "Consequences," he finally managed.

Lucid shook his head. "Fuck the consequences," he said, his voice getting louder. "Let's go, now!"

Russell staggered to his feet like a drunken toddler who had just gotten into trouble. He grabbed his sword belt off the chair next to him. His fingers failing him, he finally got it strapped it around his waist. He took a deep breath to steady himself. When he finally met Lucid's eyes again, he saw that they were hard and determined.

"Please don't let him kill me," Russell said as he started toward the door.

"I won't let him get anywhere near you. And neither will Father," Lucid assured his friend.

It took Russell a moment in his current state, but the weight of those words finally dawned on him, and he visibly relaxed. He would be well protected.

Daryl and Jon stepped out first to scout, looking up and down the street and listening for the slightest noise. Lucid gave Russell a cup of water and had him stretch a bit as had been drilled into all of them as boys. Finally Russell got his feet under him, and he and Lucid followed Daryl and Jon, but at a staggered run, lagging behind the others before they even reached the beach. When they arrived, Lucid allowed for a small break so they could catch their breath.

Russell immediately bent over and vomited the dark wine he had been drinking. Lucid looked at his shadowed friend as the liquid poured out of him, appearing black in the darkness of night as the waves crashed heavily behind them, signaling high tide. Despite their slight holdup, the timing was perfect. As Russell stood up to catch a few ragged breaths, he smiled and nodded. "Much better now," he said with a thumbs-up.

Lucid knew the run would be easier on his friend from here on out with his stomach now emptied of Percy's wine. As his breathing steadied, he looked over the condition of his friends.

"You guys ready?" the prince asked. They all nodded. Lucid took off south down the beach, toward Altheia.

Before they'd even taken five steps, Lucid heard an extremely ragged and wet inhalation from just beyond the tree line. He was clearly the only one who'd heard it. He stopped, and the boys following crashed into him. They all went down in a tumble. Then there was another wet, raspy inhalation, closer this time. Lucid sat up and heard a faint voice calling.

"Help," it said, just above a whisper.

Lucid rose to his feet slowly and quietly crept toward the tree line, his friends following silently. Where the sand ended and the dirt began, Lucid spotted a glimmer of moonlight illuminating a small, dark pool and a shadow resting directly in the center. It was a man, he realized, lying in what looked to be entirely too much blood with a hand raised straight toward the sky.

"Help," the man rasped again.

Taking another step forward, Lucid got a better look at

the familiar-looking man dying on the ground. They had just come across this man earlier, carrying a dead dog. He was clad mostly in black with a veil hanging loose about his throat. He was pale, sweating, and struggling to keep his eyes from rolling back into his head. He was not a particularly large man, but he stank of skill and death. Whether it was because he was dying remained to be seen.

"I know you!" Russell shouted at the clearly soon-to-be corpse, startling everyone.

The man snapped his head around, his eyes looking at each one in turn, lingering on Lucid for and instant and then settling on Russell. The man coughed a bloody spray and said one more time before he passed out, "Help me."

When Lucid looked over at his friend, bloody tears were streaming down his anger-filled face. Russell said, "He saved my life tonight. He cowed Percy to abandon the beating he was giving me. He was just passing by—saw a boy in trouble and did something." Russell's voice was growing louder as he spoke. "I don't know this man, but he was willing to stand up for me when no one else in Drondos would—a fucking stranger. And now look at him! That's how the world is, you know. This is what happens to good people." Russell approached the near-dead man and inspected him slightly before attempting to hoist him up. He failed in his mission, falling to the dirt.

"Russell," Lucid said carefully as he approached, "we did not account for this. If we attempt to save this man, we will never make it back before sunrise, and that is what I promised my father: in and out in the cover of darkness. One night, one chance, was all I was given. Forget my father's wrath. If Percy is to come home early and discover you missing …" He left the rest unsaid.

"I don't give a shit. Help me lift him or I am not leaving," Russell said firmly.

Lucid cursed and ran over to help his friend. Jon and Daryl followed suit. After looking the man over, Daryl disappeared into the woods for a few minutes. When he returned, he was dragging a makeshift sled made from small branches woven together. It was not ideal, but it was something. Soon it seemed the healer had the man bandaged as best as possible with their sleeves and any spare cloth available. Lucid and Jon loaded and secured the man with lashing made from palm leaves and began their long run home.

"You know there is a chance with his wounds that he will be dead by the time we get back," Lucid told Russell as they ran.

Russell took a glance back at the man, then back to the path ahead, and said, "He will live."

Hours later, by the time Altheia came into view, the sun was beginning to brighten the sky. Lucid stopped to rest one last time, checking on the man, who was now barely breathing and still unconscious, then pushed hard to finish the trek. Lucid stood guard with Jon, scanning their surroundings, as Daryl and Russell deposited the man as carefully as possible onto the bed in the royal fishing hut on West Beach. No one used it anymore except Lucid and Jon, so the prince figured the stranger would be safe here. Daryl volunteered to stay with him, dressing the wounds and stitching him up. Russell said he would stay as well, but Lucid shook his head.

"Too dangerous. You will stay in my chambers until all this settles down and passes. No one will ever find you there," Lucid told him. Russell was reluctant to leave the man until Daryl assured him he would live.

"He may never walk again—the knife slid right next to

his spine—but he will live," the healer said. Russell nodded, clearly satisfied.

"Go to my chambers and get some rest," Lucid told him.

"You're not coming?" Russell asked. Lucid shook his head.

"Have to see my father first and tell him everything went according to plan."

Lucid glanced at the injured man as Russell asked, "What will you tell the king about him?"

Lucid stared a few moments. "Nothing," he said, looking at the other boys in turn. "That goes for all of you. As far as this world is concerned, he died on that beach."

CHAPTER 8

Brynn awoke as the sun came streaming into her window, her cat Daisy curled up next to her face hogging her pillow. Brynn wrapped herself tight in her blankets and rose, shuffling toward her wardrobe. She chose two outfits, one for school and one for the formal evening meal. She liked to be prepared and absolutely loved clothes.

She always took special care to rise early so she could sit in and listen to the morning meeting with her father and the councillors. She was only eleven but was a princess, so the high-ranking members of the community always looked the other way at her ritual intrusion. After several years of this, her father had honored her with the responsibility of keeping Altheia's citizen count and doing the census.

"If you're going to be here every day, then you will have to work like everyone else," Normin had told her the day he handed her a large stack of folders.

Brynn did not mind and even found she enjoyed the task. It helped her to stay unnoticed as she sat among the highest-ranking members of the community, and she relished the information and gossip the old men produced. She thought herself the most informed on current events around town and liked that the best.

As Brynn dressed, Ella entered to help her and began her morning routine. "Good morning, Princess," the girl greeted. Brynn smiled, giving her a small wave.

After Brynn was presentable, she headed toward the council

chambers, yet on her way she spotted her older brother on his way out, stinky, filthy, and with spots of blood on his tunic. His sleeves were missing as well. The sight of him ragged and filthy brought back a memory of when she'd found him after he'd fallen out of a tree. He'd looked much the same then, only now all his limbs seemed intact. He saw her looking and placed a finger to his lips.

"Are you hurt?" she asked, despite her agreement to stay quiet. It was still her big brother.

He shook his head and smiled. "I'm fine, Sis," he said as he approached and planted a stinky kiss on her forehead.

That melted away all her concerns. She smiled, pivoted, and headed for the royal council chambers. As usual, she was the first to enter, so she had the serving man add some logs and stoke the fire in the hearth. Then she began helping to set out the councillors' breakfast and drinks. The servants relished the help and absolutely loved her for it, but for her it was nothing, just something to occupy her time until everyone arrived.

When the high-ranking members and elders of the council had all filed in and began to eat, the sound of utensils on plates, of drinks being poured, and of blissful chewing was the only noise.

Then finally her father said, "Lucid's mission to retrieve Percy's boy from Drondos was a success. Russell is officially a protected citizen of Altheia."

He paused, apparently to let that settle in, before he continued. The fact that he gave credit to Lucid and let him handle everything told Brynn much. It appeared to Brynn, at least in her father's eyes, that Lucid was officially a man.

"As I briefed you before, every detail was meticulously planned, and they had a clean getaway. As promised, it was accomplished in the span of one night, using darkness to hide.

For all our sister city will know, Russell simply disappeared. If God is with us, Percy will not even notice or else will be grateful to be rid of his burden," King Normin finished.

It was the leader of the scholars who responded: "You are not worried about retaliation if Drondos were to find out? A dead guard is no small thing. No one has ever killed between cities before. Ivan will not take it well. Or what if Percy actually does care and wants his punching bag returned?" asked Master Wyndell.

He was an ancient man, stooped and frail with a receding hairline of white hair and with a beard of ridiculous length, yet he was easily the smartest man in Altheia. He maintained the curriculum for the schooling. Brynn did not fail to notice how attentive her father was when the old man spoke.

"That was indeed my thought as well, yet Percy is not the one to be feared. If this grabs the attention of Ivan, then he may seek to retaliate. Word is, his troop numbers are growing at an alarming rate. Any suggestions as to why or how? We are an older city, and we had many times their numbers only thirty years ago," the king said to the room.

"I believe I have determined the cause of growth," said Master Blake.

George Blake was the leader of the craftsmen and always had his ears open for information. Absolutely everyone needed something built or fixed at some point. Brynn knew that the man was never shy about conversation. Plus, people came from all over the city simply to lay eyes on his beautiful and brilliant daughter, Alisha.

Normin rolled his eyes. "I have heard your opinion, George, and I just do not think it plausible. Ivan is a wretched man, but even he could not possibly consider enslaving his own people."

The master craftsman just shook his head, returning to the

last of his breakfast. George was never one to argue with his king.

Normin caught the move and added, "All right, keep your ears open and maybe inquire quietly for more information, then come back with some firm evidence. I don't think it's possible, but it never hurts to be sure."

George smiled and bowed his head. "Of course, my lord."

Normin sat up and drained his orange juice. "Is there anything else?" he asked, indicating a close to the meeting.

Brynn left the council chambers to find Catrina, her best friend. She hugged her tightly. The girls began their daily walk to the adjacent school of Altheia. Cat was the daughter of the city's clothing maker. Her mother, Rebecca, could weave the most beautiful and lightest summer dresses and also the strongest, most flexible armor. Everyone bought her wares, and that included the royal family.

"How did it go this morning?" Cat asked Brynn as they walked.

Brynn shook her head. "Just normal, boring business. Except …" She looked at Cat with a mischievous grin. The girl stopped and grabbed her arm.

"What? What is it?" Cat asked anxiously.

Brynn knew well how much the girl wished she could be in there with them; she loved nothing more than gossip. "Lucid got Russell back," she told her in a whisper. Catrina's eyes went wide.

"Your brother is nuts," she said simply as the girls began walking again. "You think he was able to accomplish it without causing trouble?" she asked Brynn, who nodded.

"Lucid is nothing if not good at sneaking around," she said. They both laughed.

"I wonder how it went," Cat said, causing Brynn's mind to

flash to the picture of her brother dirty and bloody as he was just a little bit earlier.

She smiled. "Now that I think about it, I don't think he can do it without causing trouble. He *is* nuts," Brynn said. Both girls laughed.

CHAPTER 9

Normin sat with his wife in the royal dining hall. As busy as the couple were with their separate responsibilities in running the kingdom, they never failed to meet every night to dine together. Their long schedules never permitted them to eat at a decent hour, and tonight their dinnertime was late as usual. Normin did not mind though; the bulk of the servants and petitioners had long since retired at that time of night, and it allowed the two their privacy.

"Lucid's been spotted sneaking around at night," Alice told her husband as they were finishing their dessert. Normin wiped his mouth with his thick cotton napkin and sat back, eyeing his wife wearily.

"Are you worried?" he asked.

The king had to suppress the smile threatening to break free. His wife, Alice, was just as stunning sitting there now as she'd ever been. She was a stubborn woman, fierce and impossible to argue with, especially with her beauty as a weapon. But she absolutely loved her children and constantly "overmothered" them, as Lucid liked to say. Although Brynn did not seem to mind. The youngest was Alice's only girl, and the poor thing loved all the attention her mother smothered her with—for now.

"I am a mother. Of course I am worried. As good as he is, Jake still spots him all over the place. Need I remind you what happened to Michael?" she asked. Normin only smiled.

"Is that amusing to you?" she asked angrily.

"First it is I who worries over our son, and now it is you.

Life's little circles," he told her, chuckling. "Our children are strong, dear, physically and mentally. Our training prepares our people to push the boundaries of body and mind. Now that Lucid is finished with his schooling, he should have no problem with the burdens of the real world. He doesn't actually have to do anything for years; that is why I am giving him his space. My father gave me that, and his father gave him the same. Lucid needs time to live and enjoy life. He needs to know what he is and what he is protecting and why. He has already built many positive relationships, like his smith friend. I want him to do so for all our people," Normin told the queen confidently.

The worried look on Alice's face did not ease at his words. "I am just being silly, I know, but he is my only son, and part of the problem is letting go. He will be a man soon, expected to marry, father a child, and rule a kingdom," she said.

Normin leaned forward, looking into his wife's beautiful brown eyes. "I understand, Alice, but my faith in our son outweighs any doubt I may have. Plus, I do not plan on leaving him the throne just yet," he said with a wink.

Alice smiled. "All the same, I'd like to go for a walk if that is okay with you," she said.

Normin frowned. "Why you like going to that dirty tower and climbing all those steps I will never understand," he said.

"Yes you do," she replied.

"The view," the two said in unison. Alice rose and kissed her husband.

The grain silo was the highest structure on the island, and Normin was very familiar with his lover's obsession with the beautiful, unmatched views from the top room of the tower. He knew it was not all about the view though. She had farmed all her life before Normin took her as his wife, and he knew there was something comforting about the smell of grain and being in a place where she had put in so much hard work as a younger woman. As he watched his wife leave, he finally let the smile reach his lips. He was lucky to have such an amazing queen and wife who was such a great mother to his children.

As Alice climbed the steps of the tower, the all too familiar ache in her legs began, and a thin sheen of sweat covered her cheeks. It was midsummer and always brutally hot in those months, even after the sun went down, as was the case now. She did not mind, however. The little bit of stiffness and the sore muscles the morning after her visits were a welcome reminder that even after more than forty years, her body was still strong and toned. She paused a moment to catch her breath and wipe her glistening face. The smell of grain was always a wonderful and painful reminder of her father's death.

She was but a child when he died, but the ache of losing the man she idealized was still there, if not a little more faint. Normin, a skinny, cocky boy, had saved her and brought her up what seemed like a lifetime ago. Now here she was, thinking of her own son becoming a man.

Life's little circles, she thought.

Just then she could have sworn she heard scuffles of boots on stone. Alice held her breath, trying to be as silent as death as she paused on the stairs to listen.

It's nothing, the wind, she thought as she began climbing again. She was so high on the stairway, she convinced herself there was no way she could hear noise from the ground floor.

Lucid needed no more overmothering from her. Normin was right as usual; her son was intelligent, strong, and brave, perhaps too much so. His boldness still frightened her at times, but she also knew him to be more than capable of positive decision-making. It did not hurt that Jake had told her Lucid was the best fighter in the city, with the exception of Jon of course. "Possibly better than Normin," he had said. Still, it was painful to let go fully of her oldest child. It reminded her of the day he had asked her to stop eating breakfast with him every morning. She had cried then and now found the same tears clouding her sight.

When she finally reached the top of the stairs, Alice could immediately feel her clenching muscles relax as the sea breeze coming in from the open window touched her glistening skin. There was something special about the top of the grain silo. It had always been her place of peace, contemplation, and relaxation, ever since she was a girl.

As she approached the large open window on the eastern edge of the room, she closed her eyes and breathed deep of the sea air. The smell of salt always seemed stronger up here. The silo was just outside the LD on the northwest corner, giving her an amazing view, upon opening her eyes, of the three standing monuments of Altheia and the city surrounding. The cathedral on her right was quiet, prayers long finished for the day, and its bell tower on top dark and quiet. The school adjacent to it looked much the same, its huge wooden double doors closed for the night. But the palace and the LD shone from that height like flickering stars or interspersed candles burning in windows. In front, the statue of King Jerald stood tall in the night, and around his feet were perfect rows of buildings and roads. Alice turned to her right and looked at the dark woods, only able to make out the tops of trees against the moonlight, gray cliffs poking their heads up in the distance as if to say hello.

The view of the tower was so familiar to Alice that she could draw it in her mind at any time. If she went blind that very moment, the sight of her kingdom from the top of that tower would be burned into her mind forever. With the slightest glance behind her, though, she could tell something wasn't right. The grain housed in the tower was gravity fed, and someone at the bottom had opened the chute and was emptying the kingdom's stores. This action immediately struck her as odd, as it was so late in the evening.

Why would Bruce be moving grain now? she thought. As she looked out the window and down, she could just barely make out figures. The men, wearing all black it seemed, as they looked like nothing more than ants at this height, were loading small carts.

The grain! Alice thought. *They are stealing our food!*

As the realization dawned on her, she felt like she was floating above herself while running toward the stairs as fast as her swift legs could carry her. When the queen began her quick and fearful descent, taking the steps two and three at a time, it quickly became apparent to her that the silo was burning.

The smoke drifting up the stairs began choking her and obscuring her view just a few flights from the top. By the time she was near to the bottom floor, her eyes stung. It was very difficult to see where she was going. She began coughing sporadically and pulled her sleeve over her face in a pathetic attempt to block the smoke. Just as Alice thought she might die in that tower, her feet fell hard on the bottom floor, tripping her, and she went sprawling to the ground.

She immediately rose and began to run for the exit when a large black shape, almost invisible in the smoke, stepped out in front of her. It was one of the black-clad men she had seen from the top of the tower. Before she even realized what was happening, she felt cold steel slide into her body, accompanied by the most mind-altering pain she could have ever imagined. Shock and confusion struck her as she looked down at the hilt of the sword and the hand gripping it. She looked up, took a shaky breath, and collapsed.

As Normin sat contemplating his next move with Drondos, he could not help but think of the *Hope*. Inder seemed determined that it was ready for longer journeys, exploration even. But where? And why? They had an almost perfect life here on this island. Some of Normin's ancestors might wonder why in the world they would leave this place. The most distant relatives may even curse him for attempting such a thing.

He looked around himself at the opulent dining room in which he sat, the same room his ancestors had carved directly from Jacques Ravine. It certainly would not be permanent; Blysse was his home. No matter how many worlds he explored, he could always return home. He was startled from his thoughts as a light from the window grew very bright, as if someone had just walked into a dark room holding a lit candle.

He rose slowly, walked toward the brightening window, and screamed, "*No!*"

He bolted for the door and ran hard for the exit, ignoring the shouts at his back. When he arrived at the bottom of the tower, he ran headlong for the crowd that had gathered, thinking to barrel his way in and save his love, but someone stopped him. People were all around him like a wall and he could not move, could not power his way to her. People were shouting all around him. Someone was screaming Alice's name loudly and violently, attempting to get her to answer, Normin supposed.

But he knew; he felt it. She was at the top when the fire started, and now she was dead, his beautiful, beloved wife, the only woman he had ever loved. His eyes stung and his face was soaked. It was not until his eyes finally focused on Inder, who was shaking him and asking if he was okay, that he realized everyone was silently staring at their king, and he was the only one screaming.

CHAPTER 10

L ya awoke to a magnificent blue sky. Beautifully shaped clouds floated by as she realized she was lying on her back. When she stood up, she noticed her surroundings. It was a place beyond comprehension. Unmatched beauty surrounded her and almost brought her to tears.

She was standing at the center of what could modestly be called a shrine of some sort. Seven exquisite statues of incredible size and detail stood in silent vigil all around her. She was standing on smooth stone with intricately painted runes in odd yet familiar patterns. As she turned to admire the towering men carved of stone, she noticed each. One man stood in full battle regalia with a sword pointed straight at the sky. The look of fierceness on his face was terrible to behold. Another man, ancient-looking with a long, sweeping beard and a half-bald head, was holding a huge book in one hand and reaching toward the sky with the other. Just as Lya realized all the statues were reaching skyward, she saw a man standing just a few feet in front of her. At this point she was not sure what she was seeing, but she was almost positive this was a dream.

"Yes, Lya, this is a dream. But that means nothing. Dreams are just as real as your shackles," the man said.

He was a tall, cadaverous-looking creature. Pale skin stretched over his bones, yet something comforting drew Lya to take a step toward him as if he were an old friend she missed dearly, yet she had no clue who he was. She lifted her hands and was met with the familiar clank and irritating chafing of her bracelets.

"Who are you?" she asked. "How do you know my name? How did you know of my shackles?"

"I know everything about you, Lya, and your parents and their parents before them. I watched as you took your first steps, just as I was watching when Tr'vastious kicked your face. I was watching when your mother and father died. I watched as your ancestors were taken, driven into slavery by brutes with the power to quench your energy. None of that matters now. There is a war coming, ultimate destruction of our people. You *must* survive. Run, escape, get away while you can, and help the enemies of your enemies. Now."

Lya awoke on her straw cot, her head pounding. She lay there staring at the thatching of her hut and thinking of the dream. It was so real, and this time it was as if she had just been there. For once she remembered absolutely every tiny detail. She was not sure if it was the power and realism of her dream, or the fact that she'd remembered it for the first time, or her fear that Tr'vastious would brutalize her more, but she made her decision that very moment as she lay in the darkness. In her mind, it was absolutely final.

She would wait for Lucid to return and make him take her away. That was her best hope as she had no clue where this other place was, where he came from, or how to find it. She had lived almost her entire life in this village, only vaguely remembering coming here with her parents from … she had no idea from where. Yet it was very clear to her that now was the time to make her move.

A week went by, then two. She was just beginning to think she might never see him again, when one day she had another dream of the thin man at the shrine. He said nothing this time and simply pointed over her shoulder. When she awoke, somehow she knew it was up to her. It could not have been simply chance that brought a handsome stranger here at the exact moment when her dreams would become more; it was fate.

For many reasons, she had never considered escaping before. First and foremost, it had never been an option as she honestly thought they were alone here. Lya could have done this years ago. She could have been planning since her parents died and been much more prepared, yet only with the elderly man's words and with meeting Lucid, learning of his people, had she found the courage.

One evening when she awoke and began her duties, she started to form a plan and kept a watchful eye on Kinetrius. She wanted to be certain of every move the sentry made for the night, what route he walked, and which sections of the village he patrolled more often. After three nights of watching, she assumed she was ready.

When Tr'vastious woke the slaves on the fourth evening, Lya rose quickly. The world seemed a dark, faraway place. As her duties flew by with her mind racing, the time finally came. This was it; the culmination of all her planning had led her to this moment. It was either make it or die trying. After playing over the meeting with Lucid in her mind a hundred times, she was sure of her direction of travel. She had to assume his and Jon's path was fairly straightforward and that if she went far enough, surely she would find it.

As soon as she saw Tr'vastious enter the woods for the nightly hunt, she started walking, slowly at first so as not to arouse any suspicion, then more briskly as she glanced back over her shoulder one more time. Then, dropping her fruit basket and hiking her dress, she ran. She ran faster than she ever had, dodging fallen logs. Holding her hand in front of her face did not seem to help as the branches still whipped at her. Soon she was breathing hard, the sweat pouring down her face and running into her eyes, blurring her vision. Still she ran, trusting in her choice of direction and praying to the gods she would survive this night.

After some time she stopped to breathe for just a minute, inhaling huge gasps of air. She pulled the small waterskin from her pouch and drank sparingly. As she rested, she noticed a very narrow walkway of sorts where the brush and trees seemed just clear enough for one small person to walk through. Curious as to what may have made this path and coming to the conclusion that Lucid surely must have made it, she tucked her waterskin away and began running again.

Hours passed as Lya tried to follow the trail that disappeared and reappeared throughout the woods. Her running had slowed significantly, and her legs and back burned with the strain, yet still she persisted. It was either run forward or go back and die. The choice was simple for her to make. But as she jogged through the woods, gasping for air and struggling to keep from falling, she wondered if she had made the right decision.

How far can it be? she thought as she stopped again for felt like the hundredth time to get some air. It seemed as if she had been running for days. As she breathed, she heard nothing, absolutely nothing, not even the usually ever-present noise of the insects. As she realized this, the hair on her neck and arms stood up and she shivered even though she was dripping with sweat.

Lya glanced around slowly and quieted her breathing as much as her exhausted lungs would allow her. About a dozen yards away she spotted a small, dim light among the brush.

She stared, and as she did so, the light shifted and she spotted two, low to the ground and attached at the head, of the biggest jaguars she had ever seen.

She began shaking and thought her heart would simply stop. It thundered in her chest. Tears streamed down her cheeks as she just sat, or had she fallen? She did not know, but she felt the cool, damp leaves under her hands and the soft dirt beneath. She had no weapon, and even if she had, the jaguar would still kill her. She felt an overwhelming sadness, so deep she thought it might consume her.

Not because her life was over and not for the jaguar that would shortly tear her to pieces. That would be a quicker and more merciful end than Tr'vastious would grant her. She was heartbroken because she had failed the kindly man from her dreams. But also she would never see Lucid again, never find out exactly what unseen force had drawn her to him.

As she cried, head down in her hands, she felt a cold and wet muzzle nudge her forehead. She looked up quickly to see the jaguar inches from her face. She gasped sharply and drew her hand to cover her mouth, but the cat only smelled her fingers. When it did, she very slowly drew her hand to the jaguar's fur at the shoulder. It was warm and unbelievably soft. The cat licked at her face, and she laughed. Its tongue was rough and dry. She asked softly, "What is happening?"

The big cat's only reply was to plop down at her feet and stretch out, yawning. Lya was amazed. She shook her head once and pinched her leg just to make sure this was real. She still expected the thing to get up and eat her at any moment, but she took the blessing for what it was and said a quiet prayer to the gods.

She sat back, resting on her elbows and admiring the beautiful creature for a time. Then its head popped up, and it growled wickedly. She was so scared, she got to her feet abruptly. The moment she did so, a spear took the majestic animal in the side of the neck, and it collapsed with a horrifying gurgle.

Tr'vastious came into view, and Lya realized her peril too late. She started to run, but a huge rock struck her in the back and she fell, the pain blossoming up her spine. In an instant, he was on her, raining savage blows that began around her midsection and eventually rose higher. Soon her eyes and cheeks were swollen and bloody. After what felt an eternity of vicious punches and kicks, she mercifully fell unconscious.

CHAPTER 11

As Terrence and his band of raiders led the pack of slave-pulled carts, all he could think about was the woman, well-dressed and beautiful, obviously some high-ranking member of the community. He had retched heavily after the deed, having never killed a woman before. It sickened him still to think about it. He would never ask any of his men to do something so stupid, so he had put torch to tower with his own hands, and for that reason he had come face-to-face with the woman.

The king should have given this assignment to Luke, he thought.

Still, Ivan had been very clear when he told Terrence, "Absolutely no witnesses."

In that adrenaline-fueled, frantic moment, Terrence reached the realization that it was either him or her.

After hours of trekking, they were about halfway back, leading the carts through a small game trail, when one slave went stumbling and fell, causing the cart he was pulling to come to an abrupt halt. Terrence cursed and went to see what the problem was. When he reached the large slave, the man launched himself at Terrence, grabbing for his sword.

The commander stepped aside easily and put the slave on his back, blade at his throat, and immediately the slave relented, hands held up in submission. It all happened so fast, but in the silence that followed, Terrence heard small, quick strides running away. It was too late; the distraction had served its purpose, and there was now an escaped slave running toward Altheia. He plunged his blade in the man's throat, and when his lover, or so Terrence assumed, came rushing forward screaming, he silenced her as well, to his horror making it two women in one night.

He was breathing hard, and the world spun. He was just so angry all this had happened under his command, on his first actual danger-filled mission, that he could not help himself. He cursed and drove the slaves harder. With a line of corpses at his back, the easily noticeable trail left by the small army, and an escaped slave on the loose, time was limited. Surely Normin would send someone after them, maybe an army of his own.

It was midmorning by the time Drondos came into view. Relief washed over Terrence as they pushed hard through the last few miles. When the caravan entered the main gate, Mason Grant hailed Terrence and fell in beside him.

"Was the fire really necessary?" he said in a low tone. "It's one thing to steal their food, but this? They will retaliate. I would bet anything on that," Grant said.

"Orders" was Terrence's only response.

"Fucking idiot," Mason said under his breath.

Terrence ignored the insult, mostly because he could not disagree.

"Ivan won't be happy when he hears of the boy who escaped," Mason added.

Terrence scowled but said nothing. How had it come to this? The plan to steal food out of the mouths of Altheians to feed it to slaves Ivan intended to use to wipe out Altheia and take over the city was beyond insane. Ivan was going to get himself killed, and his city along with him.

When the king and Terrence were boys, there had been peace between the cities, each going about their business without the slightest thought of the other. Drondos had been prosperous then with plentiful food and the merchant district thriving.

Anything you could possibly need or want was displayed in the long avenue of shops and merchant tents. That was until fat ass took the throne and decreed all the craftsmen now worked for him and would be doing nothing but making weapons. Pots, pans, knives, and all other sorts of everyday items became very hard to get over the years.

Then it was the boys. Ivan decreed every boy who reached the age of twelve would be taken into the barracks and trained, living and fighting among other boys and allowed only limited interactions with their families. The Carters had fought this, unwilling to simply give away their son to be brutalized and turned into a soldier. William had refused the king. Ivan had him killed with haste. Then Mrs. Carter died mysteriously. And finally the boy died.

Terrence remembered the time when Ivan's father, Wayne, was still alive. Ivan seemed a completely normal kid. They swam together, grilling fish on the beach. They chased the women in the same circle of courtesans. Ivan smiled often and laughed loudly, unashamed of his thick-set body and uncomely features.

When Wayne died, Ivan changed, slowly at first, just keeping to himself and not going out very often. After that a more pronounced change was noticed by all. He often made harsh decrees, and his punishments were vicious and brutally unnecessary. He caught one man stealing a sword from his armory and had him tortured publicly. It lasted a fortnight. Then Terrence had stumbled upon him in his chambers, blood-drenched from fingers to elbows, dissecting what looked to be a human arm. Horrified, Terrence had excused himself quickly, but he still caught the wicked grin painted on Ivan's face. Ivan was the king, however, and his word was law.

This decision though, this raid on Altheia, was the first of its kind. Never before had either city so boldly stolen from the other. But the fire—the fire was a message directly to Normin; Terrence was sure of that. What he was not sure of was the possibility of Drondos winning an open war against Altheia. In fact, he was sure Altheia would win. That was most likely everyone else's thought as well.

Terrence waved the general off and headed straight for the royal manse. He was done with Ivan's brutal political games and did not wish to do anything else for that selfish pig.

"I'm done," he told the king when escorted into his chambers.

"That is good news! How much grain did we get?" the king asked excitedly.

"You misunderstand me, sir. *I* am done. I officially retire as first commander," he told Ivan.

The king narrowed his eyes. "Why?" he asked simply, suspicion in his tone. Luke stepped from the shadows just one pace, as if Terrence did not already know he was there.

"I have reached the age where I cannot physically do what needs to be done, regretfully," the commander said.

Ivan frowned and said, "Come on, old friend, you just had the most successful mission in our city's history. This story will be written and will be retold for centuries. You are a hero!"

Terrence just shrugged. "I appreciate you saying so, but again I must retire. Digner is more than capable enough to take my position. I will instruct him on the details of his duties."

The king shook his head, but he just threw his hands up and said, "Fine, after what you accomplished, I can deny you nothing. Go find your peace, Terrence."

Terrence bowed to his king one last time and exited quickly.

Brynn awoke early that morning, knowing it was up to her

to be strong for her family. She knew the condition of her father and was determined not to be overwhelmed on such a sad day. She went through her normal morning routine, but as she left the palace and entered the courtyard, something felt wrong. Perhaps it was just her mind playing tricks on her, but the air felt unnaturally cool that morning.

Lost in her thoughts of her father and the oddly mild weather, she almost missed a small foot protruding from the bushes on the left of the pathway that led to the cathedral. It was so caked in dirt that it was hard to spot. It was even harder to imagine the person the foot was attached to.

She stopped and cleared her throat loudly. Nothing.

"Hello?" she said, but the only response was the small foot edging deeper into the bushes.

She bent over and peered in and was absolutely shocked at what she saw. Slivers of sunlight penetrated the foliage, and she could see him clearly, a boy, a young boy so dirty that she could not tell the color of his skin, which was so tight against his bones that she wondered how he had not starved to death. She gasped. He must have seen her looking because he bunched up like a hare getting ready to flee.

"Wait," she said before he bolted. "It's okay. I won't hurt you."

Still, the boy did not relax. His chest began heaving up and down, breathing in short but silent gasps.

"What's your name?" she asked, but still he just stared at her, too frightened to move or speak.

"Okay, my name is Brynn," she said as she sat down on the ground in front of the boy's hiding spot. "Are you okay? I don't think I've seen you before. Who are your parents?"

Still nothing.

She frowned and glanced up at the sun. "Are you hungry? I can get you food."

This finally rewarded her with the slightest relaxing of his muscles and a small, almost unnoticeable nod. She rose slowly and waved him on.

"Food! Great! You look starved half to death. Does nobody feed you?" Brynn asked.

He shook his head slightly, looking at his feet as he rose from the bushes, and moved toward her, but Brynn was not quite sure what he meant by that. She had been joking; surely someone took care of this boy, although looking at his condition, there was no way to tell.

She led him to her chambers, where she'd left her breakfast untouched. If they hurried, she knew they could make it before Ella cleaned up for the day. It may not be a hot meal, but at least the poor boy would not starve and they would avoid being spotted by anyone of authority. She felt the need to find out more about this boy.

As they walked, the boy behind her with his head bowed, she looked over her shoulder and asked, "How old are you?"

The boy just shrugged. That was very odd. If he did not want to share that information, that was one thing, but he seemed as if he did not know.

How is that possible? she wondered.

Brynn decided to save her questions for after the poor thing had eaten. Once they arrived safely to her chambers, she led him to the uneaten meal on her small dining table and gestured for him to sit. He slowly sat and looked longingly at the plate, but then glanced sharply up at her.

"It's okay. Eat," she said as gestured once again.

This earned her the first glimpse of a smile as he began stuffing the cold breakfast into his mouth so fast that she thought he would choke. In an instant, it was gone. The boy sat back and sighed.

"Any more?" he asked. Brynn shook her head sadly.

"Now that you know I am not going to hurt you, maybe you could tell me your name?" she asked hopefully.

He nodded and said, "My name is Coy."

Brynn smiled and asked, "And who are your parents, Coy? Surely they will be worried about you."

The boy just looked down at his empty plate. She was just about to ask another question when he said only one word, just above a whisper: "Dead."

Brynn's heart began beating a little harder and her throat tightened.

"How long?" she asked, trying to keep her thoughts together.

"Two nights," he said.

Brynn's mind raced, running over the most recent death reports she could think of. Had his parents died in the same fire as her mother? She did not think so, yet it might still have been too early to tell if everyone was accounted for. Brynn's sharp mind tried to make sense of it all. Why hide in the bushes instead of going to the king?

In Altheia, if a parent died, it was very sad, but nothing was done about the children because the surviving parent was expected to either continue raising the child or formally request royal help. If both parents died, however, her father, the king himself would choose who would raise the newly orphaned child. Had one slipped through the cracks? If that was the case, it certainly was surprising considering the circumstances, but other than her mother, the only death Brynn was sure of was that of an old tailor whose heart had stopped in his sleep. The man was ancient and had children and grandchildren, of whom Brynn was sure this boy was not one. As this information ran through her head, it slowly dawned on her. She struggled to keep calm.

"So I suppose I can assume you are from Drondos?" she asked. The boy nodded, eyes still down looking at the plate.

Suddenly a memory of the council meeting from the other morning struck like a slap to the face. Brynn's throat closed and, hard as she tried not to, she began to cry. Huge tears streamed down her cheeks as she looked at the slave boy across from her. It was true, Drondos kept slaves. And this one had escaped.

Coy looked at her curiously as her tears slowed. She wiped her face angrily as she stood. She sighed, glancing at the widow at the steadily rising sun.

"I have to go for now," she told him. He looked up at her with a frightened expression. She gestured to a cold and slightly used tub of bathwater. "Rinse the first layer of dirt off yourself, and get some rest," she finished, heading toward the door.

"Wait," he said as she reached the door. She stopped without turning around. She thought if she looked at the poor boy again, the tears would follow. Just when she was about to turn, she heard him say, "Thank you."

Brynn hurried down the palace steps and rushed past the school. She glanced up at the cathedral, getting closer, as the bells began to ring.

The opulent chamber the city gathered in was a huge dome carved of rock like most of the main buildings in Altheia. Four pillars rose skyward, touching a ceiling so high that Brynn could just barely make it out as she entered just in time for the ceremony. Benches surrounded the center in a circular pattern, rising with every row so that everyone could have a view. In the center of the pillars, where the royal family was gathered, lay her mother.

As she lined up next to Lucid and her father, she glanced at each of them. The king did not look well; he looked like a dead person standing there as Minister Tiller began last rites and prayers. His eyes stared at nothing, and he appeared to be distracted as Brynn was sure he heard none of the minister's speech. Glancing at Lucid, she thought that her brother looked much the same. Both men had shadows under their eyes, and their exhaustion was palpable. Brynn bowed her head and prayed for the men, for her mother, and for herself.

CHAPTER 12

Normin had not been the same. He was having trouble keeping his thoughts together. What kept running over in his mind was the many ways he could end that miserable old man's life. He could not stop thinking about revenge. Ivan had ripped away half of him, and he intended to repay the favor. Maybe he would literally cut him in half, although it would take several swings. Ivan may not have done the deed himself, but that did not matter; he may as well have.

When Normin was a skinny twig of a boy strutting around the island as crown prince, he had stumbled across Alice by total accident. He was on his way back from a fishing trip with some of his friends when he had seen her working the fields, a young woman with beautiful dark hair. Her body was so tanned from the sun and so athletic from her work that he thought he had never seen anything so beautiful. Undaunted by his status and influence, she saw nothing but another boy attempting to woo her. Every day he passed by that farm, even after all his family told him she was too low born for the would-be king, his father going so far as to tell him his younger brother Don would replace him as king if he chose to marry a lowborn. Normin did not give a shit. "Let him have it," he had told his father, convinced that a life with Alice would be preferable to being king. But the Lord works in mysterious ways as Don had died when they were boys and Normin was allowed to marry whomever he wished. It was simply expected of him to marry a highborn, but the opinions of others had never bothered him.

He persisted in taking Alice flowers and fancy foods from royal meals. She was never impressed, and on more than one occasion he had brought home with him the item meant for her. It was not until her father had passed that Normin took action, a gesture he knew she would never forget. Her mother had passed giving her birth, and Alice was an only child, so when old man Freeman died, Alice had no one. She attempted to step up and do her duty, but grief and the workload soon overwhelmed her. After watching all of this, Normin went to his father and begged him for help.

"Ben Mathis just lost his wife. He has no kids and needs something to do, someone to love. He is a good man and would be a perfect fit to help Alice on the farm," he had said.

And so Normin set into motion not only the saving grace of Altheia's most fertile farm land and Alice but also the law his father would pass just a few months later giving orphaned children the right to a new guardian.

After that, Alice had given in to Normin's requests, letting him take her fishing and hiking and even to the palace to dine and meet his parents. At first he knew it was just to show her appreciation and gratitude. Normin knew she was well aware of what he done for her, and he hoped that it would earn him a special place in her heart, one that would last a lifetime and beyond. He would have gotten his wish had his wife's life not been cut short by that fat, selfish pig.

When he looked up, people were looking at him expectantly, and he mindlessly did his duty and said some words so everyone could leave.

He had plans for that man, oh yes. It was all he could think about. Normin obsessed about it. The clear winner up to that point was the plan to choke him to death. He could draw it out slowly and look at that son of the devil right in his eyes just as

Ivan realizes his life is over. Although a nice, long slice to the throat might be just as satisfying, listening to his bloody gurgles. He would still choke to death technically.

When Normin looked up again, most everyone had filed out of the cathedral, and the rest were on their way. Lucid and Brynn stood there looking at him, along with Minister Tiller.

"Are you okay, Daddy?" Brynn asked him. She looked so much like Alice that Normin had trouble looking at her. He gave a false smile and a shallow nod. "I'll be okay, dear, thank you. You guys just go on home to bed and get some rest."

They just glanced at each other. "Dad, it's morning," said Lucid. "Are you sure you're okay?"

Normin just nodded again. He hugged each of them, then turned on his heel and exited the cathedral.

Lucid watched his father go, worry increasing in his gut. He looked to his sister. "You will be watching him, right? Make sure he's okay and has what he needs."

She nodded. "I'll keep a close eye on him."

He just looked at Brynn, only eleven years old yet brilliant and able to handle such stresses on top of her grief. He realized in that moment looking at her just how deep his love for his sister ran. Maybe because he was getting older now and began seeing things differently, but in that moment he would have literally done anything for her. She looked up at him when he hesitated, and he saw the sadness there, hidden by a child's stubborn refusal to seem weak.

"And how are you? You okay?" he asked.

Her eyes filled with tears, and then the tears streamed down her small cheeks. Lucid embraced her tightly, tears of his own matching his sister's. The huge, empty room served as a private grieving chamber where the two wept for their mother.

A short time later they separated and wiped their wet

faces and red eyes. Brynn's expression turned angry after a silent thought. "Drondos keeps slaves, Lucid," she said without preamble.

He was stunned. "How do you know? Are you sure?"

"A slave boy escaped. I found him hiding in the bushes this morning," Brynn told him. Lucid ran a hand through his hair, blowing out a long breath.

"Where is he?" he asked.

"In my chambers for now. I would like to assimilate him into school, but I thought I'd ask Father first." She glanced at the door. "Don't think he is in any shape to make decisions at the moment," she said.

"To be honest, Brynn, I am not sure what to do with this information. It doesn't have much impact on Altheia. Do what you have to about the boy, and get him into the correct classes quietly. Father does not need any extra stress. Outside of that ..." He just shrugged.

Brynn looked at him for a moment, and before she even opened her mouth to speak, Lucid knew what she was going to say: "We have to save them."

Lucid chuckled mirthlessly. "What do you want from me, Brynn? We storm Drondos and free their slaves? We don't have the troop numbers, for one thing. And again, it's not our problem. Besides, we have other issues to contend with," Lucid told her.

Brynn's face darkened. She shouted at him, "Tell that to the starving slave boy with dead parents living in my room!" She turned and strode out angrily.

Lucid sighed and headed for the door himself. As soon as he exited, Jon fell in beside him. With everything that had happened, and even though Lucid was not the king yet, Jon refused to be more than two steps away. Lucid loved him for it as his mind was in no state to constantly scan for threats.

"I need to see her," Lucid told Jon.

"Good God, man now, is not the time. With everything that's happening, don't you think we need to be here? I love your father as I do my own, but he is in no condition to run this city. Who does that leave?" Jon said. Lucid said nothing. Jon stopped him, grabbing hold of his arm and looking into his eyes with an intense expression. "I need you here. We all need you here, now more than ever before. Stay focused on keeping us and our people alive. She will be fine without you for a short time."

Lucid nodded, knowing his responsibilities well. It took every ounce of his being not to give away his intention in his expression. Jon knew him way too well.

"Okay," he finally replied.

Vincent awoke with sunlight streaming into the small windows of a tiny hut in which he lay. Groggy with heavy eyelids and limbs like jelly, he lifted his head, which felt like a boulder, to look down at his midsection wrapped tightly in fresh bandages. When he turned his head to the side, he noticed someone sitting there watching him. This person's skin was dark like the color of fresh-turned soil, and his hair was short and neat. He had a pleasant face and a kindly swagger about him.

"Hey," Vincent said weakly. The young man smiled, showing surprisingly straight white teeth.

"How are you feeling?" he asked as he moved over to Vincent and began probing around his midsection, looking for telltale winces and grunts.

"I'm alive," he said between winces. Vincent realized then that he knew this boy as his brain began to clear. It was

Lord Reginald's son, Daryl. Reginald was the master healer of Altheia, so Vincent knew he was in good hands with this one. *Best keep that to myself,* he thought.

"When we found you, we thought you would die right there as we watched. We all agreed to just leave you, all except Russell," Daryl said.

Vincent nodded. "I remember. I saved him from a bully earlier that night," he said calmly.

After a moment, Daryl nodded. "That wasn't just a bully; it was his father. And we weren't there to save you; we were there to save him." Vincent just digested the information calmly. "What do you know about Percy Chavez?" Daryl asked, suspicion slowly creeping into his words.

"Nothing, I have never heard that name before. I simply saw a man beating someone and did something about it," Vincent replied. Daryl stared for a moment then sat back and nodded.

"Can you tell me where I am?" Vincent asked.

"A fishing hut in Altheia," Daryl said. Vincent thought he feigned surprise well enough. If he were to give any indication that he knew this man, his father, and this place, Daryl was smart enough to put the pieces together.

"Can you tell me what it is that you do in Drondos?" Daryl asked.

"I am a craftsman. I make weapons," he lied.

Daryl looked at him skeptically. "So someone literally stabbed you in the back and left you for dead over … what, an unpaid debt? Didn't finish a blade fast enough?" Vincent only shrugged.

"Right," Daryl said at length. "You are alive because of us. The least you can do is be truthful."

Vincent hesitated and glanced down at his bandaged midsection. Then he sighed and said, "My name is Vincent

Joice, and I am an assassin and a thief. I had a mission to steal Altheia's grain silo key. When I went to make the exchange, I got betrayed, and that is where you found me." Daryl's eyes went wide in surprise, but he said nothing. Vincent continued, "I know you, Daryl, and your father, Reginald—not personally, but I know much about Altheia. I was born here as Effram Dillon." This time, Daryl's surprise was too much, and his mouth dropped open.

"You went missing and were presumed dead. I remember reading something about that. It was a huge deal as a death had never occurred where the body went missing. There have been animal attacks, but always a piece of the body was found. What made you abandon Altheia?" he asked.

Vincent fixed Daryl with a knowing look. "You know this city better than most. Any need for a thief assassin? Ivan is a better client by far and keeps me working," he told the healer.

Daryl crossed his arms and mumbled, "Maybe we should have let you die."

"I'm right here. I can hear you. Besides, no one gets hurt or looted unless I get paid well for it. I don't do this kind of work for fun," Vincent told him.

Daryl frowned. "Yeah, that justifies killing people. At least you are paid. Why do it at all?"

Vincent just shrugged. "It's all I've ever known. Growing up here, I was obsessed with fighting and knew the only way I would be able to do it for a living was in the shadows."

Daryl thought for a moment. "So what can you tell me about Drondos?" he asked.

Vincent shrugged again. "Anything. What do you wish to know?"

"Who stole our grain and burned the silo?" he asked with no preamble.

"Ivan. Well, not him directly. I stole the key for the king's personal bodyguard, Luke, which is why I'm lying here with a hole in me. But most likely orders such as those would be carried out by Terrence, the king's first commander," Vincent guessed.

Daryl nodded, filing the information away for later. "You know that little raid by Ivan cost him his life? The queen was caught in the fire, and Normin has that crazy look in his eye. A blind man could see he seeks revenge for his murdered wife— and most likely sooner rather than later. Normin isn't a man known for procrastination."

Vincent nodded gravely, looking down for a minute, before raising his eyes to meet Daryl's with an intense expression. "I am very sorry about your queen. Had I known what would happen …" He trailed off as Daryl waved his hand in dismissal.

"You did not kill the queen or set fire to our silo. I believe you were just an unwilling pawn of Ivan in this mess. Still, it would be best to keep the details of your last mission to yourself. The whole city is in an uproar and looking for someone to blame," Daryl stated.

The small wooden door to the hut opened. Russell entered and grinned widely when he saw Vincent's eyes open. "He lives!" He walked up and reached his hand out. "Russell Chavez. Thank you for saving me that night. I believe my father wished to take the beating to a new level, and who knows, had you not passed by, I might not be here."

Vincent shook his hand and smiled. "It was nothing. Anyone with half a conscience would do the same."

The look on the young man's face changed to anger quickly. Vincent was afraid he'd said something to offend him. "No they fucking wouldn't. You'd be surprised how many people in Drondos have seen that and just kept on going about their business." As Russell pulled up a chair next to Daryl, the healer began filling him in on Vincent, repeating his story with Vincent's help.

Russell shook his head and whistled. "An assassin and thief with a conscience? Drondos's minister didn't even try to stop Percy from beating me, and here you are, a thief, a killer—nice guy. The world is weird and fucking backward." He looked into Vincent's eyes and asked, "So, what now? I suppose you can't go back to Drondos?"

Vincent drew a breath, winced, and blew it out slowly. "I honestly have no idea. I cannot go home and would not want to anyway. Also I do not imagine I can stay here with my being accidentally to blame for the death of your queen. I suppose I will have to live in the woods until Ivan dies. If what Daryl says is true, that might be sooner than I expected. Either way, I am finished with my line of work. I like this hut. Maybe fishing would suit me. Still get to kill shit. It would just be fish instead of people."

They both laughed, and Vincent chuckled and then cringed. Daryl stood and rummaged through the items on a shelf before bringing Vincent a vial of some sinister-looking liquid. "This will dull the pain significantly. Might knock you out, but I figure sleeping would be preferable to the pain. You will be safe here," the healer told him.

Vincent nodded, taking the vial. He pulled the tiny cork and took a sniff. Then as he looked at them, he said "Cheers" and emptied the contents. "Thank you, boys. You two are good people. Trust me, I can tell. Living in Drondos so long, I forgot there were actually decent people in the world." Just a moment later, he slipped into a deep sleep.

CHAPTER 13

Lucid opened his chamber door slightly and stuck his head out for what felt like the hundredth time. This time, thankfully, the light was out in Jon's chambers down the hall and nothing but darkness was visible around the outline of his door. Lucid was the prince and Jon the future head king's man, so their chambers were in the same wing of the palace. Lucid loved his best friend dearly, but Jon would never let him enter those woods alone. Plus, this way, if things went poorly, the consequences would fall on Lucid alone.

It mattered little though. Something nagged at him inside, and he found the need to see her face to be overwhelming. That fact alone was odd enough as he had never had feelings such as those about any woman. But the current situation, hers and his, was just as queer and unpredictable.

As soon as Jon's chambers went dark, Lucid was on the move. He crept down the stairs to the main entrance and out into the courtyard. Jerald stood there, silent guardian of the quiet Altheian streets. Lucid crept past the statue and onto the path behind the huts, hugging the grassy west side of Jacques Ravine. He took a different route to the woods this time, being extra careful so that Jon wouldn't find him and try to stop him.

When he finally entered the thick jungle in his usual spot, he broke into a jog, not a full-blown run but setting a nice pace. He wanted to get there more quickly so he would have extra time to talk to her. With silence usually being his only worry, his feet ate up the miles as wind whipped his face. He stopped suddenly, almost going sprawling over a dead log as he caught sight of a spear standing straight up in the air like a lone fence post.

He thought that odd in the middle of the thick trees, halfway between Altheia and the gvorlocks' village. There should have been nothing man-made out here. He moved closer and saw that the spear was protruding from the side of a jaguar's neck, a huge beast as cats go. He reached down and felt the blood pooled around it. It was still warm.

That's odd, he thought as he raised his eyes to his surroundings.

Lucid inhaled slowly through his nose to slow his breathing and to smell the jungle around him. Looking around, he spotted blood on a bush a few yards away and headed toward it. Then he saw more blood on the ground and yet more on some foliage. The gore made a trail of sorts, and Lucid began following it. As he did this, the blood seemed to be fresher and fresher, the last bit still dripping off a small bush about waist high. He stopped and bent to inspect it, and as he did so, he heard faint footsteps coming from somewhere ahead of him.

He picked up his pace and increased his stealth, calling on every bit of training and experience he could muster to muffle his steps. When he finally had a clear line of sight, he saw a huge hulking form and what looked to be a slender body slung over his shoulder like a doll.

Lucid just snapped.

There was simply no other way to explain the quickness in this change from curious and worried to incredibly angry. When he recognized those beautiful golden locks marred with blood, his face burned as if it were on fire. His teeth grinding intensified a thousandfold when he got close enough to see the blood dripping from her face as it bounced limply with the giant's steps. Before he knew what he was doing, he had his blade out and was charging the beast. He must have kept silent enough because the gvorlock did not even react until Lucid sliced deep gashes across the backs of both his knees.

The giant bellowed a deep growl and dropped Lya, who landed hard and did not move. She landed on her back in a patch of moonlight that breached the canopy, and he got a better look at her face. It was swollen and bloodied, and she was unconscious—no doubt from having been beaten. Lucid was filled with blind rage, and his mind and vision darkened. He stepped back just fast enough to dodge a slow backhand blow from the gvorlock as he turned, and he swung his sword down, separating the giant hand from the giant arm. The gvorlock screamed again and clutched at his missing appendage, dark liquid squirting in waves down his remaining hand.

The creature still managed to choke out, "We will destroy your people for breaking the treaty. You will not …"

His words were silenced when Lucid drove his sword right into the middle of the gvorlock's neck, after which he twisted it and it yanked out. The big beast fell face-first into the dirt. The prince never said a word, lost in his emotions, until he approached Lya with his heart pounding. He knelt by her, praying to God she was alive. He looked her over and brushed the dirt and leaves from her head and hair, gently shaking her.

"Lya?" he asked, his voice cracking and his eyes beginning to water at the sight of her face up close. She looked much the same as Russell had when he found him drunk and beaten.

"Oh please no, Lya!" He shook her a little harder. Lucid felt a huge weight lift as he saw her chest rising and falling, but he knew it might not be all well just yet. Who knew what type of injury she could have sustained internally. He gathered her up and did his best to sling her over his shoulder the way he had seen the gvorlock carrying her. He was not nearly so large or strong, but he still got her balanced well enough to manage a decent trot.

As he ran, his thoughts flashed back to what Jon had said: "Now you want to steal their women." With Lya slung over his shoulder and a dead gvorlock at his back, that is exactly what it felt like. His heart sank. This time, his actions may very well get him and every one of his people killed. The gvorlocks would want revenge, and who knew what the small population of giants were capable of. Lucid had no idea what would happen now that the treaty was broken, because clearly it had never happened before.

There had been a lot of firsts on the island in the last few weeks—Drondos openly stealing and attacking Altheia, and now this. The fact that what Lucid had just done might have been worse than the attack on the tower that killed his mother sickened him. However, just like the steps of his run, he would put one foot in front of the other.

Tackle your problems one at a time. Get Lya home safe first, he thought.

He picked up his pace as the edge of the tree line came into view. The last leg of his trip was a blur as his tired legs and back were on fire and he could not seem to get enough air into his lungs. Next thing he knew, he burst into his chambers. Russell was startled awake from his burrow of blankets on the floor.

"Get Daryl now!" The urgency of Lucid's voice sent Russell off at a run. Lucid laid the limp girl on his bed and began checking her for deep cuts or other visible wounds. Soon after, Daryl entered with none other than Jon coming in behind him.

"Heard the commotion. What the f—" Jon trailed off and his eyes went wide as he saw Lya lying there. "What have you done?" he asked in shock.

"She is from Drondos," Lucid said harshly with a look at

his friend that would brook no argument. Jon shot his prince a sharp look, but Lucid continued, saying, "I found her and she is hurt. What more is there to know?"

Jon approached and, upon seeing her condition, seemed to soften slightly. "She cannot stay here," he said bluntly. Lucid frowned.

"Where else? She will be safe here," Lucid told him as he looked to Daryl, who was running his skilled fingers over her midsection.

"Too dangerous. With Drondos acting a fool and Russell just now getting settled in, it's just not the right time. She can stay in the infirmary," Jon said.

Lucid fixed his friend with a knowing stare, and Jon threw up his hands.

"I will talk to Alisha. She can stay there," Daryl interrupted.

Lucid and Jon both looked at their friend in shock. Alisha was a hard woman known for her inability to put up with bullshit, and their crazy antics had always been in that category. Taking a strange woman to stay with her while she healed would likely be asking for a pummeling.

"It's fine," Daryl said. "I will take the heat. In the meantime, I need both of you to get out or shut up. She is bleeding internally and has a few broken ribs. Her jaw is broken as well, so I have my work cut out for me. Now let me focus," the healer finished.

Upon hearing of all the injuries the poor young woman, had sustained, it took everything Lucid had in his reserves of strength not to show on his face what he felt inside. Still, Jon seemed to have caught the look and edged toward the door, scooping Russell up on the way.

"Come on, bro, you can sleep in my chambers," Jon told Russell, who yawned and followed.

"Got anything to eat in there?" Lucid heard Russell ask as the pair moved down the hall.

Lucid watched the horror of cutting, stitching, and bandaging that followed for quite some time before Daryl stood and wiped his hands on a clean rag. "She is as patched up as she can get. We just have to pray she will be okay. I am slightly worried that she has not regained consciousness, but she is breathing normally. And to be honest, I have seen worse. Can you carry her?"

Lucid nodded eagerly. He had run with her weight for miles; carrying her gently downstairs sounded much better. He gathered her up gingerly this time, as if carrying an infant, and followed Daryl through the palace to Alisha's chamber. When they arrived, Daryl pounded on the door so hard that Lucid could already imagine the outcome. He edged a little farther away from Daryl and shifted Lya's weight in his arms. The door flung open. A very naked Alisha came flying out and punched Daryl hard in the stomach, crumpling him to the floor.

"What the fuck are you banging for? Do you know what time it is?" She looked up and saw Lucid standing there, an unconscious woman in his arms, attempting to avert his eyes at her nakedness.

"Hey, Lucid." She greeted him with a small wave, brightening a bit. "What have you got going on there?" she asked, gesturing to Lya and not seeming to notice her boyfriend taking huge gulping breaths on the floor while clutching his chest.

"Need your help. Think you could stay with him for a while?" Lucid asked.

"What is going on? Is everything okay? Who is that?" she asked.

Lucid just shook his head and looked down at Daryl, who was standing up and beginning to breathe normally.

"I'll explain later. Just trust me ... please?" She stared at him a moment, then nodded.

"I trust you. Let me gather some things," Alisha said, turning back to her chambers.

"Clothes, maybe?" Lucid called after her, and she huffed. After the couple made their exit, Lucid sat in a high-backed chair next to the bed and watched Lya sleep for a time. The moment he laid his head back against the chair, he fell asleep.

CHAPTER 14

As Coy walked to the training yard that morning, none other than Derek Inder bumped into him. This was quickly becoming a daily humiliation as the large boy always seemed to cross paths with Coy. This time it was only a single punch to the face, but it still sent Coy sprawling backward, hitting the ground. He rolled over onto his stomach, waiting.

"Watch where you're going next time, *slave*." Derek spat the last word with disgust as he walked away laughing.

Coy just stared at the ground, where the blood was pooling from his nose. When he heard footsteps retreating, he stood. The bullies may be huge and vicious, but he was simply biding his time. The training of the Altheians was nothing like what he had experienced in Drondos. He was sure he soon would be able to beat them.

If slave fighting was a humming tune, then Altheia fighting was a symphony, graceful, agile, and brutal. Coy could not pump the knowledge into his brain fast enough, and when he did, bullies like Derek Inder would pay dearly.

And the whole of Drondos will pay, pay for my parents' deaths, for my life, and for the lives of my aunt and all others.

He blew as much of the gob of blood out of his nose as he could, wiped the excess on his sleeve, and gathered up his heavy schoolbooks that had fallen all around him in the fight. The moment he entered the training yard with all the boys his same age, Jon Trigo saw his bloody nose and shook his head.

"Again?" he asked. Coy just stayed silent, knowing what

was coming. Coy knew the older boys were trained by the head king's man and Jon's father, Jake, but the younger boys' training fell to Jon.

"Take a lap," Jon said at length while swirling his finger in a circle to demonstrate. As if Coy did not know every blade of grass and pebble surrounding the training yard. "You will win or at least fight back, or you will run every day!" Trigo yelled at the boy as he dropped his books and took off.

Coy did not mind. He could literally feel the effect the training was having on his body. He felt strong for the first time in his life. Well rested and well-fed, he began putting on weight and turning it into muscle. Princess Brynn had put him up with a wonderful farming family who treated him very well, but the change was shocking at first. Three meals a day and a soft bed to sleep in was so alien to him. He still slept on the floor most nights.

As he ran, he thought about his parents and their sacrifice for him. Tears ran unchecked down his face as he plotted his revenge against the killer, which made him push his body harder. He would become a great fighter, then return to Drondos and kill every last slave keeper and free his people.

By the time he came around the yard to the end of his run, he was breathing hard and sweating, but Jon gave him a slight nod. Coy stood straight at the head of the gathering children as Trigo took the class through the warm-up stretches. It had taken him several sessions to earn that nod of respect as his fighting skills had been severely lacking.

After the stretches, the boys lined up in rows of five, five deep, and began going through the combo of low block, high block, high sweep, and lunge. Over and over Trigo drilled it into the boys. As Coy went through the motions, he felt more motivated than ever. Jon switched to a feint and riposte combo, and sweat began pouring down Coy's face in the morning summer heat. His nose aching, sweat stinging his eyes, he relished the pain and turned it into even more motivation.

When the practice was finished, everyone replaced their heavy practice blades in the small armory shed and lined up where Coy had begun the class. Running laps was always the closing to the practices, and even though he had already taken one lap as he did every day, he expected no breaks and lined up with the rest. Trigo said running shaped bodies and minds and built endurance, so it was as much a part of training as swinging a sword.

When the laps ended, Coy gathered up his books and headed up the wide steps to the school. He entered the huge foyer filled with children running to and fro. He spotted Brynn and her friend Catrina, and the princess shot him a small wave when she saw him. He smiled despite his rocky morning. She always made him feel nervous and unsure of himself. Coy told himself it had nothing to do with her being so pretty, but he was not fooling anyone. She was like a dark-haired goddess. He waved back and shook his head as he headed for Mr. Redkey's classroom. If the talk he had overheard was true, Brynn was one of the councillors of the kingdom, in charge of thousands of people and countless responsibilities, yet here she was, not failing to miss school no matter what was happening.

She really is an amazing girl, he thought. He could not be more grateful to her for what she had done for him. He was nobody, a nothing, yet she gave him a life with a wave of her hand. He walked through the giant hallway, turned at the first set of stairs, and began climbing. Older kids, young men and women, were on the first floor. The younger kids like him were on the third floor, the even younger children were on the fourth floor, and so on. Coy loved being here; it reminded him just how old and well established Altheia was, like an impenetrable fortress. He felt safe. And learning from the men in this place was a rush unlike what he was used to. He had never learned much as a slave, but now, as the knowledge flowed, he found he was hungry for it. After a short time he'd discovered just how powerful knowing things was. The more he learned, the more powerful he would become.

"The brain is just like your sword arm; it needs to be worked and practiced," Mr. Redkey had told him after Coy had let slip just how much he loved to train.

"Knowing how to strike someone down is fine, but outsmarting them, I think you'll find, is much more satisfying," the teacher had said.

That was where their agreement ended. Knowledge was power, sure, but Coy expected there was nothing so sweet as plunging a blade into the people who had hurt you and yours, watching them die as they realized their mistake.

As with every morning, Coy was the first to arrive to Mr. Redkey's classroom. Other kids wandered the halls or gathered in groups talking and laughing with each other until class began, but Coy was always first in and first out as he had no friends, except Jerry.

Jerry was a pet of the family who had adopted Coy. "A beautiful and smart golden lab," Mr. Mathis had said of his dog, and Coy found no words to be truer. Jerry had taken a liking to Coy quickly, and he was unsure if it was because Coy liked to sleep on the floor—something they had in common— or simply because Coy loved the furry animal, and Jerry could tell.

"Another fight?" Mr. Redkey's words snapped him out of his thoughts. Coy had chosen his usual desk in the back of the class and looked up to see his teacher wearing the typical tan and white robes of the teachers, along with a worried expression. "Please do not let one bad apple spoil the whole batch, I always say," Mr. Redkey said.

Coy looked at him confused, and he clarified: "Do not let the actions of one spoiled bully affect your opinion of us Altheians. Most of us are decent folk just trying to live life and be happy, same as you," the teacher advised.

Coy nodded but stayed silent. Soon the other kids began filing into the classroom. Knowledge followed, and lots of it, so much that Coy always thought, *There is no way I'll remember all of this tomorrow.* Yet somehow the information always stayed. Reading and writing, math, science, plants and animals, ethics and economy, and he even heard talk of a class for older kids called psychology, whatever that meant.

When finally his classes ended and his brain hurt, Coy left the school and walked through the LD to his new home. People still gave him looks, and some treated him with disdain, but these were things he could endure easily. It was the blow to his pride that Derek struck at him every day that was something unforgivable to him. Coy would earn the older boy's respect by beating the jerk out of him.

He arrived at the farm and had just enough time to set his books down before he could hear Bruce's whistle signaling which field he was harvesting that evening. The Mathis family lived in a huge home. At least to Coy it was almost as if he had the whole of the slave quarters in Drondos to himself, only this was much more comfortable, and there was food. Made mostly of wood, the house was two stories tall and so perfectly square that he wondered at the skill of the builders. A large barn that housed the cows and chickens sat next to the home. Coy entered the barn to retrieve his scythe, and armed with his wicked harvesting blade, he went and opened the back door to let Jerry out.

Coy set his tool down to give his friend a proper rubdown. With his tail wagging and his tongue out, the hound followed as Coy picked up his scythe and headed for the south field. Mr. Mathis would grumble something about the dog getting in the way, but Coy knew the old farmer did not mind. It amused Bruce that Coy and Jerry were the best of friends. The man clearly appreciated it.

Muscles stiff from training and his nose now at a low throb, Coy said nothing as he got to work mowing down large sections of wheat. Jerry would nip at his heels and jump around at him during the walk to the field, but once the scythe started swinging, the dog always found a nice high spot to lie in the retreating evening sun and watch the two men work. After all the days they had performed this routine, Coy still marveled at the intelligence of the beast.

After hours of cutting, binding, and hauling the wheat to Bruce's wheeled cart, Coy was exhausted and his limbs felt like the jelly Mrs. Mathis served at breakfast. Still he said nothing as the two pulled the cart back toward the barn. But by the time they reached it, he was sure his legs would give out, shakily walking inside to wash before supper. He would not dare complain, knowing what his people were facing on a daily basis.

"That is the hardest-working person I have ever seen, and look at the size of him. I worry one of these days he will just collapse, poor thing." Coy heard Mr. and Mrs. Mathis speaking quietly as he exited his room and headed downstairs for supper. He paused to listen.

"Then give him a break. God knows he needs it. Comes home with a fresh bruise or busted lip about every day. Give him a week's rest," Mrs. Mathis replied.

"Cannot do it, dear. I truly wish I could, but with our stores stolen, we need to pick up the pace, not the opposite," the farmer said.

"I don't mind," Coy cut in from the top of the stairs. They both looked up sharply. "Honestly, I don't. You people are so good to me, I would do all the work myself if I were bigger and stronger. I am getting there."

Mrs. Mathis's eyes grew wet. She excused herself to get supper. Bruce just looked at Coy with that intense stare of his. He watched as the boy slowly made his way down on shaky legs, limping slightly. Both his eyes were beginning to blacken from the blows he'd received earlier, and he could just barely lift his arms.

All I need to do is lift food to my mouth, he thought as he sat and looked up at Bruce, who was still watching him.

"I can see you are struggling. You are young and still untaught about the ways of the world. You do not owe us anything, Coy. You do not have to be so damn …" He paused and looked at Coy, who remained silent. Bruce sighed and said, "I just want you to have a good life here. We can give that to you, but you are not required to work like a, ahem …" He paused again and looked uncomfortable.

Coy thought this whole conversation backward as this man and his wife had already done so much for him in such a short time that he would do anything they asked of him without question or delay.

Mrs. Mathis entered with their supper, and Bruce just sighed and sat up in his chair, beginning to fill his plate in silence. They ate without a word, and when the meal was done and Coy was finally in bed that evening, all he could think about was how happy he was to get to wake up tomorrow and do it all again.

CHAPTER 15

Terrence sat reading in his home in the abandoned merchant district of Drondos. After the king had stolen the craftsmen and shut down most of the businesses, Ivan had some of the buildings on the street cleaned and converted to living quarters for his most trusted advisers and soldiers. They were important folk, but not important enough to live in or around the royal manse. Terrence's residence was two buildings down from the palace to allow for quick response, but now that he had no call to which to respond, he was thinking of relocating.

Terrence received a knock at his door. He was enjoying being lazy so much that he dreaded having to mark his page in the book he was reading and get out of bed. *Retirement suits me,* he thought as he laboriously hauled himself up and stretched. He reluctantly set his book down on the table next to his small feather bed.

Stories of the ancient past were so very interesting. When King Normin's ancestors first landed here, they wrote down everything. It was a large book taking Terrence many hours to get through, but it was a wonderful read. The bottom floor of his large home was all Terrence needed, one open room with a fireplace for cooking and warming himself in the winter and a bed for sleeping. He moved toward the door, his bare feet slapping against the wood floor.

He opened it to see Smith standing there, out of breath and looking half dead. The scout pushed in quickly. Stan closed the door behind him, locked it, and immediately began checking the windows.

"What the hell, Stan?" Terrence asked the scout.

"You are not going to believe this shit. I followed Lucid as you asked." The scout sat down at the small table next to Terrence's fireplace, looking dumbfounded and a little terrified. He just sat staring at Terrence, and when he spoke, it was just above a whisper: "We are not alone here."

Terrence frowned and said, "What do you mean, Smith? There is no one here but you and me."

Smith shook his head violently. "No, I mean we are not alone *here*," he said, gesturing to the ground. Terrence still had no idea what the man was talking about. "On the island, I mean," he added.

"Of course not. There are thousands of people in Altheia. What are you babbling about, son? Spit it out."

Stan took a shaky breath and began his story: "I found the site where Lucid enters the woods each night when he leaves, so I camped near there, hoping to catch him and follow. I just wanted to see where he was going. When he began his trek, I followed for a few miles or so, struggling to keep up because he set a brutal pace. Soon, we caught up to one of them—a huge beast, white as paper and not human. It was carrying a girl over its shoulder ..." He trailed off when Terrence cut in.

"What do you mean, 'not human'?" he asked Stan.

"I've never seen a man like that. Easily three feet taller than me and three times as wide. No hair whatsoever, and a bright green glow to his eyes, easily spotted with its being so dark. And that is not even all of it. When Lucid saw it, he killed it and took the girl back to Altheia," Stan said.

The scout sat back with an even more frightened look than before and added, "The thing was huge and scary, and the prince killed it without even breaking a sweat. When Altheia comes after us for stealing their grain, they will kill every last one of us."

Terrence sat down at the small table across from the scout, digesting all of this information. "How do you know there are more of them?" he asked.

Stan shrugged. "I am just guessing. The chances of there being only one such beast are slim. We know very little about the thickest-wooded areas of the island."

If there were beasts of some sort on the island, how could Normin not know? Surely he did know and kept it a secret. That man knew everything about every person, every grain of sand, and every blade of grass on the entire island. Had anyone else in Drondos discovered this? Did Ivan know?

He looked at Stan. "Have you told anyone else of this?" The scout shook his head. "Good. Keep it that way for now. I would like to find out more. Can you lead me deep into the woods and back out again?" Again Stan just nodded numbly.

"If there are more of these beasts, I believe I need to see for myself. Go get some rest. We leave at sundown."

Terrence dressed and gathered the necessary supplies for a weeklong trek. He placed these into a satchel and set it next to the door. *So much for retirement,* he thought. He knew he should not be doing this type of shit anymore; it simply was no longer his problem. Still, he could not help himself. This was something completely unexpected and a little frightening. Stan's behavior now made much more sense. He figured if they were to hike all night through thick woods, he needed rest as well, so he lay down and attempted to sleep. There was just entirely too much going through his head, so sleep never came. Hours passed as he lay there thinking, until a knock startled him out of his reverie.

He rose, threw on his satchel, opened the door, and began to step out then hesitated. It was not Stan who stood there in his open doorway but a tall figure dressed in black with a veil over his face and a dagger in his hand. The man immediately swiped at Terrence's neck, but despite his age, the ex-commander was quick to throw his head back out of the way and take a step back. In the blink of an eye, he had his own sword out. The men circled each other.

"Did no one teach you? Never bring a dagger to a sword fight," Terrence growled as he lunged, going for a quick thrust to his adversary's heart. But the tall figure surprised Terrence, parrying his blow smoothly, and delivered a slash to his bicep so quickly that Terrence barely saw him move. Terrence grunted and stepped back, clutching at his arm with his free hand. He expected the killer to rush him and attack, but he only stopped and turned his head slightly toward the door. Fear washed over Terrence as he realized too late what he was listening for.

"Stan!" Terrence screamed, but it did not matter. The second his frame blocked the door, the man in black turned and threw his dagger, which landed right in the middle of the scout's throat. Stan collapsed with a thud, and the black-clad man ran for the door, seeing his advantage slip. As he did, though, Terrence caught a long downward stroke across his attacker's back as he retreated. The would-be killer pulled the dagger from poor Stan's throat and kept running.

"Luke, you fucking coward!" Terrence screamed. His right bicep was on fire, and he was having trouble closing that hand. He tore strips from an old tunic and wrapped it tightly, tying with his free hand and his teeth. He took one last sad look at Stan, said a silent apology, and stepped over his corpse into the night, alone.

As soon as Terrence crossed the tree line, the world went

shockingly dark. The wind in the trees sounded like ghosts whispering all around him. The hair on the back of his neck and his arms stood up. A twig snapped close by, and he whipped his head around to see nothing but shadows. His visibility was limited to just a few feet, so he paused and tried to let his eyes adjust. Minutes went by as he stood there listening to a mix of unknowable sounds. Terrence trekked a small distance through a haze of brush and trees before deciding it would be easier to navigate in the sunlight. He found a nice large tree with a hollow spot around its roots and drifted off quickly.

The next day he awoke with the sun and began moving in the direction he thought most appropriate. Deeper and deeper he hiked through the woods, trying to keep a good heading by tracking the sun through the small holes in the jungle canopy. The jungle was thick. In some spots Terrence struggled just to find a way through and eventually began hacking limbs and brush with his sword. He stopped suddenly, looking at a particularly large tree rotting on the forest floor.

I know I passed that just a bit ago, he thought.

He shrugged it off and kept hacking his way toward this mysterious beast. *What will I find?* he thought as he cut through a low thornbush on his right. Maybe his name would be immortalized for not only finding something nobody ever had but also possibly befriending this creature. As the woods around him began to darken once again, he cut through a particularly thick set of vines blocking his sight, and he gaped. Again, sitting next to the path he had just cut earlier, was the same dead tree lying on its side, rotting and mocking him.

"You should never have come," whispered a voice.

Every hair stood this time, and Terrence froze, looking around himself frantically. It was getting too dark now; he could not see very far.

"Who is there?" he yelled at the forest.

Nothing. He was lost, going in circles, and it was once again too dark to navigate. Above all, exhaustion was causing his mind to slip. He put his back to a tree nearby, slid down, and passed out.

Normin sat in his chambers, a week's stubble on his face and shadows under his eyes. Sleep eluded him. It had been over thirty years since he had slept in a bed without Alice, and he found it impossible. The lack of sleep was beginning to play tricks on his mind, he knew. The king supposed it was about time to plan out his attack on Ivan. If it did not go well, Lucid would make a great king. The door opened after a light knock. Normin did not need to look to see who it was.

Brynn had been checking on him regularly throughout the days following Alice's death. Normally he would have been profoundly proud of his brilliant and mature daughter for taking care of her daddy during his time of need. But Normin was beyond such things, beyond any emotion. All he cared about was balance. A life had been taken, and to balance the universe once more, another must be taken.

"How you doing this morning, Daddy?" He looked over and gave her a false smile and a small nod. She sat down next to him and just stared, so long that Normin finally turned to look at her. "You haven't eaten in days. Is that yesterday's breakfast right there?" she asked.

Normin glanced down and shrugged, then continued looking out his window. Brynn kept staring. It was beginning to annoy him.

"What?" he asked. She frowned.

"I am not leaving this room until you eat something," she replied.

He looked down, grabbed whatever was on the plate, and stuffed it into his mouth, chewing quickly. It tasted like day-old pancake. Brynn slammed her hands on the table as she rose and stormed out.

Jake poked his head in and said, "I understand you are grieving, but that is your daughter, Normin, and she is only trying to help you."

Normin waved him away. Jake stepped back out and left the king to his thoughts. Normin must have drifted off, because next thing he knew, he was walking home from fishing with a handful of flowers and a beautiful flounder he had caught. When he presented it to her, she smiled and his heart burst with excitement. He gave a start and realized he had drifted off for some time as he glanced to the darkened window. He wanted to stay in that dream forever and drink in his wife's beauty.

Why is it that she is gone, yet that bastard continues to insult me with every breath he takes? He rose and dressed, his blacks including a veil. Then he changed his mind, leaving the veil. He would want Ivan to see his face as he ended that pathetic excuse for a man. He went to his chamber door and lay his ear against it, listening. He heard Jake shift his footing and knew that he would have to be extremely stealthy so as to not arouse suspicion. He took some old clothes and made his bed look as if he were sleeping in it. It would not fool anyone who got close, but if they glanced from the door, it would serve well enough. He only needed an hour or so; that would be more than enough time to put enough distance between him and his city that no one could stop him. Knowing Jake as he did, he would probably try to talk him out of it for some stupid fucking reason.

The king of Altheia slipped out the window, calling on his climbing skill from his younger years to inch his way down the exterior of the royal wing. *Why the hell did my ancestors have to carve it directly out of the rock?* he thought as he struggled to find footholds. Mercifully, after a short time, his feet touched the ground and he sighed and stretched his arms. Normin was between the side of the palace and a row of huts, the statue of Jerald looming over the roofs. He looked each direction and decided to go toward the huts. If any citizens saw him, they would not dare try to stop him. This way there was less chance of Jake finding him as well. Quietly he made his way to the beach, and when he arrived, he thought hugging the tree line would be the smarter choice. It would make for a longer and tougher walk, but there would be no tracks in the sand to follow.

Lost in his thoughts, walking in a sleep-deprived stupor, Normin did not even remember the trip. Next thing he knew, he was walking right through the front gate of Drondos, his heart pounding with excitement. The cocky asshole did not even bother to close it.

"Hey, you! Who are you, and where do you think you're going?" came a call from his right side as he passed under the archway of the gate and into the city.

Normin immediately turned toward the two guards and drew his sword, murder and revenge in his eyes. One of the men managed to at least get his sword out, but Normin was highly skilled and even more highly motivated. He cut right through the neck of the first guard. It was a clean cut, his anger powering an already strong swing. Before the poor man even knew what was happening, his head was in the mud. The second guard was a little faster at realizing his peril, but Normin's original swing had so much force behind it that it carried through and took the other one in the ribs, the sword wedging deep. Normin's left fist came up and connected hard with the guard's temple. The man crumpled unconscious as

Normin yanked his sword out and spun abruptly, continuing his walk deeper into the streets of Drondos.

Every step took him closer to his vengeance. By the time he was walking around the side of the royal manse, he had begun to feel slightly normal once more. It felt right; his actions had purpose, and he felt good about it. The climb up the side of the building was much easier than his earlier climb down from his palace because of the shit craftsmanship and lack of maintenance of the manse. When the king reached the top, climbing from one windowsill to the next, he took a peek inside the window on which he hung. In the darkness of the room he could just barely make out the form of a tall, slender man with bandages wrapped from neck to waist, fresh bloodstains on his back. *That's not him,* he thought as he shimmied over to the next window. *It has to be on the top floor.* When he checked the next window, he made out a large bulge in the middle of a huge bed. He very quietly opened the window, his eyes never leaving the sleeping king. Normin quietly pulled up a chair next to the bed, pulled his bloody sword out, and laid it across his lap. He cleared his throat loudly and kicked the bed for good measure.

The king of Drondos awoke, sat up in his bed, and rubbed the sleep from his eyes. Normin saw shock and fear wash over the man's face when their eyes met.

"Let me explain!" Ivan said quickly, holding out shaking hands. Normin noticed a growing wet spot around his midsection and scowled.

"I had planned a speech for this moment, played it over in my head a hundred times, something grand about going on to a better place, possibly given another chance in the next life." He stood. Disgust washed over him as he looked at the terrified king. "You are pathetic. Your life is worth even less than that puddle you just made, you fucking coward." Normin sneered.

He grabbed Ivan roughly by the front of his shirt, pulled him from his bed, and dragged him to the center of the floor. He began pummeling him with his hilt and kicking at his head, turning his face into a bloody ruin.

"You killed my wife!" Normin said, continuing to beat on the helpless king.

"No!" Ivan choked. "I didn't know! It was an accident!" The fat king cowered, covered himself, whimpered, and begged, but Normin heard none of it. When Ivan rolled onto his fat belly and attempted to crawl away, Normin walked up behind him and grabbed under his chins with one hand, the other cocked back and ready. He sliced the man's throat in an explosion of dark liquid, silencing his pitiful cries. Then Normin released the king of Drondos, whose royal head fell limp. He stood up, wiped his blade on Ivan's oversized tunic, and sheathed it. Normin looked over at the table and saw a full jug of wine. He went over to it and drank heavily. He dumped his waterskin and filled it with the dark liquid from the jug. Just then, someone tried to open the door to the chambers. Then there was a pounding.

"Sire, are you there? Is everything okay?" called a voice from the other side of the door.

Normin belted the wineskin and quickly exited through his window, climbing down and heading for his city. Enough men had died tonight to satisfy his hunger for revenge. He would avoid being seen from here on. As soon as he climbed the outer wall on the beach side of town and exited Drondos, he took out the wine and began drinking, slowly at first, but as he walked down the beach, his thirst crept up and he drank more. Soon he was stumbling through a hazy night with a full moon. As the trees went by in a blur, the sound of the waves crashing steadily threatened to cause him to succumb to exhaustion. He tripped over a rock, or was it a limb? He had no idea but did not care to look as he lay there, his head spinning. He turned his head and retched.

He awoke to the sun in his face. *Oh shit!* was his first thought as he sat up. And then the blinding headache was all he could think about. He blinked at the sun, which was surprisingly high in the sky, and tried to take a sip from his wineskin, which was empty. He growled and threw it into the woods, rising shakily to his feet. He put a hand out to shade his eyes, glanced about for a direction of travel, and then began walking. He retched twice more as he walked the beach and remembered the days when he and Inder first discovered wine.

They were just ten years old, and Normin had managed to trade a cask for some of his father's stolen smoke. They started having the best night of their lives, clinking cups and downing whole glasses. At one point they laughed so hard that Inder very nearly pissed himself. Until it hit them both, neither one of them knew what their limit was, and they had drunk entirely too much. They were both sick for days. Since that time, Normin only drank beer, and even that was on the rare occasion.

Before long the crest of the royal wing could be seen in the distance. The reality of what he had done was beginning to sink in. He had killed men, his first—and not just any man but the king of Drondos. His actions could very well be the end of that place. Who knew how Ivan's people would react to Jason becoming king at such a young age?

When Normin finally stumbled to his own chamber door, Jake was still standing guard just outside. He said nothing as Normin walked by. The king thought that odd. After all, Jake had not seen him leave. But it all became apparent as he opened his door and there sat Brynn with a worried look painted on her small face. When she saw him enter half drunk, with sand and blood all over him, her face darkened into something Normin had never seen of his little girl.

Those eyes, the ones that looked just like his Alice's, were incredibly angry as Brynn stood and stormed over to him. Normin was beyond shocked when she placed a front kick directly at the point of his sword belt where the hilt protruded upward. Her intention was immediately clear as the belt snapped and went flying across the room. The kick, however, grazed his hip and he went down to one knee, bringing father and daughter eye to eye. Brynn had never struck him; surely she had never even thought about it. Bloodshot, anguished, and with tears streaming, these were the eyes of his little girl, and he found it very hard to believe. A child he had rocked to sleep every night when she was an infant was looking at him as if *he* had killed Alice.

"He killed your mother, my wife," he said in defense before she uttered a word.

"Do you honestly think that demon swung the sword himself? Put torch to tower with his own hands? If that is what you think, then you are a fool. Bunch of angry-headed, violent, unthinking beasts! Do you feel better now!" Brynn seethed, screaming at him as never before. "Did killing a person bring Mom back? The rumor is true, Father: Ivan has slaves. Does even that justify what you have done?" Her voice had turned into a shrill yelling that made Normin cringe. She took a shaking breath and began to slowly back away from him, a strange calmness washing over her tear-streaked face as she came to some decision. "You are no better than he is. You are a murderer. I hereby invoke law 57. You are no longer the ruler of this kingdom," she said as she turned, quickly snatched up his sword belt, and strode out.

She slammed the door behind her and from inside. Normin could hear her yell, "What?"

There was no response from Jake—or anyone for that matter. Brynn continued, "I want two men on his door and two watching his window. And send a runner to find Lucid. I need to see him immediately," she said fiercely.

"Yes, ma'am," Jake replied.

CHAPTER 16

Jason just stared. It was difficult for him to grasp that it was his father lying there facedown in a massive pool of blood.

We are all just bags of liquid, he thought.

He had never seen so much blood in his life, and it was all he could focus on. It finally started to sink in, and Jason struggled hard not to smile. This may very well turn out to be the best day of his life. This would fast-track his plans and cut out at least six months of bullshit. Vincent was just the first step.

After Jason had seen that boat, that huge beautiful boat sailing majestically in the sea on the north side of the city, he had been planning constantly. This was simply a very convenient shortcut. He was pretty sure Vincent did not care for his father much, except the pay. Still, Jason could not risk that man actually siding with Ivan. He was just too dangerous.

Vincent is dead, and now I am the king, he thought as he looked around at his father's councillors, Luke, Brett, Richard, and …

"Where is Terrence?" were the first words Jason spoke after finding out that his father, the king, had been murdered. He supposed he should have said something nice or mournful for the man, but he just did not care. He was the king now, and he had not particularly liked his father anyway.

"Um, I am not sure," said Richard. He was head of the crafter's guild and a ridiculous excuse for a councillor. Jason knew for certain in all of his fifteen years in this world that he had never met anyone so stupid. The only thing the man was good for was making weapons, and Jason was sure that his grandson Zak was just as capable in that regard.

"Shouldn't we, you know, have your father's body removed and prepared for a funeral?" said the head of the healers, Brett Kince. He was grotesquely old, and the little skin flap under his chin disgusted Jason.

"Funeral?" Jason said, incredulous. "You are our top healer, best in the city, yet here I am looking at my dead father. How is it you could not save him?" Brett opened his mouth to reply, but Jason cut him off. "Because you are too old to move fast in an emergency, my father's life spilled into the floor as you waddled your way here for a few hours. And you!" he said, turning and pointing at Luke. "You are supposed to be his bodyguard, his shield protecting him at all times, yet here you stand, barely—because you are injured—able to stand, much less fight off a murderer. You are relieved of your duties, all of you. Get the fuck out."

All three began speaking at once, Brett even going so far as to begin shouting. Jason simply went over to the peg on the wall where the king's sword hung, picked it up, and unsheathed it. They quietened immediately, and he said softly in the silence, "Are you disobeying your king?" Jason glanced at each of them, daring them to challenge him. They all knew the punishment for such things, and he knew the only one in the room who had even the slightest chance to defeat him was injured and wrapped in bandages. They said nothing as they began filing out, bewildered looks on their dumb faces.

"Wait. Take this with you," he told them, indicating his father's corpse by kicking it. "Smith!" he yelled. The young man entered.

Jason had made him wait outside; he was not important enough to witness what had transpired. A cousin of his father's scout, Randy looked much like Stan. The young man was tall for his age and thin with long, dark hair and the beginning of a youth beard. "Your cousin is dead," Jason said simply, looking him in the eyes, searching. Smith said nothing and just shrugged. Jason smiled. "Nice to know where your loyalty lies. Fetch the new council and Percy. I don't give a shit if he's drunk or sleeping; tell him his king needs to speak with him." Smith nodded and ran off to do Jason's bidding.

Percy may have been a traitorous drunk, but his "lightning," as he called it, was incredible. The fool had stumbled across it accidentally when trying to cook fermented corn. He claimed that was how he came to make the strongest drink in the city, really strong shit. It burned all the way down. When the drunken idiot burned his face all up and lost half his hand and an ear in an explosion, Jason immediately began thinking of ways to use the volatile liquid.

When Smith returned, Jason had the rest of his small council assembled. Frank Digner was his capable captain of guards. Jason knew him well; he would be the perfect replacement for Terrence. He was a strong stocky man with a good head on his shoulders. Tim Meadows, Jason's best friend, the new head of the chroniclers, and the best healer he could trust, was also assigned the role of scribe to record and document all of what was to come for the new histories. Plus, Tim was an artist when it came to torture. And of course, there was old Brett's grandson Zak Kince. Extremely capable with both blade and hammer, he was large around the arms and shoulders and had bright red hair that always hung wildly about his face. Jason had come to rely greatly on the large boy over the past months of planning.

"In two weeks, I want to send a raiding party to Altheia to soften the edges a little. As dumb as it was, my father's burning the tower and killing their queen was an excellent start. Let's keep up the pressure until the time is right. Percy, I want you making lighting, as much as possible. I will give you whatever people and resources you need. Zak, I want your catapult positioned on the parapet above the manse. I have something special in mind for that."

Randy spoke up. "There is one more thing," he said. Jason looked to his scout, who wore an uneasy expression. "I think Vincent is still alive," he said, cringing as if he had just stepped on glass.

Jason frowned. "What makes you say that?" he asked.

Randy took a breath and replied, "Tim and I went back to dispose of his body so your father wouldn't find out." He paused and looked to his king. "We could not find it. All the blood and signs of a fight were still fresh, but no body."

It was Percy who spoke up for once: "He is in Altheia."

Jason looked to the old drink maker curiously. "And how do you know that?" he asked Percy.

"My boy disappeared the same night. I am sure the prince and his little gang of brats had something to do with it. Let me take care of it. I will not let you down," Percy told his new king.

Jason hesitated while looking into the man's eyes. He saw anger there and was not sure if he should let this volatile drunkard attempt to settle the matter. "I am sorry, Percy, but I do not believe you are capable of killing Vincent."

A small amount of shock registered with the drink maker's scowl, and it was at that moment Jason realized Percy may not have been referring to taking care of Vincent. "I can do it, I swear. If Randy is correct and he's laid up full of holes, then it should be nothing to kill an injured man. He may be dead already. I will find out either way," Percy told him.

Jason was shaking his head before the man finished. "Frank, send one of your men," he said to the captain. When he looked back to Percy, the man was a picture of barely contained rage. "What do we do about Terrence?" Jason asked the room, still looking at Percy, daring him to threaten him.

"Nothing. I believe he is too old to pose a threat to us or our plans. Leave the man to his retirement," Frank said.

Jason frowned. He knew the two men had been colleagues for years and probably had somewhat of a relationship. "Fine, but at the first sign of disloyalty, I will end him," he said. His captain nodded.

Lya awoke in a beautiful stone room in a bed so soft that she was immediately sure she was dreaming. She blinked and sat up slightly, rubbing the sleep from her eyes, and she was met by the familiar clank of her shackles and an unfamiliar pain in her ribs. She felt her face; it seemed larger. She tried to lick her lips, but her jaw would not open.

Definitely a dream. She looked over, expecting to see the now familiar and somehow lovable face of her old man in the hood. What she saw shocked her, and she sat upright quickly and took a few breaths. One of her eyes was swollen shut, but she was positive that was Lucid sitting beside her. She tried to speak, but still her jaw would not open. What came out was a pitiful moan. Fear gripped her, and the memories of the run came back in a flash.

Am I dead? She was so scared that she began shouting, or what she thought would be a shout turned into more moans and grunts. Lucid had been sleeping and immediately snapped awake at her braying. He stood over her.

"Shh. It's okay. You are okay." He had such a huge smile on his face that she was confused and terrified.

"Mm," she moaned, pointing to her jaw. She probed with

her fingers and began shaking when she felt metal attached to the front of her teeth.

"It's okay, Lya. It's just a device to heal your jaw. It was broken in two places, and for it to heal properly you will need to wear this for a time."

She relaxed a bit yet had so many questions. The obvious *How will I eat?* came to mind first. As if reading her mind, Lucid stepped back and grabbed a large cup with a tall stick poking out of the top.

"You have been out for a while. You must be starving," he said as he brought the cup to her lips. "This is food," he told her. Her skepticism must have been apparent in her expression because he chuckled and said, "I mashed it up and blended it into a liquid. Try it." He told this to her as he sat down on the bed next to her. Her heart started beating faster. She had never been so close to him, not consciously anyway. Her lips were swollen and cracked, but she was starving, so she took the cup and tried a small sip. It was unbelievably delicious. Her eyes widened. She had never tasted anything so good. Soon she had an empty cup and a full stomach. She handed the cup back to him, and he smiled.

"Good, right? Just tomatoes and carrot with some fruit. Wish I could grind meat, but so far that level of liquefying food has eluded me," Lucid told her ruefully.

She tried to smile but found that difficult in her condition, so she settled for an enthusiastic nod. His Lockian had improved much in their time apart. He brought her a smaller cup with another hollow stick, and the cool water was everything she needed to feel almost normal again. He sat back down in the chair next to the bed, which appeared to have been moved so he could be closer to her. She liked that and found herself staring at the handsome man. She had never seen him in full light. He was so perfect that she felt such a mess sitting before him, unable to speak with her face bashed to bits.

"Oh, sorry. I suppose you will not be able to speak for some time, so I can provide the conversation. It will give me a chance to really master your tongue, and it just might help you feel better to hear about all of my problems." She leaned back into the pillows, making herself comfortable, and continued staring—and not just because he had her attention. It was hard to look away.

"I am not sure how much you remember, so I will just start fresh," he told her as he slid down in the chair slightly and propped his feet up on the side of her bed. "I have been going through quite a lot lately. Probably evident to you because, as you know, I have not had a chance to come see you. I would have come every night if I could." Lucid's face colored at that, but he continued quickly. "I had made the decision to sneak off without Jon. He is my best friend, but he told me it was foolish to go when our kingdom is in such turmoil. Probably was, but I did not see it that way. I found you being carried by a gvorlock, so I …" He hesitated. He looked down at the floor, and when he finished, he spoke much quieter: "I killed him."

Lya was absolutely stunned. *He killed a gvorlock? Impossible,* she thought.

Lucid caught her look and added quickly, almost defensively, "I couldn't help it. I saw you slung over his shoulder like a dead deer, your face all beat up, and I just snapped. I'm not sure what came over me. I have never killed anyone before. But what he did to you …" He stopped and stared at nothing for a moment before he continued, his face taking on a sadder quality. She felt for him. "Our people, us and the gvorlocks, we have lived in peace for hundreds of years, maybe thousands. I broke a treaty that has been in place all this time because I was angry." He shook his head. "What I don't understand is, why are you there? You are not one of them, or are you? Is that just what their infants look like? Are you an infant?" he asked, panic growing in his tone. She shook her head, and he seemed to relax. "What is it then? Do you serve them?" he asked, and immediately he seemed surprised by his own question as something in his brain clicked.

Lya nodded and raised her arms, showing him her shackles. They were made of unbroken metal. On each wrist were two flat metal bracelets connected together by tiny chains and wreathed in tiny symbols. The metal was dull, almost like stone, and the symbols seemed to glow of their own light. They did not seem like shackles at all, just bracelets marking her as a slave as the separate rings on each wrist were not connected, binding her hands together as with normal chains. Lucid looked dumbstruck, so much so that Lya thought he might fall out of his chair.

He sat back, still looking dazed, and mumbled, "She was right." Then he looked up and continued, "I guess it does not matter. You are under the protection of Altheia now; no one will touch you. Although now that I have killed a gvorlock, I don't know how much protection I can offer. And don't get me started on Drondos." She looked confused. He sighed and said, "Let me just start at the beginning …"

Over the few weeks he told Lya everything, or at least he told her about so many things that she struggled to keep it all together. He told her of the start of their culture here on the island they called Blysse, the split of the two cities, and the tensions growing between them. He told her stories of his childhood and of his family. He told her in detail about all his friends and the nature of their relationships, among those a young woman named Alisha who was Daryl's girlfriend and the owner of the room in which they lived.

Days went by, evidenced by the cycle of blissfully uninterrupted sleep and delicious liquid meals. Over all of this time, Lucid never left the room. He had one person he gave orders to, and that person brought food and drink and anything else they needed, including a large book of gvorlock words and their Altheia tongue counterparts, the latter of which Lya began learning. It was not until the fourth day that she learned that particular helper's name was Russell and that he was recently rescued from Drondos, a close friend of Lucid's from his childhood stories.

Lucid and Lya grew closer as the days went by. At least Lya thought so. She was unsure exactly when it had happened, but somewhere between him breaking his arm falling out of a tree and him and Jon almost drowning in a whirlpool, it struck her that she was in love with Lucid. What was worse, she was nothing but a slave, whereas he was a prince. There was a huge social chasm between them, and the more he revealed about himself and his position in this city, the more it broke her heart at the realization that someone like him would never be interested in someone like her. She was just a girl in trouble and he'd done the right thing and saved her because he had a soft heart.

He would have done the same for anyone, she had thought many times. Still, she marveled at her new life, days spent listening to Lucid go on and on as he helped her recover, nights spent sleeping peacefully. She felt alive for the first time. Every day that she awoke to Lucid's smile, she silently thanked the man from her dreams.

Over the time Lya spent recovering, Lucid's friend Daryl

stopped by every few days to check on her progress and make an adjustment to her metal mouth shackles.

"It seems to be healing well, and at an alarming rate," Daryl told them one afternoon as he inspected her jaw and the metal within. "In fact"—he shot a glance and a tiny half smile at Lucid—"I believe it's time to remove the brace."

Lya smiled broadly, or at least as far as the brace would allow. *Finally!* she thought as Daryl stood, walked to the table near the entrance to a small but sturdy bag, and began pulling tools out. Some of those were wicked-looking weapons. She sat up quickly and began rubbing her hands together nervously. She should have never been worried, however, as he simply pulled a small gripping tool of sorts with two tapered pieces of metal bound in the center and two tiny grips. He stuffed everything back in the bag and sat down on the bed next to her.

"Open," he said, gesturing to her lips.

She was so excited that this was finally happening, she used her fingers to open her lips as far as possible. Immediately her face reddened as she realized Lucid was watching her. Her eyes drifted to his chair, but he had gotten to his feet and was pacing around the small room, giving what little privacy was possible. *Has there ever been anyone so thoughtful and considerate?* she thought as Daryl began his delicate yet surprisingly gentle work.

The gvorlocks were emotionless brutes with absolutely no consideration for one another, much less their slaves. When one of their own died, no one cared because there was always a numbered male to replace him. They simply dragged the poor creature to the sea, tossed the huge corpse into the ocean, and made jokes about how stupid or ugly the dead gvorlock's family was all the way back. That tiny gesture of Lucid's, simply getting up and looking away, spoke volumes. Lya's heart started beating much faster as everything began to process in her mind.

She would be able to speak to him.

With all the time they had spent in this room, she knew absolutely everything about him. She knew that grilled cow meat was his favorite food. She knew that when he was fifteen, he had stolen smoke from his father for the first time and he and Jon had snuck off to the beach, stayed up all night talking, and awoke late the next morning with the worst sunburn of their lives. She also knew that once Lucid's father, the king, passed away, Lucid would be the ruler of the whole city. What would she tell him? What could she tell him? She was quite literally, compared to him, a nobody, nothing, a slave whose whole miserable life had amounted to working the gardens and getting beaten and brutalized. A sickening feeling crept up in her gut, and suddenly it was difficult to see as she blinked tears away. Her hands being preoccupied, the tears fell freely down her cheeks.

Just then she felt a small snap and a release of tension in her jaw. Daryl, who had been digging around her teeth with his gripping tool, slowly pulled out a long length of wire. Relief washed over Lya as immediately the tension holding her mouth released and she began flexing her jaw. Daryl saw her tears, but she assumed he took them for tears of relief and so said nothing. Lucid had told her that only the king knew about the gvorlocks, and she had yet to practice their tongue even though she had been reading Lucid's book, so she simply smiled at Daryl as he got up and began gathering his things.

"Can she walk?" she heard Lucid ask.

Daryl nodded. "Leave the bandages on until she feels no pain in her ribs. Other than that, she will make a full recovery quickly."

She understood few of their words, but after Daryl's reply, Lucid glanced at her with a huge smile. After a few more exchanges of words, Daryl exited the room, leaving her alone with Lucid.

"Thank you—for everything. I know now what you risked to save me, and I am so grateful," she told him, her own voice sounding strange and unfamiliar. He sat in his chair next to the bed and got comfortable. "I think I need you to help me with your language. If I am to pose as a runaway from Drondos, my speech would be a dead giveaway. The book is wonderful, but practice will help."

Lucid nodded and thought a moment. "You will have plenty of time to study where we are going," he said.

She looked at him curiously, and he continued. "First of all, how do you feel? Think you would be up for a short hike and a boat ride?"

She had no idea what "boat ride" meant, but going anywhere with him sounded wonderful. Lya smiled. Getting out of this room they had been stuck in for what felt like months was exactly what she needed. Lya nodded, swung her feet off the bed, and sat up. She was a little stiff and sore, but she had been pacing the room over the past few days—with Lucid's help—so she felt strong.

Lucid got up and wandered to the large chest filled with clothes and drew out two cloaks. He brought one to her and slipped on his own. She stood and did the same, realizing they both had head coverings attached to the upper backs of the garments. He pulled his to rest on his head, and his face was mostly hidden. She understood. She mimicked him, and he reached out to her, smiling and looking into her eyes. She could have just stood there taking in that image for days.

Touching someone, even simply hand-to-hand contact, was something alien to her. Her parents had died when she was so young that she hardly remembered any sort of physical affection. The only other experience she had was patching up her fellow slaves' wounds. With Lucid, it was a whole new level.

Could he possibly share these feelings? she thought.

She reached out and took his hand. It was rough and strong but warm and surprisingly gentle. Her heart was pounding as he said, "Just a couple of stops to make first," and turned to go. They exited the room together, hand in hand.

CHAPTER 17

Brynn sat in the royal council chambers amid all her father's top men, including Jake, whom she wanted sitting as an equal at the meeting rather than standing in the shadows. Over the last several days she had come to rely greatly on the head king's man as he had proven himself fiercely loyal to Brynn since the night she caught her father returning from the murder of Ivan. With Lucid still missing, she knew Jake had to be on her side.

It was a serious problem, her brother's disappearance, as she needed him at this moment more than she had ever needed him before. To evoke law 57 legally, it must be the firstborn child to make the claim, and that child must be considered at the age of majority. Without Lucid, her father's councillors may not side with her, but she had to try. Her father had crossed a line from which there was no going back. He had taken a person's life. A vile person? Of course. Did he deserve it? Brynn could not say. But the fact that her father had done such a thing was ... She pulled herself out of her thoughts and stood to address the room.

"Thank you, gentlemen, for accepting my summons. Let's just get right to it. I am sure you have all heard, but for those of you who have not, my father is not well. He has killed Ivan, the king of Drondos." Brynn paused, looking at their faces.

Shock passed over some of those faces, but most took the news as if she had just told them the cattle count for this summer.

This is not going to go well, she thought before she continued.

"I do not need to remind you gentlemen that we have very strict laws about murder here in Altheia. With the murder, coupled with the behavior of my father over the grief of losing his wife, I believe it is time to evoke law 57."

The men around the room rose and burst out with angry chatter immediately.

"Impossible."

"That fat idiot deserved it."

"Absolutely not."

"Ridiculous."

"You are just a child."

Jake let this go on for a few seconds before he stood abruptly and slammed his fist down on the table. The room quieted instantly, and the head king's man yelled to the councillors, "Sit down and be quiet. You will all hold your disrespectful tongues and listen to what she has to say! You forget yourselves. This is our princess, and she has been through more in the past few days than any of you could handle." He paused and looked around at them. "Despite her age." He sat back down slowly.

She nodded and continued. "Lucid is missing. I have had king's men tear the royal wing apart, and similarly the rest of the city, and no one seems to know where he is. If anyone here has any ideas where he might be hiding, speak up now." She paused briefly and looked around at the men, but they all looked bewildered. "I thought so. Once again I ask you, let me evoke law 57 and relieve my father only until Lucid is found or Normin recovers."

It was old Master Wyndell who spoke first. "No disrespect, Princess, but that law was put in place 126 years ago because your great-great-grandfather went"—he paused and cleared his throat—"mentally insane. The law states, 'Any king or otherwise leader of our people who appears to be mentally unfit may be temporarily disabled as leader pending further medical evaluation. If the master healer justifies that the ruler is no longer able to run the kingdom, the throne shall pass to the firstborn of adult age,'" the old master recited.

"The way I see it, there are many problems with your proposal. The first and most prominent is that Reginald has not yet given the king a proper mental evaluation. Also, Lucid must be found, as the law clearly states 'firstborn of adult age.' And again, no disrespect, Princess, but you are neither of those things," Wyndell said.

It went on like that for some time, old men arguing against an eleven-year-old. Brynn held her own respectfully because she understood these men were extremely loyal to her father and she could not fault them for that. However, neither did she let them walk all over her. The hardest part was convincing them to let Reginald evaluate her father at all. In the end, her wits prevailed, and they all agreed the kingdom must have a ruler at all times no matter the circumstances. Still, as they filed out when the meeting was over, their general aura was one of disapproval.

Brynn sighed and sat down after the men had exited, looking at Jake, who had stayed seated. He waited patiently while she brooded. How was she to hold a whole kingdom together when she could barely convince a handful of old men to go along with her? The obvious answer was that she could not. Lucid had to be found immediately.

"I need you to do something for me," she told Jake. He sat up, looking intently at her. He always wore that expression. "I need you to stop shadowing me and find Lucid. Whatever it takes."

After the meeting, Brynn exited the palace into a beautiful sunny day. It was so nice that she decided a walk on the beach would do her wonders. She took her time, winding her way through the lower dirt paths and speaking to the people in the lower dwellings as she went. It helped keep her mind off the inevitable. Jake's replacement, Gerald Dane, stayed a step behind and said nothing but kept a watchful eye, his head constantly turning and scanning for threats. There was no need as the people, at least Brynn thought, enjoyed speaking with their princess and adored her for taking time to check on them.

After some time, she finally cleared the last row of huts and reached the white sand and beautiful blue water of Altheia's beach. She walked right up to the crest of the tide and closed her eyes, breathing deep of the sea air. When she opened her eyes again, she just stared out at the endless blue. Such a peaceful place for her, it allowed her to finally relax and place her thoughts.

Brynn was overwhelmed with responsibility. With her father struggling to keep his wits and Lucid missing, she despaired how she might hold the kingdom together. The lowers seemed to be fine, but the very foundation of the Altheia royalty had been rocked over the past several weeks. If not for the council, morale would have begun to decline quickly. Normin had held these people together for years; they prospered under his leadership. How was Brynn to be expected to fill *those* shoes? If Jake failed to find Lucid and her father was diagnosed and found to be incapable, she could never expect to achieve the same level of respect and leadership. She was just too young in the eyes of the kingdom. Her thoughts got her feet moving; she began walking down the beach.

Seriously, what the hell is Lucid's problem? She understood he had his own life now, and as the history went, as long as the king was still alive, then the prince was given freedom to do as he wished. Her father had done it; now, her brother. She was unsure if Lucid knew about their father killing Ivan, but how could he just leave right after their mother passed? It was still so fresh for Brynn whenever she thought about it. She had been so busy that there had not been much time to dwell on her mother. Yet in moments like this, it was like prying open a wound that had already healed closed.

Tears fell as she walked. Thankfully Mr. Dane was walking a few yards behind her. It would not do for anyone to see their potential ruler as weak; it would play into the councillors' point that she was too young—and she refused to let the kingdom see her as a weak little girl.

As she progressed down the beach, it struck her that she recognized her surroundings. Her father's fishing hut was just around the next bend. Blysse was an irregular-shaped island, which led to many right turns when walking the beach, and it has many curved inlets with cliffs overlooking the water. There was a more direct path to the little hut through the high city, but Brynn had never been there from this direction.

As she followed the curve of the water, soon the brush maneuvered itself inward and the hut came into view. She decided she would stop there and rest for a little while, her small legs tired from the walk. Her family had spent a lot of time there as fishing used to be one of her father's favorite hobbies.

Normin would swim out into the ocean with his reel in hand, so far that Brynn could just barely make out the top of his head. He would cast his line from there and swim back quickly to get set. She must have seen him do that a thousand times from the little chair under the window of that hut. But the huge fish he could reel in were impressive. She tried not to think of the hundreds of grilled fish her mother had cooked on the little pit just outside as she passed it and approached the door, Dane still trailing silently a few yards behind.

Brynn opened the small portal and froze, mouth agape in shock. The hut was not empty.

Lying unconscious on the little bed was a thin man wrapped chest to waist in bandages. That did not shock her quite as much as the masked man with a dagger standing over him, looking directly at her. She screamed, and poor Gerald came rushing forward just in time to catch a savage thrust. The dagger looked to have pierced his heart because the effect was instant. He managed a bloody exhale as he vainly attempted to bring his sword up, but it was slow even to Brynn's untrained eyes. The killer yanked his dagger out quickly, and Dane fell dead, a pool of blood spreading out around him at a rapid pace. Brynn was shaking and frozen in place with fear. It was like a nightmare where she could comprehend everything that was happening but could not get her limbs to react. When she peeled her eyes away from her guard and looked up to the masked man, he took one half step toward her.

This is how I am going to die, she thought.

However, at a glance she noticed the bed with the injured man was now empty. In the blink of an eye, the bandaged stranger snuck up behind the killer and wrapped his arms around the man's head. With a grunt and a disgusting snap, the killer's head spun completely around to face the opposite direction with the body staying perfectly straight. Given the speed at which all of this had taken place, it was a moment before Brynn realized what had just happened. When it hit her, the world went dark.

CHAPTER 18

As Normin dressed himself that morning, there was a knock at the door. He already knew who it was, knew this moment would come. He did not really believe Reggie intended to give him a mental evaluation—the man felt more like an older brother to the king—just a conversation in which Normin intended to convince his friend that this plan might work. However, learning of his ancestors' slow descent into madness had stuck with Normin over the years and always seemed an overly uncomfortable topic.

As expected, Reginald stood there when the king opened the door. As the master healer saw the rags his king had dressed himself in, the look on his face was pained and a little frightened.

"Come on in, Reggie. I will explain," Normin said.

Reginald Wilkins was at least a decade older than Normin with dark skin and pure white hair cropped short. His light brown eyes held a seriousness few could match. Reginald was dressed in the typical white robes of the healers, long sleeves rolled up to his elbows to allow for less hindrance to his work. He was the second-smartest man in the kingdom, and Normin always took his council seriously.

The king's chamber the healer had entered was huge and lavish with smooth rock walls covered in beatific art in a circular pattern and a fireplace directly in the center with a double open face. On the east side of the room was a table with a set of chairs under the opulent window, placed there to catch the first rays of the sun each morning. Reginald sat, and Normin did the same, the men facing each other.

"You know why I am here," Reginald said simply. Normin nodded.

"The council has …" Normin began.

Reginald waved him off and looked deep into Normin's eyes as he sat forward in his chair. "Your daughter. Lucid has gone missing, and Brynn has already begun taking the proper steps to ensure the safety of the Crown and the people," he told his king.

Normin was immediately perplexed and very proud. Lucid was a bold kid and inclined to do as he wished. The king also knew of some kind of nightly expeditions but did not pry too much into his son's personal life, mainly because he himself had more than his fair share of mischief at that age and took those experiences to be helpful in the big picture. Also he considered his son a man and tried to let him make his own decisions. But pulling a disappearing act when the kingdom was on its head was more than troubling. For an instant, Normin doubted his mad plan and began to reconsider. That it was all his fault did not elude him; neither did the fact that Brynn was doing what was needed in her brother's absence. He had always known she was smarter than other children her age, but over the past few years it had become apparent that she would be smarter than he and his father before him. The thought filled him with pride.

"Lucid is not 'missing.' He would never just outright leave. He is becoming a man and has his own life, but he will turn up eventually," Normin said.

It mattered little; Brynn would do a fine job, he knew. The memory still haunted him, yet it was the very reason he was able to continue and snap back to reality. Brynn's eyes were the very picture of her mother, and in those eyes the king saw disappointment, shame, anger. In her eyes, Normin saw that Brynn's father, her idol, her infallible king, had betrayed her. He shuddered.

He looked at Reginald and gestured to his clothes. "I know what this looks like, but I am not crazy, Reggie. I may look like I am spiraling here, but just let me explain." He leaned forward and set his elbows, looking deep into his friend's eyes. "Do you trust me?" he asked simply.

The man answered without the slightest hesitation, "Absolutely."

"It's true, Reggie. George's rumors of slaves is true. Drondos has a host of them—been breeding them for years like a pack of fucking hunting dogs! I do not know what his intentions were, but it does not matter now. What does matter is, what do you think that spoiled little shit Jason would do with an army of slaves? I have singlehandedly given Drondos and its slave army to a young boy. I don't like it one bit, so I intend to do something about it. Maybe it will make up for taking a man's life, at least in the eyes of God."

Reginald gave him a reproachful look, and Normin raised his hands in defense. The old healer removed his glasses and massaged the bridge of his nose, eyes closed. When he opened them, he said, "What you propose is suicide. You are the king. Without you, we fall into chaos. I cannot let you attempt to save them."

Normin slammed his hands down on the table, shouting, "Then who will?" He let the silence answer.

"I cannot ask this of any of my men. I would not risk any of their lives for this mad plan."

He had discovered the hard way that vengeance was not as sweet as could be expected. As horrid of a person King

Ivan was, killing him brought Normin no satisfaction—and no matter how much he washed, the blood was still on his hands.

"Trust me now, old friend. Let Brynn and the council work things out until Lucid turns up. I have complete confidence in my children and my advisors to hold the kingdom together until my return." Normin stood and raised his arms to his sides, a tiny grin tugging at the edges of lips. "Do I look like a deserter, a … slave?" he asked.

Reginald looked at him with that intense stare of his for a moment, then replied, "Yes, yes you do." Reggie stood. They both walked toward the door. But before exiting, the healer turned to the king and asked, "What am I to tell your children, Normin?"

He put a hand on his friend's shoulder and said, "You tell them what you must … unless it's the truth. Do you understand?"

The healer nodded grimly and made to leave, but just before he could open the door, Normin put his hand on it, stopping him.

"Thad and Edward seem like they could use a small break," he said quietly, nodding his head slightly toward the guards posted outside his door.

"Understood," Reginald said.

Normin closed the door behind Reginald after the latter had made his exit and returned to his chair to think. He felt good about his decision; it felt right. In his daily prayers he always urged God to keep him on the right path, and as usual, things seemed to begin to fall into place. It was a little terrifying to leave the comforts of his kingdom to intentionally become a slave in a city where he had just murdered the king. He knew his day would come, however, and it mattered to him much less now when that day would be. This was something that needed to be done, *had* to be done.

Tensions between the cities had reached an all-time high, and something drastic was required to keep the peace. Very drastic.

Normin rose and readied himself for what may very well be the single most insane act of his life. He opened his chamber door and looked around to make sure Reggie had done his duty. No one was around, so he exited quickly, locking his door behind him, and hurried through the halls and out the palace doors. Dressed as he was, no citizens seemed to notice who he was. He passed smoothly through the edge of the LD and out into the woods on the north side of the city.

As he walked through the woods to Drondos, he could not help but think of his children. Lucid would be an extremely capable leader—if Brynn could track him down, that is. What mischief Lucid was up to finally piqued Normin's curiosity, and he wondered what the hell his oldest was doing at that very moment. As long as he stayed away from the gvorlocks, it did not matter. Was he staying away from them though? Normin stopped walking and started to turn back, thinking that the gvorlocks' village may very well be the destination of his son's little expeditions. Lucid did take the meeting with D'matrius much better than Normin had when he was Lucid's age.

No, he thought, *one foot in front of the other. Drondos first. Trust in Lucid.*

He turned back toward his goal and kept walking. As he walked, he began planning his slavery takeover. Earning their trust would be key. They must trust him if they were to follow him blindly into freedom without fear of retribution. The promise of protection and life in another city just might do most of the work for him. Still, the fact that no slaves had escaped and come to Altheia begging for aid told him they were locked down tight and were possibly watched all hours of the day and night.

This is so stupid, he thought as he continued walking. Still, it seemed to be the only way to make up for what he had done. He knew what type of kid Jason was and had no intention of leaving these people to his mercy. Nor did he like the idea of that little brat having an army of slaves.

When the main gate of Drondos came into view, Normin stepped off his path, found a nice moist mud puddle, and finished the job of making himself look like a filthy beggar with nothing to live for. It was not that difficult to assume that role. A month's worth of not shaving or trimming his hair would do the rest. Hopefully anyone who knew his face would not look at a slave so closely and no one would recognize him. As he approached the main gate, he noticed it was closed this time. No surprise there as their king had just been assassinated.

"Help!" he yelled up at the ramparts.

A moment later a guard peered down over the edge. He looked him over and scowled. "What do you want?" he asked.

"Please, sir," Normin replied, "I am just looking for a place to live. I'm very hungry and ran out of water days ago. Please, may I enter?"

The guard leaned against the rail and said, "Deserter, eh? Had enough of that pussy King Normin? Sure, let me just open the gate." He disappeared, and a moment later the gate began opening. Two guards came out to greet him, and as they got close, they did not slow down. Next Normin knew, he was facedown in the dirt, hands being shackled behind his back. He tasted blood in his mouth as the guards hauled him to his feet and half escorted, half dragged him through what looked to be an abandoned market of sorts. They each had one of his bound arms. As they pulled him, he noticed lots of empty shops, each with a living quarters upstairs that also appeared to be empty. There was hard-packed dirt used for what could modestly be called a road, lined with abandoned buildings in different stages of collapse.

"What happened here? Where is everyone?" Normin asked of his captors.

"Shut up, gutter rat," one of them replied, complementing his remark with a little shove, which caused Normin to drop to his knee. It hit hard. He heard a pop and grunted at the pain. He had no time to dwell on it, thank God, as he was immediately hauled back to his feet, continuing down ghost town road. Soon they approached a large building, possibly a warehouse of, or at least at one time it may have been used as such, but now the building looked as if it might fall right where it sat. The whole thing leaned slightly west, made of wood, he thought. It was cracking and peeling so badly, it hardly looked like wood at all. The only thing covering the window holes other than stone bars were different-colored clothes that blew slightly with the wind. The heavy door was solid, however, and two more guards stood watch on either side. What also stood out, next to the disheveled warehouse, was a freshly built fort made solid with thick logs lashed together.

Guard shack, he thought. *Ivan may have been a wretched person, but he was no fool.*

The two door guards opened the door to the warehouse, and Normin was thrown roughly to the ground just inside.

"Look alive, you worthless pieces of shit. Better be ready," the soldier said, raising his voice to the gathered crowd. "We're doubling your training hours." He paused, taking in all the slaves' faces. "We raid Altheia in one week."

And with that, the door slammed shut behind Normin. He

heard the sound of a heavy bar close and lock. His heart sank at the words. How could he have been so bold and impulsive? Perhaps the death of his beloved Alice really had played with his mind.

This was so stupid, he thought again.

What would it be like to fight against his own people? He would have to hide his face and do everything necessary to prevent loss of life. He stood and looked around the building, and gaped. A huge number of people, perhaps as many as a thousand, stared back at him.

CHAPTER 19

Terrence awoke as if struck by lightning. The pain came hard and sudden. Someone had punched him awake. He gasped. His stomach felt as if there was a blade in it. He realized his hands were lashed together behind him, tied very tight to a large post of some sort, as he could not move anything but his head. The pain coming from his left eye, which saw nothing but blackness, was excruciating.

Memories began coming back slowly. He recalled wandering the woods. He'd gotten lost after only two days; he definitely remembered that. Then, nothing. He didn't remember how he had come to be unconscious or, as he looked around, where he was.

He was in a small thatched hut made of long limbs interwoven into walls. He also noticed that he was face-to-face with a large, bald-headed man. The fog in his mind began clearing a little more, and he focused on the man with no eyebrows. When he realized what he was looking at, Terrence's own eyes went wide with shock and more than a little fear. His bladder failed him instantly. A nightmarish green glow burned bright in eyes full of hatred and anger. The thing punched him in the face, and it rocked his whole head backward, causing it to strike the post. Agony rocked him to his core as the pain migrated to all his other wounds, and his body and voice screamed as one. He saw stars for a moment before getting another punch to his stomach. In an instant, he had zero air in his lungs as he gasped and coughed.

"Who did it? Was it you?" the behemoth shouted in Terrence's face, almost close enough to touch noses.

It was odd hearing a normal question from the creature, as if Terrence had expected it to grunt and yelp like a monkey. Agony washed over him as he tried to breathe. He felt something hard in his mouth and spit out a gob of bloody teeth. He had no idea how to answer the question, even if he'd had the air to do so.

Terrence gasped a few more times and managed to say, "I don't know what you're talking about."

Again the thing struck him across the face, dizzying and disorienting Terrence and clouding his thoughts.

"We will destroy your people for this. Just remember that when you are standing over your cold, dead children, it was *you* who broke the treaty!" the creature shouted.

With a murderous gleam in his wicked eyes, the huge man walked behind Terrence's post, grabbed one of his tied hands, and said, "I am only going to ask once more: Who killed him?"

Still dazed from the blows, Terrence hesitated. The giant took a strong hold on his little finger, twisted savagely, and pulled it off. The pain was unlike anything Terrence had ever experienced. His body shook with agony. He screamed something primal, vomited, and passed out again.

When he awoke, once again only one of his eyes opened. And the pain—he was sure that was what woke him. Pain everywhere. Again he looked around at his surroundings slowly. He did not see the giant. His heart began beating a little faster.

This may be my only chance, he thought.

It seemed he had reached that moment before death when he refused to give up, when he was resolved to fight no matter what, and the natural instinct to live took over. He hovered over himself like a ghost, watching as he wriggled one of his hands free, the one that lacked a finger. It seemed with one missing, the width of his hand had shrunk a fraction. He wiggled it painfully out of the rope and began, even more painfully, untying his other hand. He started sweating and gritted his teeth as he worked. Blocking out the pain was becoming increasingly more difficult as he worked with the rope. Finally, with his vision beginning to go dark again, he felt the restraint fall to the floor. Without the rope holding him, his legs failed and he sprawled painfully in the dirt, followed by an immediate head rush. The world spun around him. He was so dizzy that he had to wait before attempting to stand. After a moment the room leveled off once again, and he looked at his hand. It did not look right all covered in blood and missing one of its appendages.

A wave of nausea struck Terrence, but he forced himself up once more and went to the gourd of water by the door. He poured some on his hand to rinse it, then drank deeply and paid for it a second later as he vomited it up. He drank slower, and after he'd had as much as he could handle, he headed for the door of the hut and listened for a few seconds. Silence. He ripped off a section of his pants, wrapped it around his missing-fingered hand, and stepped out.

It was daytime. He saw no one around, which he thought odd, but he did not question his luck. He chose a direction at random and took off running. He made it about twenty yards, mostly on adrenaline, and then stumbled and fell. His legs felt like they had been pierced by a hundred needles. His hand and eye throbbed with horrible pain, and he was so weak from hunger that he had no idea how he had even made it this far. He glanced back to the hut prison he had escaped. The simple structure of woven branches still looked so close; he'd barely made it anywhere. With a clench of his jaw and a determined growl, he stood and began moving again, walking this time.

At a pace just slightly faster than a snail, Terrence made his escape and marveled at how easily he had just walked away in broad daylight.

Time and trees went by like a dream. He had no sense of direction and felt as if he were severely drunk, but he continued to stumble forward. After some time, he must have fallen again because he realized he was sitting. He struggled to pull air into his lungs and despaired that he would die right where he sat. Terrence was not a religious man; no one in Drondos was—they simply lacked belief. Altheians were fiercely devoted to their god, and Terrence had read a copy of the holy text, but as with most Drondosians, he simply lacked faith. Still, he sat there, sick, weak, starving, and bleeding to death, hopelessly lost. He looked up. "I don't know if you are up there, but if so, then please hear me now. I am Terrence Williams, and I am not ready to die. Please help me," he prayed.

He felt tears on his face and an overwhelming sense to just lie down and give up. He took one shuddering breath and began to lie down right where he sat.

Splash.

The sound came from somewhere close. Terrence turned and held his breath. There it was again, another small splash not far from him, off to his left. He must have lain down—he did not remember—so he crawled toward the sound and was absolutely dumbfounded to find a group of frogs splashing in a small pond just a few feet away. One leapt toward him. With his good hand he snatched it up quickly. Without a second thought, he bit the head off, spit it out, and began tearing into the legs. The warm meat was very good. It had been so long since he'd had food. Fresh tears appeared and fell as he chewed. Then, as he realized what had just happened, he was stunned. He had prayed for help, and the god of Altheia had answered. He had been given a second chance at life by a god whom he had never given any thought to and honestly didn't think existed. In the depths of his misery, he devoted his life right then and there to the merciful deity that had saved him.

After the frog, and two more after that one, Terrence felt revitalized. He was still in a tremendous amount of pain, but as he stood, he felt new energy surge through him. He began walking again.

Where will I go? he thought as he slowly worked his way through the thick woods. Drondos was out of the question, as Luke had tried to kill him once, and Terrence was positive the king would not stop until he was dead. Why? He did not know, nor did he care, as that realization left him only one option. But how would he find it? He only knew the way from Drondos, and even that route he knew only vaguely. And even if he were to find it, he would never be accepted by those people because he had killed their beloved queen.

Maybe someone will know, he thought as he walked.

With no other choice available, he just kept moving. He was unsure how long he had traveled when the light from the sun began to fade. Suddenly, he heard the waves crashing on shore faintly; never before had it sounded so beautiful. The end of the tree line came into sight, and just on the other side lay a large swath of wheat stalks.

Farm, he thought as he stumbled on.

When he finally found the house, his vision began to darken again and his head was spinning. Dizzy, he fell and found the world spun so much that he could not open his eyes again.

He awoke in a very nice bed in a neat, clean room. He rubbed the sleep from his eyes and sat up to get a better look. Then he remembered making it to a farm. The farmers must have gotten him to bed and patched him up because the pain was everywhere but manageable for the first time in what felt like an eternity.

"Thirsty?" asked a small voice filled with malice and hatred.

Terrence looked over to see a small boy holding out a cup of water. His face betrayed his true intention.

"Do I know you?" Terrence asked without taking the cup. The boy's sneer indicated that the cup may contain more than just water.

"You don't remember me?" the boy asked as he set the cup down and walked to the bed to stand over Terrence. "I suppose you wouldn't. I am a bit thicker now. Been actually eating thanks to these nice people."

Terrence felt this might be leading to something, and he was in no mood for games. "What is ..." he began. The boy backhanded him, causing pain in his missing eye to flare up and the room to spin.

"You killed my father," the boy said, his voice cracking. "Then you killed my mother."

The escaped slave from the raid, Terrence thought. Fear washed over him. It would be ironic if this boy were to kill him after everything he had been through.

Please, God, not now, he prayed.

Terrence's fear and his desire to live must have been written all over his face because the boy smiled viciously and said, "Don't worry, I will be patient for now. I will wait while you heal. I will eat; I will train; I will wait. Just know that when the time comes when you can hold a sword again, I am going to kill you." The seriousness and determination in the boy's livid eyes were unnerving.

Terrence simply nodded. The boy left, slamming the door behind him. Terrence let his head fall back into the pillow.

"Great."

CHAPTER 20

It was a beautiful, warm morning on the *Hope*, Captain James Inder thought as he stood atop the aft castle, looking out at the nothingness of the ocean. The sky was a particularly deep blue that day. Inder always thought the sky held different shades of blue depending on the time of year and the level of moisture in the air. He had mentioned it to his son Bryan once and received a chuckle in response.

What would we find if we just fucking kept sailing? he thought as he took a breath, which smelled of fresh air and salt. He loved that smell. The sea was fairly calm that day, thank God, so the light journey around the island was smooth. It had taken many months before James had earned his "sea stomach," as Inder called it. Something about being on a rocking boat for any length of time tended to lead to a horrible illness, and for hours afterward, back on solid ground, it still felt as if he were rocking.

Captain Inder shouted his orders to Aimes, his second-in-command, as the *Hope* crested the eastern edge of Blysse. The orders were repeated down a line of men, and soon the ship began a slow turn, leaning to one side slightly. Inder spread his stance to keep his balance through the turn. *Perfect*, he thought of his achievement. His father, Jordan, may have begun the monumental task of building such a thing, but it was he who finished it. His father had the right idea, but after a few design changes over the years, Inder had everything perfect in his mind. The tough part had been telling George exactly what he needed built and then having it crafted to the proper specifications. George Blake was an incredible craftsman, the best. But Inder felt as if there was a language barrier when they spoke of scale, material, and the overall design. All that was in the past as he sailed comfortably through the blue waves, keeping the coast to his port side. He noticed the ship was approaching Drondos as he thought about what Normin had told him before.

"Keep it under wraps that she is sea ready. I do not want everyone to know and have word get back to Drondos," his king had said.

Inder was constantly amazed by Normin. It was as if he knew tensions were rising between cities, even though nothing had happened yet. Altheia was the blood coursing through the king's veins, and he could feel the slightest cut. James said a silent prayer for the royal family. The captain supposed it was not a great idea to sail right next to their rival city, but it was such a small window where the royal manse could be spotted that he figured they would be okay. Most of Drondos was hidden by the cliffs on the north end of the island, but for a few short minutes, King Jason could potentially spot the huge ship. Just as Inder was about to come into view of Drondos, he decided it best to keep to his king's advice.

"Turn her about, boys. Let's bring this bitch back home. Fuck!" he yelled. He could hear Billy next to him repeat the order.

Billy Aimes was Inder's second-in-command, a tall and lanky fellow with long arms and a good head on his shoulders. Aimes had a commanding voice, which he currently used to shout orders to the men. Billy ran to the port side of the vessel to holler down to the men to get their asses moving, and the *Hope* began a slow turn back toward Altheia. Just as they reached Shadow Cove and slowed the ship to a stop, Inder spotted a small canoe in the distance with two people heading toward the cliffs on the south side of town.

Nice day for it, he thought. "Aimes, gangway," he ordered.

His men hopped to it, placing the large walkway in between rails on the port side. They dropped it on shore with a heavy thud.

Inder was the first one across. He needed to speak with Alisha. There was one more addition James felt the ship needed, and if what he had heard about Alisha's bow was anywhere close to accurate, she would have no problem with the task. He stopped first at his chambers in the palace to retrieve the current blueprint of the ship. When he entered his room, however, he smelled something awful coming from his son's chamber next door. Derek was most likely outside getting into some mischief, but his twin, Bryan, was no doubt the source of the horrid stench. The captain went one door down and opened his boys' chambers to find Bryan sitting in front of a comical amount of glass vials filled with all sorts of colored liquids, the origins of which James could not begin to grasp.

His son glanced up when he entered, and he put a stopper over his tiny stone fireplace that he had made himself for just this purpose. The bubbling stopped quickly, and he turned in his chair. "Father," he greeted.

"What the fuck have you got going on now, boy?" James said as he moved over to a glass with a liquid so deep purple in color that he couldn't help but lift it to get a better look.

Bryan got up quickly and moved over to him as if he held a blade to his own throat. He eased the vial slowly out of his father's hands and muttered, "Had to pick that one," setting it down slowly on his worktable. "It's extremely volatile. Had you dropped it, we would have both been dead."

Inder frowned and opened his mouth to protest such a

dangerous liquid, but Bryan was faster to answer his question. "I am working on a new sedative for Daryl. He asked that I make it to certain specifications. What can I do for you, Father?" he asked as he looked down at the parchment James had in his hand. "Need help with something?"

"Actually, yeah. How easy do you think it would be to raise the mainsail at the pull of a lever? Would something like that be possible?" He moved over to a large worktable where his son had other parchments spread out without any sort of organization and laid out the drawing.

"We already have this release switch here that drops the sail at a pull of this lever here." James indicated on the paper. "But I want something that can do the same going back up just as quickly."

Bryan looked over the drawing quietly for a time. "Well, gravity is what takes care of it coming down. You would need a power source to pull against that. As it is now, your men's arms are that power source. Maybe a small generator powered by the movement of the water, similar to those ancient water wheels we read about."

Inder smiled widely. "Goddamn, you are one smart little fucker." His son smiled back at him timidly and moved to go back to work. "No, boy," Inder said as he caught the move, "you are coming with me to give Alisha directions. I do not want this getting fucked up."

Bryan looked sick at the thought, and Inder knew he was not happy. The kid just abhorred being outside or around unfamiliar people and preferred to spend all his time buried in books and vials of dangerous liquids. "Alisha is no metalworker. You will need someone with knowledge of metals if it is to be done correctly," Bryan told his father, making no move to follow.

"Then she will have help. Just get your shit and come on," James commanded.

Bryan sighed but obeyed. Soon the two of them were walking through a beautiful summer afternoon toward Alisha's little shop in the LD. After a short explanation pried out of Bryan at the tip of a sword, Alisha promised she could handle it with a little help from Rusty, the royal smith.

"Give me two weeks and a couple of strong backs," she had said.

Inder believed he was on the right track for once. He dismissed his son to get back to his vials, but he grabbed his arm before he got too far. "Do not set the palace on fire," he told him. Bryan just smiled and nodded. James headed back to Shadow Cove. He needed to make sure that while the part was being built, the officers would still drill his men and repair what damage they could to prepare for the new assembly. He should not have been worried, however, as Aimes had the men doing just that.

Three days later, the new part was still under construction but looking well. Inder was exceedingly excited. He was sure this was it, the final design of the *Hope* down to the last detail. He was incredibly proud watching the shoreline recede once again. Two generations of work had led to this moment. His heart soared as he shouted orders to Aimes, who repeated them to his men. Inder had to show Normin; his king would be proud. Inder knew the circumstances of his condition, but he was sure that if Normin knew this was the final finished product, he would definitely want to see for himself. The captain wondered at the health of his friend and thought, *Maybe I should go check on him, tell him she's finished.* "We did it! You and I can accomplish anything we put our minds to," he would tell his king, and Normin would begin to pull out of his spiral.

A shout startled James out of his thoughts. He looked up, surprised to see they were already approaching Drondos.

"Get ready to turn to port!" he shouted. It echoed across the ship. He glanced up to Drondos as they began to pass by, and Inder thought he spotted something new on the parapet of the royal manse. He had passed by quite a few times previously and always stared intently, nervous that Drondos would jump off the cliff and attack. Today, his fears became a reality. He saw it in slow motion, or at least it felt that way. The huge contraption released a gigantic arm that swung around faster than Inder thought possible. An enormous flaming ball was flying through the air, directly at the *Hope*.

"Starboard! Now! Now! Starboard!" he shouted, but it was too late. The flaming ball already had the trajectory lined up perfectly; they had been prepared. The speed at which the large flaming object flew shocked Inder. All he could do was watch as the projectile slammed into the center of the main deck, rocking the ship. Wood, rope, and men alike blazed as chaos ruled the *Hope*. Screaming men engulfed in flames ran into and shoved their comrades aside to get to the ocean. They jumped overboard. Inder did not expect to have to fish them out. All he could think, watching his men die and his years of work burn, was, *Fuck, you were right, Normin. Too risky, God damn it.*

CHAPTER 21

Lucid crept silently through the LD under the cover of darkness, hand in hand with Lya. The warm softness of her skin and the way their fingers intertwined thrilled him; he found it was difficult to let go. He wanted to keep her safe, to keep anyone from ever harming her again. During all the time he had spent watching her sleep while he helped her recover, something had been growing inside him. When they first met, she was just a beautiful oddity. But now he had built her up on an untouchable pedestal and it was becoming increasingly more difficult to tell her how he felt. Still, he wanted to impress her, to show her the beautiful side of life and his city. He'd had no qualms about how she lived until now. She was a slave and most likely had lived her entire life in that tiny village. He intended to show her the full breadth of the word *free*. When they reached a modest hut near the center of town, Lucid stopped and turned to Lya.

"This is the house of a friend of mine, Rusty Lewis. He is the royal smith, and he owes me a favor. Thought we might get those uncomfortable bracelets removed," he said.

Lya lifted her hands to look at her bands, and his hand lifted with them. She nodded enthusiastically. He smiled, getting lost in those bright blue eyes for a moment before reaching over with his free hand to bang on the smith's door. No answer. He turned and hit it a few times with a little force, and the thin wooden door rattled on its hinges slightly. He heard grumbling growing closer and knew his friend was finally up.

Rusty opened the door a crack. Lucid saw part of his face covered by his long brown hair with a single dark eye peering out. When the smith saw it was his prince, he opened the door without hesitation and waved him in with only a slightly odd glance at Lya.

Rusty was not a particularly tall man, but he was huge around the arms and shoulders from a life at the forge. His build had always reminded Lucid of a beer barrel, but despite his strong physical appearance, Rusty was a weak-minded man. Addiction had almost killed him over the years after disease took his wife and his father passed. The metalworker had no one in his life to watch out for him, and he had spiraled into depression. Three years ago Lucid had paid a visit to Rusty's shop to retrieve his first ever long sword commissioned by his father. He was so excited to be getting rid of the practice sword he carried that he paid regular visits to Rusty's shop for those few weeks it took to complete the masterpiece he now wore on his side. On his third trip to check on his prize, Lucid had found Rusty passed out, facedown in a puddle of his own piss and vomit. Lucid had saved him from drowning in his own fluids and cleaned him up. After that, he camped out at Rusty's until the withdrawal symptoms from the alcohol had lessened and finally stopped. When the head smith sobered up and even began to gain a little weight back, he had come to see Lucid and thank him for saving his life. Lucid was a bit younger then, so that appreciation had him puzzled.

"I was just helping you get well, doing what anyone would do if they found their friends or family sick," the prince had said.

Rusty was so grateful to Lucid, he declared from that day forward that anything he ever needed—not just metalwork but anything—he would be there to provide it.

"You know what time it is, boy? And where the hell have you been anyway? Your sister has the king's men tearing up the city looking for you," Rusty growled.

Lucid raised an eyebrow at that last part. "What's happened now?" he asked with more than a little frustration in his tone.

"Your dad has been diagnosed by Reginald, and …" He hesitated. Lucid took a step forward, causing Lya to step with him. "It's bad, Lucid. He says that the king is mentally incapable of ruling the kingdom. Normin killed Ivan," Rusty said, cringing as if saying it out loud physically hurt him.

Lucid knew how poorly his father was taking the death of the queen, but he was stunned at the master healer's assessment. *What is she thinking?* he thought of his sister.

"That's not possible. Sure, Father is grieving and mad at the world right now, but I cannot imagine Reggie stripping his power like that. They have always been close friends. Reggie should be covering for him at the very least while he recovers. And who cares if Father killed Ivan? He was a terrible man."

Rusty nodded. "Your sister cares. She takes law one very seriously, and she is not happy about all this. Now no one has seen Normin in days and your sister is in control of the kingdom, as evidenced by the king's men searching at every path, business, and house. She needs your help, Lucid."

Lucid frowned. "Okay, I understand. Now for the real reason I am here in the middle of the night." He pulled Lya gently forward. "I just need you to chop off these shackles— *bracelets*. They are just bracelets, but they are stuck."

Rusty looked at Lucid a moment, then looked over at Lya. He scowled but nodded. "You know you don't have to hide anything from me, boy. I keep all your secrets. Or have you forgotten your little beer incident?" the smith asked as he moved over to the wall of the hut where an assortment of tools were hanging.

"And again, I appreciated that you never told Father, but this is different, dangerous. The less you know, the better, and that is me honestly looking out for your well-being."

Rusty's tone changed immediately from a scolding parent to an overprotective dog—a dog that bites. "What's wrong? Anything I can do to help?" The smith had retrieved a pair of metal cutters and gestured for Lya to hold out her arms. She finally released Lucid's hand to let Rusty work. Immediately Lucid felt he was missing his clothes or boots.

"No, thanks. I need to work all of this out myself," Lucid replied.

The smith nodded, focused on placing the cutters just right, and clamped down.

Snap.

Both men's head popped up in fear as Lya let out a long gasp and her eyes went wide. Lucid barely heard the clink of the little bracelet hitting the ground. Rusty seemed satisfied that he had not cut her, so he began placing the cutter on the next bracelet on her other wrist. Lucid knew, however, that something wasn't right.

A multitude of things came across Lya's face in those short few moments before the smith cut the second one. First came surprise, as if seeing the world for the first time. Then came fear, the kind of fear that Lucid expected dead people experience when they realize their lives are over, the expression of fear the gvorlock had as Lucid drove his sword into him. Finally, as he stared with his own fear into the endless blue of her eyes, the amount of sadness there made his heart hurt—not heartbreak because of a lost lover, but it actually hurt his chest.

Lya's chest began heaving up and down rapidly, and huge tears began to fall down her cheeks.

Snap. As the second bracelet was cut, her eyes rolled back into her head, and she collapsed.

Rusty looked up at Lucid, horrified. "I swear, I didn't cut her, Lucid. Something is wrong with her," he said with a little fear in his tone.

Lucid stepped toward her as quick as his body would move and caught her in his arms just before she hit the ground. He eased her into Rusty's bed and, without another word, bolted out the door. He ran hard to the palace and sprinted up the steps, taking them two and three at a time. Arriving at Daryl's chamber door, he pounded several times until the healer finally opened it, dagger drawn. Alisha was behind him looking very angry, but Lucid could muster no sympathy.

"I need help now! It's the girl!" the prince all but shouted at him.

Daryl turned and said to Alisha, "Shit, I will be right back." He sheathed his weapon, and he and Lucid two took off down the corridor toward the exit. Just a couple of minutes later, they burst into Rusty's home. After a quick yet thorough examination, the young healer turned to his friend. "This is why you dragged me out of bed with, ahem ..." He hesitated and glanced at Rusty. "This late," he corrected quickly. Rusty smirked, but Lucid ignored it, shaking his head.

"She was fine one second, and then she just ... passed out," Lucid said as Daryl stood and took one last glance at Lya. Then the healer clearly headed for the door.

"Sure, she is unconscious, but her breathing is normal and her heart rate is fine. She's just sleeping," Daryl said as he took a step toward Lucid and lowered his voice. "She has been through a tremendous amount over the last few weeks, both physically and mentally. Let her rest."

Lucid nodded, and Daryl exited, grumbling something about taking a punch for him. Rusty stood. When the movement caught Lucid's attention, his friend gestured for him to take the newly vacant chair.

"Better get ready for the day anyway. If you need me, I'll be at the shop. Try to catch a couple more hours' sleep before the customers come." Lucid nodded again and sat down, dazed, confused, and more than a little worried. Daryl was right though; she just needed to sleep.

Lya awoke to an amazing sky—no clouds, and the color blue was so deep and constant that she felt she could stare into it forever. Then she snapped when she realized where she was. She stood to see the shrine with all the tall statues. This time the man was smiling when she spotted his face a few yards away.

"How is it that you are doing this?" she asked as she stepped toward him. He raised an eyebrow curiously but stayed silent. Lya looked around and gestured around her and then to herself, indicating the pair with her hands.

Understanding struck his ancient features. He said, "You would not believe all the things that our people are capable of if I told you, so we will skip that for now. This is our home. You are still in Altheia, in the company of your young lover." Lya's cheeks burned with embarrassment at that last part. The old man's smile grew, but he waved it away. "Yes, yes, I know all about the extent of the feelings you have for him, but now is not the time. Later, I swear it, I will not be in such a rush and I will be able to answer all your questions. Right now I need you to listen very carefully. Those bracelets that Lucid just had removed were not just to mark you as a slave. They are made of a very special, very rare metal that blocks our energy. As soon as they were cut, the energy from that world, its living creatures, and its emotional aura flooded into your mind. When you awake, you will need to have some basic knowledge of your energy or else you will not able to stay conscious for very long.

"First things first." He lifted his hand near his chest and took two deeps breaths. "Breathing. It's something our bodies do without a thought, yet even the simplest, most natural tasks can be impossible while your mind is overwhelmed. As soon as you feel it, close your eyes, think of nothing else, and just breathe.

"Second, it will respond to your mood, so be mindful of your emotional state. If you are frightened, the energy will be sporadic and unreliable. If you are relaxed and in control, the whole of the world will be at your fingertips. If angry … well, we will get to that later. Our energy is drawn from the world in which you reside and the living things in it. That is why the jaguar did not kill you; it knew you intimately.

"Now, last is control. There are complicated hand and arm gestures you may use to bend the rules of the world to your will, but we do not have enough time for me to teach you even the simplest conjuration, so I am trusting that you will be able to … learn by doing, so to speak. Just feel it, trust your senses. See you soon."

Lya awoke with a start to sunlight streaming into the tiny window of the small home. Immediately her senses were attacked, like being blinded and deafened and choking on smells so strong that she could taste them, but only in her head. She did as she was bade and closed her eyes and took two deep breaths, noticing as she did so that the attacks dulled. After a few more breaths, the world returned to its normal volume and smell. She relaxed and opened her eyes to find Lucid smiling at her. She smiled back at his beautiful face and then remembered the most prominent of invasions just before she had passed out, the very reason she had passed out, the pain overwhelming: his mother.

Of all the invasive and uncomfortable feelings she felt, the amount of sadness there was like looking into the darkest part of the woods on a moonless night, endless. She sensed emotions so deep and still very fresh, held in check by his capability to hide his deepest pain and by the fact that Lya was keeping his mind otherwise occupied. If he held for her even a tiny fraction of the amount of love he had for his mother, she could die happy right then and there.

"I don't know if I ever told you: I'm really sorry about your mother," she told him.

This appeared to take him by surprise as his smile faded and he looked away. He was silent for a moment, staring at the floor.

"She was a great woman. I already miss her so much." He paused and took a shaky breath. "When I was a boy, I had trouble awaking on time for school in the mornings. After I was late to my classes several times, she began to come wake me every morning, walk me to school, and sit with me to eat breakfast before classes began. As I got older I realized it was not exactly a popular decision to be with my mother so often, so I started eating with my friends. Two years later, she was still waking me in the mornings and following me to school every day. I hated her for continuing to baby me even after I'd gotten used to rising early. On the day she finally stopped hounding me, I spotted her at the door to the cafeteria, crying. I pretended not to notice, but now, every time I close my eyes,

I see her standing there with tears in her eyes." He paused and wiped his eyes.

"Now all I can think about is how I will never get to enjoy another breakfast with her again." When he looked back up at Lya, she had tears of her own to match his.

"You were so lucky to have a mother like that. I was very young when my parents died. I only have very vague memories of them. Sometimes I struggle to even remember their faces."

They were both silent for a few minutes, lost in thought and grief. Lya noticed shortly afterward that as long as her mind was occupied, the energy was not so invasive. Lucid stood up and reached for his hooded cloak and satchel.

"There is a place I like to go when I am feeling down like this. We were headed there when … Well, anyway, I would love to show you. Are you okay to walk?"

Lya nodded and stood, actually feeling really well, surprisingly well, better than she had ever felt. She moved to fetch her own hooded cloak and slipped it on. Lucid slung the satchel slung over his shoulder and reached out for her hand again. Their eyes met, and they smiled timidly at each other. She took his hand, and they moved toward the door, putting up their hoods to hide their faces.

Immediately upon exiting, things stood out to Lya in the bright sun of early morning that she had not noticed in the darkness on their way here. They walked through what looked to be the nicest and cleanest place she had ever seen. Perfect little huts with thatched roofs lined the path made mostly of stone. After a short walk through what Lucid called "the LD," they reached a spot on the beach with a narrow wooden platform protruding into the water of the ocean with a small wooden device floating next to it, waves pushing it back and forth as they rolled in and out. They walked up onto the wooden walkway.

He let go of her hand and grabbed hold of the floating wood, gesturing for her to climb in. Lya was a little scared to be on a piece of wood in the ocean, which was just huge and endless blue. But she trusted him so much already that it shocked her. She hesitated only a second then shakily stepped in.

She sat quickly on one of the raised pieces of wood so she did not topple into the water. The boat rocked one way and then the other as Lucid stepped in and sat upon the other raised seat, which had two long poles extending out to the sides. She wondered what they were for, but only for a minute. Lucid took off the satchel, grabbed the poles, and began propelling them through the water. She was amazed at such a simple piece of wood as they rushed away from the beach, rocked slightly by the waves. He pushed them with the little poles straight out into the ocean before turning to go along with the coastline. The sun was high in the sky and the day was warm, so Lya removed the hooded cloak and leaned back, admiring Lucid as he pulled the poles through the water. The prince pulled while they were submerged, removed them, and dipped them again over and over. After a time, he noticed she was staring, and he smiled.

"So where are we going? And what is this we are riding in?" Lya asked.

He chuckled and said, "It is called a boat, and the place we are going is special to me. I want it to be a surprise."

She smiled and took the hint, grabbing his satchel to remove the large book she had been studying. Lucid's language was not easy to learn and had many complicated sounds. The gvorlock tongue was harsh and clipped, like growling and spitting with words. The Altheian tongue was musical, beautiful to hear yet difficult to pronounce. Lya loved the way the *z*, formed by her teeth and tongue, sounded like a hive of bees. Also the *th* and *ch* sounds fascinated her. She had begun her study while she was recovering from her injuries and could hold small, simple conversations already.

Time passed as she got lost in the book of lovely words, yet soon she felt Lucid turning the boat. He began heading toward a rocky cliff. The waves helped push them along. Lya was surprised at the speed they picked up. Wind whipped her hair; the sensation was exhilarating. She laughed and let her fingertips graze the water as a bird skims its wings. Again she could not really comprehend that all of this was real. As if it were a dream she was afraid to awake from, she pushed it out of her mind quickly. Soon after they were climbing out of the boat onto the beach with huge gray cliffs looming above. The sight of the cliffs and the waves crashing around them was beautiful to behold. Lya paused to take it in. After Lucid tied the boat to a post on the beach, he joined her and took her hand again.

CHAPTER 22

The first time the guards came to bring food, Normin simply watched. He wanted to see why only half the slaves seemed to be starving to death while others were huge solid bricks of muscle. Normin was fairly sure he knew the answer, but he had to see it with his own eyes. He heard the heavy bar being lifted and watched from the back corner as the guards opened the door and slid a wooden cart of food just inside. The portal slammed shut quickly. Normin's suspicions as to why the guards didn't enter were proven the moment all the large men surrounded the food and the fighting broke out.

The thinnest and weakest would not challenge such large men on shaky legs and empty stomachs, but others were more than desperate enough to give it a try. Starving to death had a way of affecting decision-making. Most were beaten into submission quickly, but one starving corpse hovering near the food had stayed out of the initial fight. Normin had only been there one night, but it was already very clear who the leader of this hell was.

His name was Brighton, and he was easily half a foot taller than Normin and twice as wide. The hard life lived by these people had turned the most well-fed into muscle-bound beasts who looked like they could crush rocks. Brighton and his little band of goons controlled everything, as evidenced by his handing out what food he thought appropriate to the people he thought deserved it.

The potential thief crept up to the side and behind Brighton, his eyes on the food. Normin could see it written all over his body language before it even happened. The thin man darted in, thinking to use swiftness to get some of that glorious food. The moment he reached for an apple, Brighton was on him. He backhanded the small man savagely and straddled his prone form, pummeling him in the face until his head was nothing but a bloody mess of brains and gore.

Normin gritted his teeth but kept still. He honestly did not expect Brighton to kill him. How was it there were so many slaves in this place if they died without so much as a "Hey, don't do that" from the guards? The huge man and his goons proceeded to make fun of the dead man and his failed attempt. Then they began throwing scraps to the starving side of the room. It seemed more for entertainment purposes than anything else as what they threw was not even enough sustenance for a child, much less a full-grown starving adult. Still, the skeletons fought over the morsels.

Normin was so incredibly angry, he could not sleep that night on his piece of floor near the center of the warehouse. He seethed and planned and seethed some more. How the hell could they be so cruel? These poor souls were all stuck in this situation together. He would have thought there would be some type of family aspect here. He was wrong. It was nothing but a bunch of bullies starving their peers to death.

The next day when the food came, Normin was ready. As soon as he heard the heavy latch lift, he made his move. The door opened, the cart slid in, and Brighton took his eyes off the crowd to take in that day's nourishment. Normin was already moving, kicking at the back of his leg just as the big man turned. Brighton dropped to one knee. Normin's timing could not have been more perfect as he spun and solidly connected the heel of his foot with the man's temple. He felt the impact go up his leg, but before the move was even completed, he felt guilty. The savagery of that particular move was probably uncalled for. A simple choke-out may have worked. But he wanted to prove a point and do so in such a way that would brook no further argument. Just as suspected, the huge man's eyes closed immediately with no sound and he dropped like a felled tree. *Crash.* Then, as the big bully hit the floor, pandemonium.

People were running to and fro, shoving and kicking one another in an attempt to feed themselves in the chaos. People were screaming, and fighting broke out in several clusters. The way had been cleared. Brighton's goons fought multiple people to regain control.

When Normin was younger and dating his Alice, one of the things he found fascinating about her was her whistle. She worked the fields as a child, huge swaths of crops, where the only way to communicate was through whistling. She could blow people's eardrums out in a small, closed room. Her whistle was incredibly loud and impressive. Normin had made her teach him. After all the lessons, he still could not quite reach the volume that his love once had. He put his index fingers in his mouth as she had taught him. His whistle was loud in the warehouse, louder than he had ever achieved before, perhaps because he was angry—or maybe Alice was still with him. Everyone put their hands to their ears and froze, looking at the man who, in the blink of an eye, had taken out the unbeatable villain.

"*Enough!*" he shouted.

"Hey, you're new, ain't you?" said one of Brighton's young goons. Normin wanted to say his name was Steve or Trent or some shit, but he could not be sure.

"Yes, I am new. I am also your new leader. That man," he said, pointing to an unconscious Brighton while scanning the crowd, "is a cruel fool. Yes, I am new, but I also have many more years than most everyone here." He glanced at an older woman cowering in the corner, her gray locks hiding her face as her head was down.

"We are all stuck here together. There is absolutely no reason why we cannot all achieve the same level of misery." Normin's blood was up, and his voice boomed through the building.

The big kid stepped forward. The king could only tell he was young by the thin wisp of a mustache that was beginning to grow. The boy was thick around the shoulders and a few inches taller than Normin.

"'Cause you're new here, old man, you don't know that there ain't enough for everyone. So come on." He struck a pathetic fighting pose. "I'm gonna show you why ol' Brighton runs things."

To call what ensued a fight would be insulting not only to the men who had trained Normin but also to everyone who ever studied the art of hand-to-hand. A few seconds later, Normin had the poor lad flat on his stomach, twisting his arm behind his back so far that it was just short of snapping. He screamed and kicked, but Normin held and looked around at the shocked faces.

"Anyone else?" he boomed. Not a soul said a word. Normin could have heard a feather floating through the air. Someone coughed. Brighton's remaining men stayed silent as Normin locked eyes on them. He nodded and released the youth, and they both got to their feet. Normin moved over to the cart to get a good look, stepping over Brighton. There was a shockingly small amount of food for the number of people, but not exceedingly so. Everyone could definitely eat, small as the meal may be.

He turned and commanded, "I want everyone in a single line, thinnest to largest." He glanced at the youth and the rest of the Brighton boys with a look that said, *Get your giant asses to the back.* Everyone quickly lined up without a word, and Normin began dishing out the food in portions he thought would allow it to stretch, almost, to the largest men.

Every person who received their meal did so on pieces of wood or stone or in their bare hands. One man even used his shirt. They all thanked him gratefully, some even going so far as to drop to their knees in thanks, telling him how long it had been since they had eaten. He simply smiled and gently pulled them to their feet, handing them their meal to keep the line moving. His god was with him that day as the food ran out just as the first of Brighton's men reached the front.

"You guys could stand to miss a few meals," he said as he menacingly kicked the empty cart out of his way and toward the door, daring them to challenge. They did not. They simply walked off, heads hung low and tails between their legs.

"What about you?" he heard a tiny voice say.

Normin turned to find a small girl with what looked to be nothing but a stocking covering her upper body and a torn and dirty short skirt that did not quite fit. She was filthy and her hair was a rats' nest, but she had brown hair and dark eyes just like his Brynn. He had to bite his tongue hard to keep the tears at bay at the sight of her. He could clearly see her ribs and collarbone, she was so thin. Yet here she was, holding out a piece of bread to him. He shook his head and slapped his stomach.

"Me? Couldn't eat another bite. You eat every bit of that."

She smiled, took a huge bite of the bread, and closed her eyes to enjoy. Normin was sick to even think about how long it had been since this poor little thing had had an entire mouthful of food. He waited for her to open her eyes, and when she did he asked, "What is your name?"

She attempted to answer, but it came out muffled around the mouthful of bread. Normin waited patiently. After she swallowed, she said, "Allie." The girl took another huge bite of bread.

His heart skipped a beat and his throat tightened. "That is pretty. Is it short for something?" he asked, terrified of the little girl's reply.

She nodded, and when she swallowed again, she said, "It's short for Alice."

His heart ached at her words. He turned to take in the whole of the crowd, more to avoid looking into Alice's eyes, afraid that she might see the wetness there. So many people, hundreds of people.

"This is the way it will be from now on," he boomed as all eyes found him. "Everyone will most likely eat light, but at least we will *all* eat." He said that last part with a look at the Brighton boys, who were so full of anger that they couldn't hold his gaze for longer than a second.

Throughout the rest of that day, Normin felt the general vibe was one of content. Full bellies and the promise of fair treatment had allowed most everyone to rest comfortably for the first time in … only God knew. No one seemed inclined to conversation, and Normin liked that; it afforded him plenty of time to think as evening approached and then as the darkness of night enveloped him. After some time of contemplating his situation and planning his next move on his little spot on the floor, he dozed off. He awoke to complete silence. Someone had touched him, and he sat up quickly. With the sliver of moonlight coming in through the windows, he saw a weathered face and familiar gray locks. It was the woman who had been hiding in the corner, avoiding everyone. He was sure she hadn't gotten a plate of food either.

"You are from Altheia." she stated more than asked, just barely above a whisper, even though she was so close that he could see the age lines on her face.

Normin nodded, not sure if there was a reason she was being so quiet.

"Coy? Did my Coy make it out?" she asked, her voice cracking. She waited only an instant for a response and continued: "They died so he could make it. Please tell me he survived."

Normin had no idea who or what she was talking about. "Shh. It's okay," he said in a calming whisper as he looked around. The room was still. He could hear people snoring lightly. He scooted over and gestured for her to sit. She did so without hesitation. Normin feared he had sent the wrong message. He knew nothing of what she spoke, but she seemed desperate enough to believe his every word. "What's your name?" he asked.

"Gina," she replied.

"Okay, Gina, start from the beginning. Who is Coy? Who died?"

"He's my nephew. A while ago his parents hatched a plan that he might escape to Altheia. We'd only just heard there was another city a few months ago from a guard, see. And so they say his daddy was one of Brighton's boys, all big and everything." She looked around and added more quietly, "But he wasn't. He was special, he was." Just as Normin was beginning to think she had lost her mind and was just babbling, she said, "Last week Coy's daddy caused a distraction during a raid on your Altheia so his boy could run. They …" She paused and choked, crying for a full minute, then turned back to him.

"Did he make it?" she yelled. A few heads popped up to check then slowly lay back down.

"I do not know." He knew very little about this woman, but he found he could not lie to her.

Her lip quivered and she looked down. After a few moments, she whispered so quietly that Normin almost could not make it out, "He's special. Has to live."

CHAPTER 23

When Brynn regained consciousness, she found herself in the injured man's bed, still in the little fishing hut. She sat up, rubbed the sleep from her eyes, and glanced to the ground by the bed. The man who had saved her life was lying unconscious, facedown on the floor, his bandages sporting fresh blood. It seemed he labored to breathe normally. She looked around and did not see the dead man with the disgustingly broken neck. Thanking God, she got up, grabbed hold of her skirt, and ran.

She flew out the door after a light jump over the killer and took off toward the high city. It was a long run to Daryl's chambers, and there was no guarantee that he would even be there, but she had to try. When Brynn arrived, she beat on the door savagely after attempting to simply burst in. It grated her deeply that she was being so rude, but time was against her. Even now the poor injured man who had risked his life to save her might be dying on the floor of the family fishing hut.

Daryl answered the door, opening it only slightly. She yelled through the crack, "I need help! Now! There is a man dying in the fishing hut! Help him!"

Daryl's eyes lit up with a mixture of shock and recognition. "Shit," he cursed and turned to Alisha. "I'll be back" was all he said just before he took off running at an insane pace.

Brynn turned to Alisha to say hello quickly. They looked at each other oddly. Alisha's reasoning was obvious; she wanted to know where her man was sprinting off to. Brynn, however, raised an eyebrow as she caught sight of Alisha. She was scantily dressed, clothing barely covering her body parts and hiding none of them. That was not as surprising as the savage-looking bow she held in her hands, with a stuffed dummy across the room looking like Cat's mother's pincushion.

"Princess." Alisha curtsied.

Brynn smiled and waved before chasing after Daryl. There was no catching him, but knowing he was on his way, she did not have to rush quite as much. Still, she hurried to the small hut to check the status of her hero, if nothing else. When she returned, she saw that Daryl had lifted him back into bed and was cutting his bandages away. Brynn was surprised to see the man's eyes were open, locked on the thatched ceiling, and his jaw was clenched in pain, sweat pouring down his face.

Daryl was scolding him as she entered. "... know what kind of injury you sustained. You are lucky to be alive. I told you not to get out of bed as it is I who will have to cut you back open and check for interior bleeding. I'm sure you busted my stitches in there."

Brynn stepped up and put a hand on his shoulder as he worked. He glanced at her, his work continuing. "He saved me, Daryl. I did not know anyone was here. I was walking on the beach, and I thought I would stop and rest for a minute. I didn't ..." She choked and began to sob, remembering Gerald; his wife, Jane; and their daughter, Cara. She would need to break the news to Jane and Cara personally to retain some modicum of respect. Her heart wrenched at the thought.

Daryl softened immediately as her words spread in that giant brain of his. He stood, going over to put an arm around her tiny frame. "It's okay, Princess. It's my fault. I am sorry I did not tell anyone he was here. I just never imagined this man would attract an assassin."

She nodded and wiped her tears away, regaining control of her emotions at his words. "Who is he?" she asked as she moved to his bedside. "And why would he risk himself to save a stranger in this condition?"

The men glanced at each other. Pained though it was there was something in that look. Daryl sighed and said, "The night we saved Russell, we found him dying in the woods. Russell said he knew him, so we did what any decent folk would do and patched him up and hid him here." Daryl moved over to his heavy bag and began removing tools.

"What is your name, sir?" Brynn asked, moving over to the man.

He had been puffing his cheeks in and out in an almost comical expression of pain. He froze and looked at her with such a look of shock that she thought for a second she may have said something wrong.

"Sir?" was all he said. Brynn looked confused, but she nodded, waiting patiently for his answer.

"Vincent," he croaked.

Brynn took another step closer to look into his eyes. He had kind eyes, full of pain, but not angry or malevolent. "I am Princess Brynn Altheia, and I believe I owe you my life." Daryl shooed her over a little as he sat down and gave the man a tiny cup, which he quaffed quickly. As soon as he did, his body relaxed.

"What is your story, Vincent? Why is someone trying so hard to kill you?" Daryl asked as he worked.

"Is Ivan dead as you suggested?" Vincent asked in reply, glancing at Daryl.

Brynn's face twisted in anger, but Daryl only nodded. Vincent continued, "Well then, it's pretty obvious that the new king sees me as a threat. He's planning something—has been for a while now. I just do not know what. He keeps councillors who are all young like him, and they are loyal and quiet about their leader. I am sure by now he has either killed all his father's men or relieved them of their duties."

Brynn could hear his words slurring more heavily, and before she knew it, he passed out. Daryl looked at her with a wicked-looking blade.

"You may not want to be here for this, Princess."

She nodded, turning to go, but she looked back over her shoulder for one last glance. "Fix him, Daryl, and make him very comfortable. He is my hero and a welcome citizen."

Daryl nodded and said, "I will send Russell to fetch him after he heals a little more. Moving him in this condition is risky. He will have to call this home for now."

On Brynn's way to the palace, Coy found her. She smiled as he handed her a written message from Bruce Mathis.

"Hello, Coy. How are the Mathises treating you?" she asked.

Perhaps because this was the first time she had seen him this close since he'd cleaned up, only now did she notice how dazzling green his eyes were. It gave his tanned skin and sharp features a striking, handsome look.

"You look nice out from under all that dirt and with a little weight on you," she added before he could reply.

Coy froze. He opened his mouth to reply, then closed it again and looked down at his feet.

"Man found on my farm, not Altheian. Need to know what I should do with him," the note read.

Brynn sighed and, after a short conversation with Coy, headed to her chambers for a quick bath and a change of dress, after which she immediately headed toward Bruce's farm. On her way out of the palace, Jake spotted her and looked very unhappy that she was alone with no guard. She hadn't seen much of him since she'd sent him away to find Lucid.

"Have you found him?" was all she said as he fell in behind her.

"No, Your Highness."

She nodded. Just another thing she had underestimated. Lucid's ability to disappear and stay disappeared was annoying. *It's not Jake's fault,* she reminded herself.

"I'm sorry about Gerald," she told him, unable to meet his eyes as surely he had heard by now. Word traveled fast in Altheia.

Jake paused. A slight touch on Brynn's shoulder caused her to spin. Her tearing-up eyes met his intense stare. "Do not think for a second that that was your fault. I have taken on the task myself of finding those responsible, and I will give them swift justice. Entering our city and attacking our princess in broad daylight! I will ..." Trigo stopped himself. His voice had been steadily rising as he spoke, not loud or yelling, but seething behind barely controlled anger. She knew Jake was a personal friend, even a brother to Gerald, as the relationships of the men in the barracks were strong.

"Thank you," she said. She had never been so grateful to have such a man watching over her.

After a fair walk through the LD and down the Mathis farm's long walkway to get to the main house, Brynn was sweating and her worry building. *Who could this man be? Could it have something to do with the other Drondosians who were here lately?*

It seemed to her that crossing over between cities was becoming commonplace. Was the new king attempting to place spies in Altheia? The thought stopped her just before she knocked on the front door. She turned to Jake, more to reassure herself that he was still there than anything else, and then knocked. Bruce opened the door and waved her in.

The Mathis farmhouse was impressive for an LD home, though technically it was outside the main city. Two stories of solid square wood whitewashed to a shine sat on several acres of cleared trees to take advantage of maximum sunlight. Inside the house were nice furnishings, and beautifully painted art hung on the walls. It was no small feat to grow enough wheat for the entire population of Altheia, so Brynn's father took good care of the family who fed their people.

Mrs. Mathis showed the princess and Trigo to the large dining table. She offered tea. Brynn took a cup gratefully and had it emptied by the time the stranger was stirring awake. Bruce led her into the stranger's room, Jake trailing closely behind her, and he left them to their business.

"I'll be right outside if you need anything, Princess," the farmer said.

At Bruce's words, the man's one visible eye snapped to her. The look of his condition shocked Brynn. He had a bandage wrapped around half his head, and there was a disgusting brownish ooze covering the bandage where his eye sat under it. His left hand was wrapped as well, clearly missing his smallest finger. He looked so thin and frail that Brynn could have broken bones by the slightest touch. When he spoke, his voice was strained and raspy. He was missing most of his front teeth.

"Such a pleasure to meet you, Princess Brynn. I apologize for not being able to stand and bow." He bowed anyway as much as his sitting position would allow, and he winced to the point of tears.

"Thank you, but that is not necessary. I am not the official ruler here. What is your name?" she asked.

"Terrence Williams," he replied without hesitation.

"And how is it that you have come to our city?" she asked, pulling up a chair from the table next to the window and sitting down next to his bed. Jake took a step closer. This time Terrence's hesitation was barely noticeable, but it was there.

Looking very uncomfortable, he said, "I heard a rumor about beasts living in the deep woods, so I took it upon myself to investigate. I got lost in the woods and"—he paused to take a shuddering breath—"I awoke in chains. They tortured me, asking questions about one of theirs who was killed." He looked directly at Brynn with a pained, anguished expression, tears forming in his one eye. "I do not know anything about that, I swear. I didn't know anything, so they just kept—" He broke off in a choke, and that led to a sob more suited to a small child.

Brynn glanced toward Jake. The look on his face told her much about the truth of this man's words. She stood and smoothed her skirts while he composed himself again.

"I see that you have been through much in the last days, so I will leave you to your recovery. Please understand my need to question you as tensions between cities are rising. After the fire and"—she paused and took a breath, refusing to look weak in front of grown men—"my mother's death, we are wary of people from Drondos."

Something very odd crossed his face just then. Brynn hesitated. All of a sudden she was very interested in what else this man may know. She was just about to inquire further but stopped herself, looking him over. This man was in no condition to be put to more questions. She felt terrible about what he had endured. The princess thanked the man for his story and told the Mathis family he may be moved to the infirmary if they wished. Of course they refused, saying, "We would never put anyone out whom the princess says is okay." She thanked them kindly.

As she stepped out into the soft glow of late evening, her mind ran wild with his tale. She did not care for the look on his face when she mentioned her mother's death. What was worse and more prominent in her mind was the story of the beasts in the woods. She would have brushed it off as a fairy tale if not for the gruesome visual proof. When she was out of hearing distance, she stopped and spun, looking straight up into Jake's eyes.

"That was real, wasn't it? The beasts, the death of one of them. That is a man who has been tortured. The proof was there for both of us to see. What do you know?"

Jake tried to match her stare, but Brynn assumed he had become attached to his little princess, and it seemed he did not want to disappoint her. A war went on in his statuesque face, and finally, painfully, he said, "I have sworn to your father not to speak of it."

"How could I ever be upset at you for being so loyal to my father?" she asked.

Surprise showed on his face. He opened his mouth to speak, but Brynn cut him off with a wave.

"You are not running full speed for the barracks to rouse the king's men, so clearly you have it under control," she told him. As she turned to go, she said, "I trust you."

Brynn was sure it went both ways. She had tried hard to earn the trust of Jake and the other councillors and assumed she had done well enough. As the day wore on, however, and evening fell, she finally collapsed into her bed and could think of nothing but the beasts and the look on Terrence's face.

CHAPTER 24

The view was the most incredible thing Lya had ever seen. Except for those in her dreams with the kindly man, no landscape had ever taken her breath away so completely. She and Lucid stood side by side at the edge of a large cave high on the cliffs, overlooking the sea. The sun was just about to dip below the horizon. Beautiful orange and purple colors met the darkening blue of the sea. She glanced at Lucid, his dark hair blowing in the wind, his eyes squinting against the sun, giving him a more serious look. If not for the huge contented grin on his face, she might have thought him angry or worried.

"Do you see now why this place is special to me?" he asked, wind stealing most of the volume of his voice.

Lya did not answer; there was no need. She took a step forward and looked down the sheer fifty-foot drop, where a clearing of sorts in the rock that jutted from the ocean formed a large pool with water much more calm than the seas around it. It seemed as if the rock formation on which they stood curved in on itself as she could see only water directly below her. The rocky formation that jutted out of the sea was lined with beautiful white and gray birds that chirped happily in the cool evening breeze. The smell was intoxicating. The fresh sea air bereft of any hint of night soil or sweat, it smelled of life, of opportunity.

Is this how he has lived his whole life? So unbelievably full of possibility, so … free, Lya thought.

"I honestly did not know there was such beauty in this world," she said.

It seemed as if the gods had made this spot just for the two of them. For this moment, right now, was the reason these cliffs, this beauty, existed. She glanced to Lucid, who had moved farther back into the cave and faced her with a suspicious grin. He bolted, running right toward the edge of the cave. She cried out and tried to grab him before he ran off the edge, but he was fast and solid, and her hand slipped right off as he jumped to what surely would be his death. She gasped and held her breath as she watched him fall, and in that moment, her guard slipped.

The living energy of the world around her once again flooded her senses so much that she cried out once more, falling to her knees and clutching at her head. The words came back unbidden. *Breathing,* she remembered, and focused only on pulling and pushing air and nothing else. Soon the world leveled, and she stood, going to the edge of the cave to look down. There he was in the water below, smiling and waving her down.

"It won't hurt you. The water is too deep," he shouted up at her. She shook her head violently.

Lucid made his way, swimming toward the sandy area where they had docked the little boat to climb back up. When he reached the top, he walked right up to her and took both her hands, looking into her eyes with an unfamiliar expression that made her heart quicken instantly.

"Do you trust me?" he asked simply. She hesitated only for a second before nodding, unable to speak or take her eyes off his. Holding her hand, he led her to the edge. Lya's heart raced. She had never before trusted her life so utterly to someone like this, and she was terrified.

She shook her head again. "I can't. I'm scared," Lya admitted as she looked again at the sheer drop.

He turned to her, pulled her close, wrapping his arms around her lower back, and kissed her. Caught off guard, having never attempted something so intimate, she felt her heart beating so hard that she was sure he could feel it through her dress. His lips were soft. Her knees felt they might buckle. He pulled away, still holding her close. Bathed in the last rays of the sun, she felt again that this all had to be a dream.

How could a man so perfect feel this way about a nobody slave such as me?

"Trust me," he said again, and with that they turned and stepped up to the edge.

That kiss and the love she felt there strengthened her resolve. She made her decision: she would jump off any cliff for this man. It was odd how the world worked, Lya realized as she prepared herself. Jumping off a cliff was exactly what she felt when she had escaped and begun this new path. Their relationship had taken that leap, and there was no going back.

Gods be with me, she thought, and as one, they leapt.

Wind and exhilaration screamed at her. The feeling of falling drawn out by fear made the drop seem to last forever. She laughed as her stomach flew into her throat and the sensation of flying took over. *Splash.* Together they hit the water and went deep into the sea. She opened her eyes in the blue-green water to see Lucid looking at her. Together, still hand in hand, they swam to the surface.

When their heads broke the surf, she gasped a breath and shouted, "Wooooooo!"

Lucid smiled widely and embraced her again. They kissed once more, adrenaline fueling a passion that had been building since the first time they met, but this time it lasted longer and was hungrier, more animal, primal even. She felt herself tingling in anticipation. She wanted him now, to give herself to him as she never had imagined. She pulled away and began swimming toward the little boat dock, pulling Lucid along with her. Her mind and her heart had gone to a place it had never been before, uncharted waters, and she longed to map those unknown areas of her heart and her body. She did not remember much of the swim back to shore and even less of the walk back up to the cave.

Next thing she knew, darkness consumed them except for the small fire Lucid had built when they first reached the cave, granting a comfortable glow around them as they faced each other. Again Lucid drew close to her, this time so tight she could feel his stiffness. He kissed her deeply, and when their mouths parted slightly, his tongue entered her mouth.

Shocked, her eyes popped open, but she let herself fall, just as if they were jumping again. She pulled away just long enough to shrug out of her dress. Lucid's eyes went wide with lust and hunger. He stripped his own clothes off, faster than she would have believed possible, and soon their naked bodies pressed against each other, kissing hungrily. She pulled him down to the simple pile of sheets and blankets he had brought to sleep on. When he put himself inside her, she stopped kissing and gasped as pain and ecstasy arced through her.

"You okay?" he asked quietly as he paused.

She nodded and pulled him back to her, their faces and body parts together. Soon she felt something building, like a pile of perfectly stacked twigs that she longed to reach out and knock over to see what would happen, how they would fall. It built more and more, and soon she forgot to breathe, air coming in short gasps between moans. Slowly, very slowly, emotions began creeping into her head. At first she mistook the pleasure for her own, but as her mind was unable to focus on her breath, Lucid's feeling of pleasure and love began creeping in as well, melding with hers and creating a new emotion that was too deep, too powerful, to comprehend.

Pleasure, she discovered, was easily recognizable as it was one of the simplest of emotions. The shared love of two people, however, was much more complex, like trying to understand how a spider might spin its web by undoing it one strand at a time. It would take a lifetime to understand the full width of Lucid's love for her, but one thing was clear: it was there and it was massive, more than she could have ever imagined. For just a second, she forgot herself, drowning in that love. Then, when she realized she was actually using her power, it all went sporadic and wild. The only thing she could focus on was her pleasure and climax building—Lucid's as well. Soon, something intense struck her. She screamed, shaking at the wave of ecstasy, and she felt a massive wetness between her legs before the combined emotions, both hers and Lucid's, were too much and the world went dark.

When she awoke, two things struck her at once: it was very dark, and Lucid was not beside her. She rubbed the sleep from her eyes and sat up, looking around the cave. The fire had burned down to just embers. It took her eyes a second to adjust.

"So it was you?" She heard a voice from the darkness, and she turned toward the sound. A man screamed in agony, a familiar voice.

"We will kill every last one of your people for your betrayal." *Unfamiliar.*

Her eyes finally adjusted to the darkness enough for her to make out two huge looming figures, one holding a smaller naked man by his throat against the cave wall. Lucid gasped for air and kicked wildly, which the gvorlock just shrugged off.

Fear gripped Lya, just for a moment, before she realized they were not paying any attention to the worthless and unconscious slave girl. Her face reddened as anger built inside her, so much so that she had to bite back a scream.

This man had risked so much for her. He had saved her life and given her more in the short time they had known each other than had her lifetime as a slave. It would not end this way. No one would take him from her unless she was dead. The gvorlocks had kept her as a slave for her whole life. They had brutalized her and beaten her senseless. They were the ones responsible for the death of her father and mother. They had given her nothing but pain and misery, and all for what? As she thought this, her anger built to something she could not control. It overwhelmed her, and her vision darkened.

She rose, naked as the day she'd come into this world, closed her eyes, and held her breath. She opened herself up to the anger, and it almost overwhelmed her as she let out an involuntary growl. Waves of emotion and bright, vivid visions sped past behind her eyelids, but she pushed them away, focusing solely on the picture in her mind's eyes of the gvorlock holding Lucid. With her eyes still closed, she searched for weapons to use against them.

The fire—it was there. She could feel it like a meek child hiding in a corner. It had burned low and was only embers, but the element was there, and she grabbed at it, screaming as she did so. It was hot; it felt like her blood was on fire. Immediately she threw her hands down to her sides and slapped both thighs, almost as if she'd actually burned her hands and had to pull them away quickly. It felt natural, just like her body would have done if she had touched a very hot surface; it knew what to do next.

The effect was immediate as the gvorlock holding Lucid did

not catch fire slowly. Instead, he combusted instantly, and when the flame washed over it, Lucid dropped to his feet unharmed. They were all left staring at a smoking pile of ash and bone. The remaining gvorlock, Lucid, and even Lya stood open-mouthed, stunned.

The other gvorlock was first to shake off the shock as he quickly turned and leapt at Lya. Lucid was faster somehow and caught his leg, causing the gvorlock to hit the ground on his belly. Lucid threw himself on the creature's back, grabbed his large, bald head with both hands, and slammed it into the rock.

"Sword!" he shouted at Lya while slamming the gvorlock's head against the rock over and over.

She turned, searching frantically through their discarded clothes, until she felt his sword belt and pulled it out, removing the weapon from its holder. She turned to see the gvorlock stand quickly, throwing Lucid back to the ground with a vicious thud. Lya threw, trusting that Lucid was watching and would not be impaled by the combination of her terrible throwing skills and the darkness enveloping them. She should not have been worried. She had forgotten that he had killed a gvorlock before, so he had to be good with that weapon. Anyone who carried such a thing all day long surely knew how to use it. It turns out "knew how to use it" would be the understatement of all understatements.

Lucid stood quickly and, in one motion that was almost too fast for her eyes to follow, caught the blade at its handle perfectly. With nothing more than a flick of Lucid's wrist, the gvorlock's head fell free in a spray of dark liquid. Slowly, the body of the gvorlock realized it was missing a key component, and it dropped like a boulder.

Lya and Lucid both stood there, naked and panting. Their eyes met. He rushed to her, embracing her so tight that she thought he meant to crush her. He pulled back but did not let go.

"Are you okay?" he asked. It absolutely stumped her.

He'd almost died. Those gvorlocks had held him at their will. Imagining just how much fear had gone through him at that moment, she shuddered. Yet the first thing on his mind was her well-being. Tears brimmed and fell as she opened her mouth to speak, but no words came to her. He reached up and wiped her tears away, looking deeply into her eyes with a look of concern. She nodded. "I am fine."

"Lya," Lucid started hesitantly. "What happened to him? What did you do?" he asked with more than a little fear in his tone.

She looked into his eyes for a long moment before deciding that if she were going to give herself to this man, there would be no secrets between them.

"I have … powers. I don't really understand who or"—she hesitated, worried how much she could tell him without Lucid thinking she was crazy—"what I am. My parents died when I was so young. I don't know, I just don't know." She stopped as she choked on her words and began sobbing.

He drew her closer and laid her head on his chest, stroking her hair.

"It's okay, Lya. I am not judging you." He paused, holding her. "Thank you for saving me."

She laughed despite herself and glanced over his chest, gasping as she spotted a wound on his shoulder pouring blood. It looked like a perfect star in the night sky, only instead of the usual silver glow it was red and black and oozing blood almost to his hip.

He looked down and waved it away. "Gvorlock speared me a little. It's nothing."

She frowned and pulled away from him, going over to grab her dress and pull it on. "It's not nothing. Let me tend to it."

He nodded and put on his pants, sitting next to her by the embers from a fire that had all but died. She coaxed the fire back to life and ripped the lowest section of her dress away to clean the wound, placing a small rock she found lying about the cave into the fire.

"This is going to hurt," she told him. He shrugged.

After the bleeding stopped, she used the bloody cloth to wrap her hands and retrieve the rock.

"A lot," she said, looking into his eyes.

He swallowed, sweat beginning to break out on his forehead, but he nodded as he grabbed a clean stick from the pile of kindling and bit down. She pressed. Flesh sizzled, and Lucid screamed. The cave quickly filled with the horrid odor of burned flesh. Quick as a rabbit, she splashed a cup of water and removed the rock in one smooth motion. Lucid relaxed but was still breathing hard.

He spit out two broken halves of stick and said through gritted teeth, "I did not expect that."

She laughed and went to him, kissing him deeply. "So strong," she said gently. He sat up a little straighter at her words, his breath finally easing to a more normal cadence. "How did they find us?" she asked.

"They didn't," he answered with a sick look on his face. "They came out of the cave." He hooked a thumb at a darker section against the back wall that Lya had never spotted before. She had had other things on her mind up until this point.

She stood and went over to the gvorlock's severed head and knelt to inspect its face. A memory from years past struck her, and her heart began pounding as she told Lucid, "This isn't one of the villagers." She looked up and saw he had a puzzled expression on his face. "He's from the warrior clan. We need to leave now!" She stood abruptly, and he stood with her, confusion still painted on his face.

"The gvorlocks in your village, that's not all of them?" he asked, grabbing his shirt and vest and putting them on quickly.

She shook her head. "I never knew from where. They only come around every ten years or so and do not stay very long." She looked at him with fear in her eyes. "There are more, many more."

CHAPTER 25

J on cursed to himself as he saw the scrawny boy enter the training yard laden with books, his nose bloodied again. *You will run every day until you at least accompany that bloody nose with a victory grin,* he thought as he sent Coy off running around the training yard. Unbidden, his thoughts turned to his best friend, unsure why his thinking of Coy's daily beatings brought to mind Lucid. *Probably not a good sign.*

Time and sympathy for the princess had finally prompted Jon to confront Lucid. Possibly for the first time ever they would have unpleasant words. Lucid did not scare him in any way; they were like brothers, and they never fought. It was for that reason he would have trouble telling his prince, "You are being an inconsiderate, irresponsible jackass, and you need you to go relieve your sister now. The kingdom needs you."

It wasn't like Brynn was doing a bad job of holding the kingdom together. She was doing excellently, better than he'd ever imagined, though he also, never in a thousand years, would have imagined she would need to rule in any case. He knew she was smart—everyone did—but it seemed he and Lucid, and possibly the council, had underestimated the young woman. Still, Jon was determined to get his friend back in court where he belonged, so he had stormed over to Alisha's chambers and burst open the door—and they were gone.

If I were Lucid and in love, where would I go? he thought.

The answer was obvious: jump cave they called it, and it was his friend's favorite place in the world. After his training class of the younger boys ended, Jon headed toward the little dock they used to hold their canoe. He could walk to the cave through thick jungle and up a steep and rocky slope, but using the canoe was much easier going. Lucid would have the boat, but at least by its absence Jon could confirm his suspicion. He was right: the boat was gone. Jon cursed his foolishness. He scanned the water and spotted his friend a few miles out, rowing his way toward the little boat dock. It was some time before they drew close, and as they did, Jon noticed that Lya was pulling one of the oars, Lucid's left arm hanging limp in his lap.

That is odd, he thought. After some time of waiting in the hot sun, they pulled up the little boat, and Lucid hopped out to tie it off with one hand.

"What happened?" were the first words out of Jon's mouth, his anger falling away at the sight of his prince struggling to tie off the little canoe.

Lucid looked up unsurprised. No doubt he and Lya had spotted Jon from the water a mile or more out. "I'll tell you on the way," he said as he took Lya's hand and approached.

"On the way where?" asked Jon.

"To talk to Brynn—some things she needs to know." *Finally,* Jon thought with a wave of relief.

"Hello, Jon," Lya said with a little wave. He could not help but smile.

"You have learned our tongue well, although the accent is …" He paused, looking at Lucid. His friend turned to look into Lya's eyes.

"It's nice, isn't it?" Lucid asked, not looking at Jon. Something had changed between them, he could tell. He knew Lucid as well as he knew himself, and there was more to that look than there was the last time he had seen them together.

Jon smirked. When Lucid turned back and caught the look, his face turned bright red.

"Come on. If we hurry, we can catch Brynn before the council gathers for supper. I need to speak with her alone," the prince said.

They hurried off to the palace, Lucid filling Jon in on the events of the last few days. Jon sensed throughout his friend's retelling that he was hiding something, or at least omitting something, but he didn't pry. Jon was just glad Lucid was home and alive. Wounded by a gvorlock, and so close to the city, his friend would not have such an easy time shaking him anymore. Jon would be his shadow.

This was bad, the treaty broken just days after finding out there was a treaty. Jon could not help but wonder at the condition of his king. If Normin were to catch word of all this, it may very well bring him back to himself. He would be furious, and it would give his mind a fresh emergency to fret over.

War, thought Jon.

It was unheard of, literally. The only war Altheia knew was in books. It had never happened in all the thousands of years their people had lived on Blysse. Jon imagined no one knew the exact number as they had not formed the council and begun the new year numbering until after the building of Altheia was complete. It was said to have taken generations.

When they ascended the steps to the final floor of the palace, Lucid stopped, turned to Jon, and said, "I need you to go get Daryl for me. I want him to treat me here after the meeting. I don't want anyone to see I got stabbed and start asking questions."

Jon hesitated and began to send someone else, not wanting to leave his prince's side again. He glanced at Lya and knew it would be improper to ask her. "Daryl will ask questions," he said.

Lucid frowned. "Just avoid answering. I'll handle it."

Jon gave in. "Okay, but do not leave the palace until I return. Promise me."

Lucid smiled and nodded, turning to open the door to the royal council chamber. As he did so, Jon noticed that the councillors were already gathered, the evening meeting beginning earlier than usual, most likely because of the chaotic past few weeks. All the faces he saw wore a mix of shock and anger.

That will not be a fun meeting. Jon thought as he headed toward the healer's wing.

The healer's schooling was slightly longer than the others on the island, so in spite of his being two years older than Jon and Lucid, Daryl would be in his studies at this time of day. Jon found him in the library, buried in a comically thick book that looked as old as Altheia itself.

Jon plopped down in the chair next to him, causing a little dust cloud to leap from the book and float about them. Daryl jumped, putting a hand to his chest.

"God, I wish you would make a little noise when you walk. Just a little. I don't think that is asking too much."

Jon laughed, probably for the first time in days, and it felt good. "Hey, I don't knock you for being so fast. I saw a jaguar in the woods taking notes during our last city footrace."

Daryl laughed and asked, "What has you in such an unusually good mood?"

"Lucid is back. He is in a meeting with Brynn and the council right now. He has a small wound on his shoulder that needs tending."

Daryl frowned. "What kind of wound? What happened?"

Jon shrugged. He hated being dishonest with his friends, but secrecy demanded it. "I only spoke with him for a minute. It didn't come up. He just asked that I come get you. It's nothing life-threatening. There is no hurry. I don't think you could get into that council chamber right now anyway. I bet those old men are tearing Lucid a new asshole for disappearing at such a critical moment."

Daryl smiled slightly. "Love makes people do strange things," he said wistfully, no doubt thinking of his own love for Alisha. "All right," the young healer said, standing, "let's go see what I can do about this mystery wound."

They exited the library and started down the long hall of the school. "So what do you think of Lucid's new woman?" Daryl asked of him as they walked.

Jon just shrugged. "I can't say I know what type of heart she has, but one thing is for sure: it belongs to Lucid now."

Daryl nodded thoughtfully. "He seems quite taken with her, which is rare for him. Royal daughters have been trying to catch his attention for years, and he has not so much as glanced at any of them."

They exited into a darkening courtyard, the sun beginning to dip below the waves. "What's her story anyway? I thought Lucid said …" Daryl stopped midsentence and tilted his head. Jon had heard it too. In the silence, a large wave crested over the sand in the distance, the north wind blowing steadily through the mostly empty thoroughfares of the city. Below all of that was a dull rumble, a hesitant roll of thunder before the inevitable crash of lightning that stretched on and on, only the sky was cloudless. Jon's stomach dropped, and on instinct he turned toward the woods.

Lucid entered the royal council chambers hand in hand with Lya to find a roomful of angry and shocked faces.

"Where the fuck have you been?" Brynn said angrily. Her face was terrible to behold.

The question shocked him as he had never once in his life heard her utter a curse word. He glanced to Lya as they stepped forward together. "I would appreciate it if we could speak alone," he told her. The councillors shifted uncomfortably but made no move to leave.

Clearly Brynn had gained the trust of these men and they would no longer take orders from their prince. It was the master healer who gave voice to his thought.

"Do not get any ideas about taking over the kingdom just yet. You will need an evaluation first, and you will only take the throne if the princess decides to step down. We have found her to be more than capable of leadership in your absence."

Brynn looked just as shocked as Lucid, but she recovered quickly. "That is very kind, Reginald. Thank you. I would speak to my brother alone," she told them. Everyone slowly got to their feet and headed out the door. Jake Trigo did not stand; he stayed sitting at Brynn's left.

"Mother dies, tensions between cities are rising, Father kills a man, and where are you?" Brynn began before Lucid could take two steps. As he got closer, she saw his wound and softened slightly.

"Brynn, this is Lya," he told her with a look in his eyes Lucid hoped his sister could not miss.

Brynn stood and went over to Lya to inspect her. Lya curtsied the way Lucid had shown her. Brynn frowned at the gesture but embraced her. Lya could not have been more shocked; neither could Lucid. The princess pulled back and looked into Lya's eyes and smiled. Then she turned, eyeing

Lucid for a second with a hard stare, and slapped him. The sharp smack echoed off the large chamber walls. In the silence that followed, she buried herself in her brother's arms.

"Please don't leave me again." She pulled back, and her tear-filled eyes met Lucid's. "I'm not Mother or Father." She glanced at Lya. "I don't care what you are doing or with whom. Just don't disappear like that, not now."

Lucid felt terrible. His own eyes felt slightly moist as he said, "I am so sorry, Brynn. I promise that, no matter what, I will not leave again."

She nodded and moved to sit back down, gesturing for them to sit next to her. She wiped her face and took a deep breath, appearing to compose herself.

"Much has happened in the last weeks. How much do you know?" she asked as they sat.

"Not much, just that Father killed Ivan and that Reggie diagnosed him. What exactly did he say after the examination?"

Brynn looked pained as she said, "He told us he had seen this type of grief before, and the only way to pull out of his spiral is for him to do it alone. Reggie has ordered Normin not be bothered." She paused and looked into Lucid's eyes. "Even by his own family. I know how highly skilled he is, but that seems odd. What do you make of it?" she asked him.

Lucid waved a hand in dismissal. "The master healer knows what he is doing. Trust him. We have much more pressing matters than being able to see Father, although he may need to hear this as well." He glanced to Trigo and shifted uncomfortably. "There is something I have to tell you. You need to know if you are to rule that there is also a very urgent issue, much more dangerous than anything Drondos can muster." Jake opened his mouth to speak, but Lucid cut him off with a sharp wave and a harsh look.

"There are … others here," he continued. Brynn's face told him that she may have heard something or at least has had suspicions. "They live in the woods, huge creatures with no hair and glowing green eyes. They are called gvorlocks, and we have lived in peace with these things for centuries now. Only the king and head king's men are allowed this knowledge. And the prince, when he comes of age obviously."

Brynn glanced to Jake, whose face was stone, but he nodded slightly. She turned back to Lucid again with a worried expression.

"This," Lucid began, taking Lya's hand again, "was one of their slaves. I helped her escape, and in the process"—he paused and looked down at the table, embarrassed—"I killed one," he said softly.

"You little fool!" Jake surged to his feet, his face peppered with shock and outrage. "Do you have any idea what you have done?" he shouted.

Brynn cleared her throat. When the livid king's man turned to look, her face was stern and emotionless. Trigo took a breath and stopped yelling, but his face said he was still very angry. In the silence that followed, he sat back down, jaw clenched and face red.

Lucid went on to tell Brynn everything he felt she needed to know, feeling that she deserved to know the whole tale. It spilled out of him in fast sentences. He felt at one point that he might be overwhelming her with everything.

Brynn stood and began pacing. "That explains why the council did not mention it when I took the throne. Now the tale of the man from Drondos makes a little more sense," she said, seeming to speak more to herself than to any of them. "If you have killed one, then obviously that means the peace that was forged has been compromised. Oh God, was I too harsh on

Father?" she asked, despair creeping into her tone very faintly. "He needs to hear all of this."

"I am afraid there is more," Lucid told her. She stopped pacing to look at him.

Coy wiped the sweat from his brow as he watched Bruce rubbing his knee. The young boy pulled the waterskin out of the cart in which Mr. Mathis sat and took a long drink. He offered it to Bruce, who paused in his attempt at relief and took a drink. Bruce handed it back, gave his old knee one more good squeeze, and stood slowly. Coy helped him to his feet. The old farmer took a few steps, wincing as he did so.

"You okay?" Coy asked of him. The man nodded stubbornly.

"We will set a slower pace back to the barn, but I will be fine by tomorrow," Bruce replied.

Coy used to have doubts, but Bruce, true to his word, no matter what ailment he suffered, always seemed spry in the mornings after a night's rest. Bruce and Coy put their hauling straps over their shoulders and began heaving. They were fairly close to the barn, so Coy knew the tough old man would push through with no complaints.

As they pulled the cart into the barn, Bruce looked to Coy. "Think you could unload by yourself?" he asked.

Coy nodded and began positioning the cart just right as Bruce limped to the house. The old farmer had asked Coy to do this once before, so the boy had come up with his own easy way to empty their load cart. He positioned his canvas and ran the rope around it, Jerry sitting patiently at the entrance. Coy opened the hatch across the back of the cart, tipped it down toward himself with his weight to get it started, then hopped off and pulled. In one smooth motion, the large pile of wheat slid off into the fresh pile.

He smiled and looked at Jerry. "Pretty smart, huh?" he asked of the hound, who barked once in response. Coy stored the cart and replaced the tools. When he entered the house, Bruce and Ann were speaking at the table laden with chicken and potatoes.

"... going to need it tonight, dear. Maybe Coy would go for you," she said as he entered.

"Of course," he said without needing to know what the errand was. He sat down at the dining table and heaped his plate.

Bruce smiled. "You are a good boy, son. I honestly don't know what we would do without you," he told the young boy. Coy smiled through a mouthful of bread as he tore a huge bite.

"I don't know where you put all of that food. Must have a hollow leg or something," Mrs. Mathis told him. "We need you to run to Mr. Martin's shop and get another box of paper. I used the last sheet today to keep tallies. We will need some for tomorrow's count."

Coy nodded. After he finished his food, he hurried out the door toward town, Jerry at his heels. He did not have much time before the paper shop would close, so he walked quickly, the sun dipping lower as he went. When the LD came into view, he put on a little burst of speed and ran, Jerry racing beside him. He looked down at the animal, tongue hanging out while he strode next to Coy. He laughed as Jerry passed him just when they were crossing into the darkened streets of the lower dwellings. Jerry came to a stop at the small hut where the papermaker made his living.

Coy stopped at the door to the shop to bend down and give Jerry a proper rubdown. "Good boy. I'll beat you one of these days." The hound gave him a courtesy lick on the cheek as if to say, *Yeah, right.*

Two pieces of metal hanging over the door clinked together as Coy entered the little shop. Mr. Martin, who had been cleaning up for the day in the back, entered the front room upon hearing the door.

"Hello, Mr. Coy. Let me guess: the Mathises are out of paper?" The boy smiled timidly and nodded. "The old farmer and his wife are so meticulous in their counts that I can usually guess almost to the day when they will be out," he told Coy as he stepped around the counter with a box laden with stacks of paper. Coy handed the craftsman the pouch of coins Bruce had given him and hoisted the box.

"Make sure to tell Mr. and Mrs. Mathis I said hello," Mr. Martin said and smiled. Coy nodded and left the shop to even darker streets. Most everyone had retired for the day, so the LD was quiet.

Too quiet, Coy thought as he paused and listened. Jerry seemed to feel something as well, and that was all the warning Coy needed. The dog had been staring intently at the woods on the north side of town when Coy exited the shop. As Coy watched now, the dog's fur rose and a low growl erupted. The boy froze, mirroring the hound as they stared together.

Men were shouting distantly. Not sounds of loud conversation or anything of the sort, this was the long, low rumble of a thousand voices as one. When Coy realized what he was hearing, the box of fresh paper slipped and hit the ground.

CHAPTER 26

Normin's anxiety mounted as the large group of slaves, accompanied by a smaller group of soldiers, marched through the woods. He had made the beginnings of a plan and would attempt to stick to it, minimizing fatalities as much as possible, but it would not be easy. With the chaos of open battle, making the plan was the easy part. Once people began killing each other, all premade moves would become moot, and it would be improvising from then on.

Please, Lord, he prayed as they moved toward his city, *please help me and my people through this. Do not let too many fall.*

He knew his citizens well. Their fighting skills would prove superior to those of the slaves but not to those of the soldiers. Somehow, Normin had discovered, the nonslave soldiers had stolen fighting skills that were much the same as what was taught in Altheia. They would inflict the most damage. And there was no controlling those men. All young and wild, close friends of Jason all, they listened to no one but their king. Normin had no idea exactly what their orders were, but he was sure it included killing Altheians.

What was Jason trying to accomplish here tonight? Did he intend to attempt to take over Normin's city? Normin's body would have to be cold and horizontal for him to let that happen. He would kill that little brat himself if necessary.

The woods began thinning, and Normin's heart rate rose again. On the front line of the little army, he glanced behind himself. Brighton was there scanning the areas around the trees, his eyes wild with bloodlust. This was a man who enjoyed violence. For the first time since becoming a slave, Normin was glad Brighton was at his back. The large man had become somewhat of a follower of Normin's and watched out for him everywhere he went, although Normin could never tell anyone who he was, so Brighton was left in the dark about the undercover king's secret plan to minimize the killing. Normin had begun teaching some of the slaves his superior fighting skills in the dark of the warehouse after most were snoring peacefully. After learning just how lacking his skills were, and after finding out that Normin could help, Brighton was never more than a few steps away, daring anyone to so much as look at Normin wrong. Apparently being a good fighter was something that commanded respect, lots of it. The big man soaked up Normin's lessons like a sponge and had improved rapidly.

The tops of the high city came into view over the thinning canopy. Normin heard the shouted order repeated down the line: "Charge!"

Slowly at first, the king and the men around him began to trot. Then Normin picked up speed, matched by the others on the front line. Closer and closer his city came into view, and faster the army ran. When they cleared the trees and started over the small hill that led to a small grassy field in front of the LD, a wordless battle cry erupted from the men. Whether from fear, bloodlust, or just plain excitement, they yelled. As one, the men screamed something primal as the footfalls of almost a thousand men thundered toward the quiet streets.

To his left, Normin could just make out the top of the steps to the palace. Standing atop them, staring out at the charging army, were Jon and Daryl. Normin cursed and scanned around, looking for other royalty. To his right, a young boy he did not recognize and what looked to be the Mathises' dog ran out of the streets of the LD toward the training yard at an impressive pace. Normin pulled a mask over the lower half of his face as he charged. Curious, he watched as the boy entered the small armory adjacent to the training yard and exited, holding a blunted training blade.

Daryl ran into the palace. Jon pulled his blade and began shouting orders to anyone who could hear. Boys and younger men, being the quickest and most curious, began emerging and fell in behind Jon as he descended the steps of the palace. Bodies began pouring out of homes, and Jon began marshalling his army youths like a seasoned general. The lack of grown men shocked Normin as it seemed the youngest were the most eager to use the skills they had been drilling for years. *This will be bloody,* he thought as he put on a burst of speed toward his city.

Daryl burst into the council chambers with such force and speed, he tripped when the heavy door did not open fast enough. He went sprawling to the ground. He popped back up so quickly that Lucid thought he imagined the fall.

"Drondos is attacking!" Daryl yelled. The four jumped to their feet and ran for the door.

What they saw upon exiting the palace made Lucid so incredibly angry that he could not quite believe it.

The fucking nerve to attack my city! Doubtless these same animals killed my mother! Lucid thought as his jaw clenched so hard in anger that he thought he might break teeth. His vision blurred and his heart was pounding as he pulled his sword and ran for Jon without another word.

Jon was gathering a group into a semblance of order, lining them up shoulder to shoulder in columns, ten wide and ten deep. Lucid joined the formation beside his friend, pushing little Joe Yemen over one row to strengthen the line.

"Keep your position. Do not let anyone in your left or right gaps. Jansen, closer!" Jon finished up and turned to take the charge, backing up slightly to take position next to Lucid.

Fierce-looking men wearing expressions that said they meant to kill were running toward the gathered assembly. As the army got closer, Lucid could make out the individual screams and see the sweat dripping down faces. He tightened his grip on the sword and raised it quietly. As he watched the footfalls of the invaders, jaw clenched, muscles tense on a whole new scale, he felt tears like fire stream down his face.

It was an odd feeling, random and unexpected, like saying ouch even though whatever blow may not have hurt at all. He was not even the slightest bit sad or upset, as he had been when he saw Lya's injured face. It was quite the opposite. An anger unlike anything he had ever felt caused his chest to heave unnaturally, and his heart felt as if it might hop out of his chest.

Jason? How dare he attack us! Lucid thought.

All at once, his mind focused with a clarity he had never known. His actions following the attack on the tower were abhorrent.

They killed Mother, and what did I do?

The answer was too painful. How could he have been so blind? The once peaceful relationship between cities had been festering like an old wound, and where was he? Out playing around the island with Lya. He had abandoned his people in their most urgent time of need. He deserved every bit of this. *God rest my soul. If I should fall, watch out for Lya.* As one, the army rose their weapons and readied themselves for what would be the first ever battle.

Line left is crooked and weak, Jon thought as he walked down the line, putting his men in place.

Watch for flank. If that side falls, fold right. Will the boys even know enough tactics for that maneuver?

All of this, plus many more scenarios, worked through Jon's brain as he shouted orders. The second Jon had seen the army from the steps of the palace, realization struck and a memory came back to him in a rush.

He was eight, and his father was drilling him in their shared chambers in the palace. "Nobody else has to practice at night. I know 'cause I asked my friends."

His father had struck him with the back of his fist. Jon blocked, but it still busted his lip. "You are not some bumpkin selling your stock in the LD. We are king's men. You will one day be charged with protecting your king and your people. You will be better, you will be stronger, and you will be smarter."

All of the extra hours spent training at night, all of the early mornings spent studying extra military tactics, snapped taut like a bowstring, and the entirety of the battle played out in a hundred pictures. Everything slowed and became perfectly clear: lighting, angle of attack, wind direction, footing, ants, pillars that might be easily removed and used as weapons.

Everything.

This was his city, and he knew it intimately. The detail shocked Jon to the point of almost laughing. As he took his place at the front of the first line next to Lucid, he felt relaxed. There was no fear and no anxiety, his heart rate even as if he were about to have supper. There was only a hint of amusement and even a little excitement. He was home here; this was his place. He glanced to the prince. The look on his face made Jon sidestep away half a pace.

Lucid had never looked so angry in his life. Jon had seen him in many stages of anger over the years. The reason today was obvious: the rival kingdom had killed his mother, and here they were again, attacking his people. Jon simply felt sorry for anyone who stood in Lucid's way, which is why he gave his friend one extra elbow's worth of room. *Go nuts, my friend. The reckoning starts now.*

Normin felt sick. It was not the run, the light meals, or even fear that had his stomach roiling. As he charged, the army had shifted, heading directly toward the gathering group of men and boys. Jason's intention became painfully clear. This was simply to thin the herd. They'd been sent to kill, and that was all.

Still, that realization did not have Normin feeling ill as much as the thought of charging at his own son in open battle. It was unthinkable, ludicrous even. If someone had told Normin that one day he would be where he was right then, he would have laughed a booming, wholehearted laugh. It simply would never happen. Yet here he was.

I will carefully break the line on the right side and play defense in the back.

His plan sounded good. It would give him a small amount of control during this desperate battle. He would let no one fall on either side if he could help it. That would be hopeful at best.

Lya watched in horror as Lucid drew his weapon and stood his ground with such a large number of men screaming and running toward the city. The invaders were huge, mean-looking men armed with brightly polished blades and armored in rough leathers. She looked to the small group of defenders, and she wanted to cry. How would it be possible for such a small group of young men and boys to stand against such a force? She glanced to the princess, who wore a similar expression, countered by the look of angry determination on her guard's face.

Jake seemed like a dog on a leash just itching to get set free. Lya was sure his duty was to protect the small leader, but he looked hungry for the fight, almost giddy. He fidgeted, clenched his jaw, flexed his hands, and shifted his weight more frequently than was needed.

"Go," she heard the small voice beside her say. The man was a blur as he sprinted down the palace steps with the grace of a master dancer.

"Get inside now!" he shouted to Brynn and Lya as he went.

Brynn turned to go. She grabbed Lya's arm, but Lya was frozen like stone and resisted the small girl's pull.

"We will die if we stay here!" Brynn shouted, her fear rising in her small voice.

Lya simply took the hand that was attempting to pull her away, looked into Brynn's eyes, and shook her head. "I have to see this. Go if you wish, but I cannot leave him."

Brynn looked ready to argue, but she stood her ground and kept Lya's hand in hers. They turned to watch the battle. The attackers were close now. Just a few more strides and then …

Crash.

The initial charge was met by the defenders with such a loud clash of metal that both girls cringed. The screams of men and the ringing of swords filled the air as bodies dropped on both sides. Lya looked to the front, where Lucid and Jon fought, and was surprised to see dead bodies quickly beginning to form around the two of them. Jon was similarly talented, Lya observed. The two of them mowed over any fighter who came close. Soon a large circle opened up around them, attackers steadily testing them just to die on their blades.

It was beautiful to watch them; they worked so incredibly well, it was like watching one body with four arms and legs. This was their art, and they were very practiced.

The battle seemed to be going much better than expected. Lya had thought initially that the invaders would swallow up the smaller group as a shark eats a minnow. Jon's direction had the group holding their ground, and even the smallest of the younger boys seemed to be very familiar with swinging a sword.

Lucid picked his first target and watched his footfalls, waiting on the swing. It was not a particularly large man, especially compared to the ones behind him. He wore a mask on the lower half of his face and ran with a gait that looked oddly familiar.

The lines of screaming men ran full tilt and slammed into the front line of the Altheians, dropping many on both sides with a sound that was so loud, it made Lucid's ears ring. The half-mask had ducked his first swing and disappeared, but Lucid picked a new target quickly and attacked, trusting in the men behind. The next man was much larger, and Lucid made quick work of his sloppy strokes, finding an opening when the man lifted his foot. A small front kick put the big soldier off balance, and in that instant Lucid went low to high and caught the man's neck in a shower of blood. Another one came in, and he dropped the next one even faster with a quick thrust to his heart. More and more came. Soon he lost count, slaying any man who came within range of his blade. He did not even feel his injured shoulder; rage and adrenaline blocked everything out but the next target. He spotted Jon out of his peripheral vision and noticed a similar pile of bodies and a large circle beginning to open up around him too.

A face appeared at Lucid's side that was unfamiliar: a young boy with a training blade, holding his own against a grown man twice his size. The sight was so impressive that it distracted Lucid just long enough for an attacker to approach his side and take a swing. The training blade lashed out and caught the stroke. Lucid glanced to see the small boy stepping over his kill to execute a perfect block and parry. Lucid wasted no time finishing the man by putting a foot of sword through his chin and ramming it out the top of his head. He turned to the boy and nodded, but behind him a smaller man crept up and, before Lucid knew what was happening, sliced deep gashes across the back of both knees.

The boy cried out in pain and fell to the ground, shaking with agony. The soldier whom Lucid now faced was different from the others, younger, more fit, and better armed and armored—and much better with a blade.

"Coy!" Brynn cried out. She covered her mouth with her hand when she saw him fall. Tears brimmed as she watched him writhe in agony. Daryl burst from the palace doors, a group of healers in tow armed with small daggers and throwing knives. Alisha was at his side with her new crossbow and a huge bundle of small arrows strapped to her back. They bolted past the girls toward the fighting. Brynn was amazed at the bravery of the healers, charging right into the fray while wielding no more than cutting knives.

They worked in pairs. Daryl hit the ground at Coy's feet and rolled him over, cleaning the wound and stitching him up right where he had fallen. Daryl's partner Kennith Graice stood guard over him, and any man who got anywhere close got a throwing knife to the throat. Even as far as fifty feet away, the men threw with deadly accuracy.

Even more shocking was Alisha and her invention. The contraption fired arrows faster than the eye could follow, and those arrows punctured with such force that they threw men dead to the ground as they struck. Over and over she fired, cranking a small handle and firing again, emptying her sack of arrows much faster than Brynn would have thought possible. It seemed that Alisha alone turned the tide of the battle as men fell dead randomly in all directions, feathers protruding out slightly, marking fatal wounds.

A large man with a bald head and a wicked smile moved around the main area of fighting and began walking right toward the girls. Brynn was terrified to the point of almost wetting herself.

She was no fighter. Girls who did not wish to receive training by no means were forced into it. And so Brynn had left the training to the boys and had no desire to learn how to kill people with sharpened metal. She began to shake and tried to turn and run into the palace, but Lya still had hold of her hand. She looked to the slave girl and saw she was holding her breath and quivering with an extremely odd expression on her face, eyes closed. It was then she realized just how tight Lya's hold was. Brynn struggled to free herself.

"Let go!" she shouted, but Lya did not hear her.

Lost in some trance of fear, Brynn assumed, Lya could not be reached. Lya's eyes opened abruptly, almost violently, and her head rocked back once. Brynn's fear increased as she glanced at the menacing killer who was getting closer, then back to Lya, who seemed to be dying without the help of the incoming attacker. Just as Brynn thought this was her end, Lya inhaled a long breath and drew her hands so far down and backward that it twisted Brynn's wrist uncomfortably. Then she blew an intense exhalation as if she were blowing out a candle from across the room. As she did this, her hands flew up, including the hand still attached to Brynn's arm, in a motion fast and fluid. Brynn had no choice but to go with the move as it seemed Lya had tossed an invisible log backward and over her head.

This girl has gone mental right in front of my eyes, Brynn thought.

But before that thought came to completion, the would-be killer let out a long scream as a random gust of wind picked him up and launched him over their heads with terrifying speed. Brynn had never seen anything move so fast. It was not that shocking when his scream cut short as he slammed into the top corner of the palace in an explosion of gore. Blood ran down the palace wall as his body continued its unnatural tumble over the building and out to sea.

Brynn just stood there, frozen. *What ... just ... happened?* she thought.

She looked at Lya, whose face was a mask of shock and fear. Lya released the princess's hand; Brynn rubbed it immediately.

"Sorry," Lya said sheepishly. "Still can't quite control it."

Brynn just stood there staring, rubbing her hands together. "Control what?"

Lya just looked away. Brynn had no idea who or what this girl was, but one thing was sure: after that display, Brynn no longer feared being outside to witness the battle.

Normin ducked his son's first swing with ease in a low crouch and continued on to the back, staying low. He had made that kid, brought him into the world, and made him who he is. Guessing which swing his son would begin with was the easy part.

As he squeezed his way through the frantic crowd of young fighters, Normin caught slices across his arms and punches just about everywhere. Soon he cleared the crowd and stood straight at the back of the defenders, surveying the battle. Some had turned to engage him, but he simply stuck with his plan and deflected swing after swing.

He spotted Lucid and Jon in the front, and his heart surged with pride. His boy, the little boy who had come screaming and crying when he broke his arm, who had refused to swim in the ocean for over a year after he and Jon got caught in a whirlpool, was standing tall in front of his people, willing to sacrifice himself for those who loved him, who relied on his protection.

Now that's king, Normin thought. Between blocking little Evan Tanner's stroke and Joe Yemen's thrust, he wiped away a tear.

Normin heard heavy footsteps of a large man approaching his side. He disarmed the two boys quickly to turn and meet the new attacker.

Of course, he thought as he watched his best friend charging at him, blade held ready for a savage cross.

Normin pulled his mask down ever so slightly, not to show his face to anyone but to show Jake his eyes. That would be all he needed, he hoped.

Jake came in fast, faster than Normin would have thought possible, and he just barely got his own blade up in time. That was all it took. These two men had swung swords at each other for so many years that they could identify each other blindfolded simply by hearing the swing. The blades met, and Jake's face lit up with shock on a whole new level. Normin had to stifle a laugh.

"The fuck?" Jake said quietly as he threw another swing. This time it was slow and deliberate, and Normin had no problem with the block. The swords met again, the clash sounding more like the bell upon entering the paper shop. Normin made a quick gesture to indicate no talking, and they continued their pretend fight as they both turned to survey the carnage.

The king was a bag of mixed emotions. These were the men and boys he and his friends and peers had given the world. Trained and taught in his city, they were the next generation of leaders and fighters. On the other side, his heart was heavy. Seeing so many of his new people he had meant to free falling to blades held by people he considered family had confused him in new ways and also showed him his true path.

All men and women are equal, given the right circumstances.

No person had the right to own other people. Watching the slaves dying on Altheian blades, Normin felt much like he was losing his own people. Then he heard a familiar voice cry out.

"Coy!"

Normin whipped his head around to see his little girl standing at the top of the palace steps, holding hands with another girl he did not recognize. He followed Brynn's line of sight, looking for a boy whom he had heard much about. His heart sank. Through the crowd he spotted a boy on the ground next to Lucid screaming in pain, clutching the back of his legs. The king looked back to the palace to see a squad of healers, Alisha in tow with what looked to be a very functional crossbow, come rushing out of the palace. His tension eased as he saw Daryl run straight for the fallen boy. The healer would make quick work of patching him up. Coy may not walk again, but Normin could at least take the smallest shred of good news back to Gina.

He's alive and well, and he fought bravely, he would tell her. No need to tell her all.

Coy tightened his grip as he lined up under Jon's direction. He was scared but also a little excited as he would finally get to take revenge upon some of the men who had starved him his whole life, men who had starved his mother and his poor aunt Gina who, even now, may be dying from a lack of food.

Coy glanced to his right and saw Joe, a boy whom he trained with every day, and they nodded to each other gravely. He glanced left, and none other than Derek Inder stood there, eyeing him and his training blade critically. He said nothing and, for the first time ever, had no punch or rude comments to throw. Coy looked back ahead at the charging army.

It was close. His heart beat faster, and he shifted his stance. The extra leverage from the shift did nothing as the attackers clashed. He could not see the collision, but he felt it. He was pushed back several steps and almost lost his footing as the front line caved backward under the charge.

Men screamed. Coy was wedged in between the other boys until some of the men on the front line fell and his line of sight cleared. As soon as the man in front of him fell, a line of angry faces emerged, and he found himself in front of a man with pale skin and dark eyes. He wore old leather armor with dirty and stained linen underneath, but the blade he had drawn back was a savage-looking thing, curved and shining beautifully. Coy could not pierce with his training blade, he discovered, as he sent all of his small stature behind a thrust aimed at the man's neck.

The big man dropped his wicked sword midswing to clutch at his throat. The force of the hit put him on his back, where Derek skewered him without even turning his head fully around. Another man came at him, a smaller man who was quicker and more agile. With no weapon but a glorified club, Coy knew he would have to finish him quickly. He switched to two-handed as he'd been taught and spun. He grunted as he swung with everything he had, aiming for the man's ankles. He was met with a satisfactory yet bone-chilling crunch, followed by a scream. The man's feet flew out from under him. Coy continued his spin, raising his weapon as he spun with the circle, and came down hard with his training blade.

The attacker's face crumpled, splashing blood and brains everywhere. Coy looked up to see Lucid staring at him in shock, unaware of the thick-set monster approaching his left side with his sword raised. Coy's arm shot out and blocked, sending a jolt up his arm. He almost dropped his weapon. Lucid's shock wore off after that, and he shoved his blade up under the big man's chin. Coy smiled at the prince, but the look on Lucid's face did not match his own. Before Coy's mind could process, pain exploded across the back of his legs.

He screamed and could focus on nothing but the stark agony. Mind-altering pain overwhelmed him and everything disappeared, the fighting, the screams of the dying men, the pride of his first battle. Next thing he knew, he was being rolled over onto his stomach and someone began patching him up right on the battlefield. A hand shot out and shoved some herbs in his mouth. "Chew," said a voice, and he did as he was bade. As he chewed, the pain lessened, and so did all his senses. The world spun, and he thought he was dying right there. He looked around in a daze and vaguely spotted shadows emerging from the LD.

"Inder!" said the voice. Coy looked over to see the boy break off from the battle and head toward him. "Take him to the infirmary now!"

Derek did not hesitate to sheathe his weapon and gather up the small boy, sprinting at an impressive pace considering his heavy charge. *Is this really happening?* Coy asked himself as he bounced with Derek's long strides. He thought he said thank you to the boy, but the world blurred and spun more by the second. Before long, he was out.

Lya stood with Brynn atop the steps, watching the prince she had fallen in love with slice and cut any man or limb that came within reach of his blade. It was beautiful and scary. She'd had no idea the extent of his skill, but watching him now, she wondered why she was worried.

Slowly at first, out of the corner of her eye, she spotted shadows moving quietly out of the streets. She caught a flash of steel in the moonlight, and it dawned on her what was happening. Relief washed over her as the large group of men approaching let out a long cry when they got close enough. Then they attacked.

These were no boys. Huge men, including the man who had removed her shackles, stormed in and joined the fight. A masked man in the back of the first group screamed, "Fall back!" and the attackers immediately broke off from the fight to turn and run.

And just like that, it was over as the men receded into the tree line. As soon as they got a safe distance away, Lya ran to Lucid. He heard her coming and turned, embracing her tightly.

"Are you okay?" she asked, still holding him tight.

He pulled back and smiled. "I am now." He kissed her deeply.

They let go of each other. Lya looked around to see everyone staring. Her face reddened with embarrassment, but Lucid simply said in a loud voice that carried to every ear, "You all fought well, every one of you. I am so incredibly proud. Stand tall, and do not ever let them come to our city and win a fight!"

The crowd erupted in cheers and chants. Lucid and Jon had

put on a show with their skills, and the love and respect poured out loudly, causing goose bumps to rise on Lya's flesh.

"Lucid, Lucid, Lucid!"

The prince waited as the cheers went on. He looked at Lya with such a contented expression of pride and love that she shuddered. He kissed her again, and the crowd cheered louder. It seemed it would go on forever until Lucid waved for silence and said, "This is not over. Everyone, stay vigilant and be watchful. It seems the new king of Drondos wants to come here and hurt my people, to take what is ours. I say, over my cold, dead body!" The crowd erupted again.

"Fall back!" Normin yelled. The effect was immediate. It seemed bravery only went so far with this group, and they stormed and pushed each other to get away.

Normin looked to Jake. "Not a fucking word," he told his friend. The seriousness in his tone and in his eyes made Jake swallow hard. He nodded.

Normin ran with his cowardly little army and put on speed to get nearer to the front. He wanted to know what Jason's men would say about all of this.

As he ran, his heart felt heavy. He needed to make a move pretty quickly if he was to spare more lives on both sides. But what? No opportunity had presented itself yet, so he felt as if he were just riding a wave, carried along in whatever direction it decided to go. He needed more control, but how? Reveal himself? Maybe it was time. He could use his little slave army to move Jason out of power. Maybe he could do so without killing the little miscreant.

When the slaves approached the main gate, moonlight was bright in the main lanes of the city. With few trees about town, the visibility at night in Drondos was much better than in

Altheia. Normin could see immediately the new decorations strung on everything high enough to tie off to.

Bodies hung like banners of some sadistic celebration. He stopped at a particularly thin yet familiar corpse with gray locks. Her face was twisted into an expression that Normin felt inside at that very moment.

"He is alive," he said through a cracking voice to Gina, hanging by her neck from a post that used to house a lantern.

He continued his walk but could not remember having told his feet to move.

Who could be so callous, so brutal, so … evil?

Jason had killed every slave who could not fight. In so doing, he had thinned his herd and sent a message all at once. But was that message directed at Normin? Did Jason know he had the king of Altheia imprisoned as a slave? Normin could not be sure, but one thing was clear: this kid was merciless and possibly smarter than Normin thought.

When Normin reached the end, a much smaller corpse hung what seemed ten stories higher than everyone else. As soon as he saw it, he fell to his knees and a lump formed in his throat. He closed his eyes and let the pain wash over him. Tears fell unchecked. He found it hard to breathe.

He had no idea how much time he spent there on his knees weeping. Next thing he knew, he was being dragged to his feet and hauled away. He took one last look at the tiny girl. Her face was purple, and there was a tear of blood falling down from her left eye. She had brown hair and eyes, just like his Brynn. Starving to death, she had offered him bread that first day. Alice, her name was. It was as if Normin was losing his wife all over again. He screamed as they dragged him away, and something in him snapped.

CHAPTER 27

Jason sat with his young councillors in the meeting room of the royal manse. "I would say we did pretty well last night, wouldn't you?" he asked Tim Meadows.

At twenty years, he was the oldest and most experienced with several more years; training in Altheian fighting style. Tim was small in stature but wiry and strong with sandy-colored hair and intense blue eyes that held a hint of amusement. "Yes, Your Majesty. I don't know how the rest of you fared, but I got four kills."

Jason smiled. "Two, but I was nearer to the back, being unnecessarily guarded by Randy." He hooked a thumb at the young scout, who frowned.

"Talk shit all you want, but you are still alive."

Jason chuckled. "I cannot argue that. Did you see Normin when he saw the girl? Hilarious. You did great, Zak," he told his new head craftsman.

The thick-red-haired boy of sixteen nodded and smiled. "We were tying off the last body when we saw the army approaching the gates. It was a close one, but we got it just in time," he told his king.

Jason smiled widely. "You did excellent, and I am sure our little slave king got the message. If not, who gives a shit? I did not want to make it too obvious, or else he might have tried to escape or send word to Altheia somehow. The bow that woman held, what the hell was it? Anyone?"

No response. "Well, we need to find out and steal it or make one. Percy," Jason continued. The old man laboriously raised his bloodshot eyes to meet the king's. "Two weeks."

Jason wished there were a younger, more competent man who could do his bidding, but this old drunk was the only one on the whole island of Blysse who had the knowledge he needed. Perhaps it was time to make Percy teach someone else the craft.

"To finish your little project, you old moron." Jason looked into Percy's eyes and slowed his speech. "Do you understand what I am telling you?"

Percy nodded with a vacant expression. Jason continued to stare.

"Perhaps you should get to work. Now."

The man rose and shuffled out. Jason shook his head, scowling.

He looked to his scout Randy. "Do you see now why I do not suffer any of you drinking? It makes you stupid. Follow Percy for me. Learn what you can about his craft. I'd like to get rid of that weak old man."

Smith nodded and rose, stalking after Percy.

"All right, men, that's enough fucking around with Altheia. I want that city. It's time to plan our final attack," he said to his council.

"What about Normin?" asked Frank Digner. He was the only old man other than Percy whom Jason had kept of his father's councillors—and for good reason. He was leather-skinned, thickly built, and strong as an ox. Frank also led the slave guards and did all training for slaves and the boys themselves. He was the only elder man Jason respected.

"What about him?" he asked of his captain.

Digner frowned. "Your little show may have cost us our element of surprise. Surely he knows now that you are well-informed. He will try to escape."

Jason smiled patiently, the way a parent might smile at a child, and Frank's frown deepened. "Clearly you know nothing of breaking a man mentally. Still, he may try if he wishes. Post extra guards during the day and triple at night. He will not get away, and as long as we have him, Altheia is weakened," he said. That seemed to placate the man slightly.

"We still do not have the numbers to defeat Altheia in battle. You saw what we were up against, and that was only a fraction of the men the city can muster," said Tim.

Jason just shook his head. "It won't matter. This time we will not charge at them; we will attack more stealthily, and we will have explosives. They will not stand a chance." He looked to Captain Digner. "What were the losses of the slaves last night compared to our actual troops?" he asked.

"Fifty-two slaves were killed or injured, and only one of our troops died."

Jason smiled. "They are an effective shield if anything. It's perfect." He stood and began pacing, thinking. "Are there no back entrances into the palace?" he asked without looking at anyone in particular.

It was Tim who answered, saying, "No, the palace and buildings around it are built right into the rock of the ravine. One way in, one way out."

Jason reached the edge of the small meeting room and turned, continuing the back-and-forth with his steps and his words. He found walking always helped him think.

"Frank, what do you think about taking the beach this time? They might not see us until it is too late."

Digner nodded and said, "That could work. I would prefer the beach. It is a blind spot for anyone inside or in front of the palace. It is also the perfect angle of attack."

The meeting went on thusly for another hour or so. When

Jason finally had his plan together, he exited the meeting room and went for a walk on the parapets. He liked the cool night breeze and found sleep difficult without it blowing steadily through his window. The night was dark when he exited the double doors on the top floor of the palace and stepped onto the balcony. It took his eyes a moment to adjust, and when they did, he found the catapult standing tall in the darkness.

It brought to mind the ship, that beautiful giant boat that he had to have for himself. *What are Normin's intentions with that thing?* he asked himself. The answer was obvious.

Once again he pictured himself sailing the open seas, fighting new enemies, finding new islands, and conquering them. It was such a glorious picture, it gave him an idea. He left the palace in a hurry and went searching the old merchant district for Randy.

He found the young scout standing outside Percy's little shop, watching the man work through the tiny window on the side of the building. He stepped closer to Randy to get a better look. Smith glanced at Jason but said nothing and continued to watch in silence. Percy was putting what looked like dough around the edge of a huge metal tank that was beginning to steam from the large fire burning under it. Jason tapped his friend and indicated with a nod a location away from the shop. The two stepped away. "This ship captain of Normin's," he began without preamble. "Take as many soldiers as you need, and bring him to me."

Vincent could hear a battle raging not far away for the first time in the history of Blysse—and he was stuck in bed. The ring of metal and the screams of pain carried through his little window in the hut. Not for the first time since being injured, he wished he could stand and fight. It was an alien feeling to him, being in the care of someone else, and he found that he was truly grateful to these people for bringing him back from the dead. He would enjoy killing those who wished to hurt his new friends.

The pain was lessening as the days went by, but putting any pressure on his spine was excruciating. Standing was not an option. He could not help but think his recovery would be a little farther along if that little brat Jason had not sent an assassin. He simply could not let Brynn die. She was just a child and an unwilling party in Vincent's problems. She was more to him that just that, however.

That secret will die with me.

The sounds of battle faded. He must have dozed off because next thing he knew, sunlight woke him. He reached over to the little table next to the bed and took a piece of dried beef and ate. Not long after Vincent had finished his little breakfast, Russell came stomping down the trail to his hut. Vincent could tell who it was; Russell did not walk as silently as the rest, and also he was unmistakable because of his whistling. It seemed the young man was unable to move without blowing out his favorite tune. Either that or he was simply very happy to be free.

He entered. Vincent could not help but smile at the huge grin cemented on Russell's face. He looked thicker than the last time Vincent had seen him, almost fat. His long black hair was tied back tight, and he had on a fresh white shirt under a sleeveless vest with standard dark pants.

"Hello, Russell. What has you in such a happy mood today? I thought I heard sounds of battle last night."

Russell's smile broadened. "We won," he said simply, plopping down in the chair next to the bed.

"The fact that it is you who is here and not Daryl tells me there was great loss." Russell's smile died as he looked away.

"They will pay dearly for every life lost. And, yes, Daryl is tending to the injured still, as we speak, along with all the other healers," he said.

Vincent had to ask, "That bad, huh?"

Russell nodded. The men were respectfully silent for a minute. "The king and his children?" Vincent asked of the royal family.

Russell waved a hand in dismissal. "They are fine. Lucid is the best fighter I know, although what I heard about Jon may change my mind," he said.

"Were you not involved in the fighting?"

Russell shook his head. "I was asleep. No noise reaches these ears after I'm out. I have been told I could sleep through a hurricane. Also, I have been bedding down early these last weeks. Nice to finally get some real rest."

Vincent nodded. "What did you mean by 'what I heard about Jon'?" he asked.

Russell propped his feet up against the bed and said, "Reports from the battle last night came in quickly and spread like wildfire. Most of the accounts are the same: Lucid and Jon standing tall at the front, defending our people. But some say Jon fought like a demon, a madman—took out more of them than any two other men combined."

Interesting, Vincent thought.

Jon was the son of the head king's man, so it was not too surprising. It seemed that Russell, and possibly many others, did not quite know about the Trigo family secret. It had always made sense to Vincent that the man who guarded the king closely every day would be expected to handle a blade better than any. Still, one thought had been bothering him.

"Where was your famous King Normin through all of

this? I have a hard time believing he was not involved in the fighting."

Russell shrugged. "Honestly, he wasn't. I had the same question, but no one has seen him in weeks. And when I ask about him, I get weird, vague responses. Seems the royals may be hiding something."

That was extremely odd to Vincent. He thought he knew the king of this city well enough to know that nothing short of missing legs would stop him from fighting for his people.

What are you up to, Normin? Vincent wondered.

More than ever, he wished he could move around. He could sneak right over to Drondos or even into Normin's chambers and get his answers. He looked down at his bandages and sighed. He just needed to be patient.

"So, other than bringing news, which I appreciate by the way, what brings you here to my temporary abode?" he asked Russell as the young man stood, moving over to the shelf where Daryl kept his medicines.

"Extremely temporarily, I have been asked to take you to the royal infirmary." He turned with a very familiar flask in his hands and a smile on his face. "It seems you have made friends."

Vincent's heart rate increased slightly, and a tiny bit of sweat marked his upper lip. "Who?" he asked as Russell brought over the flask.

"Brynn. And I am under direct orders to drag you if you refuse. Although I'd much rather do that, carrying you seems more appropriate."

Russell extended the flask, and possibly more nervous than he had ever been, Vincent quaffed it. Vincent knew making that trip awake would be more painful than he cared to comprehend. But he could not let Normin find out; he would be the only one to remember. That was his last thought before passing out.

He awoke in a much softer bed, in a much cooler room with natural light filtering through colored glass that lined the upper walls. He looked over, and none other than Brynn's cute little face smiled at him.

"It's nice to see you again, hero. How are you feeling?" she asked, holding out a cup.

He took it and drank, surprised to find it was cold.

The princess giggled at the shock on his face. "We keep it underground—stays cool."

He smiled and chugged the rest of the invigorating water. He must have been out for a while because the water was too refreshing for just a few hours. "I am feeling much better, thank you. How long have I been out?" he asked.

She shrugged. "Don't know exactly. Been busy, you understand. My best guess would be a couple of days, maybe three."

Damn, Russell, he thought.

That was much more of the medicine than he usually took, but he just assumed it was to make sure he stayed sleeping during the move. Now, though, he wondered just how little the young man knew of these medicines and how close Vincent must have come to drinking so much that it could have killed him.

What's done is done, he thought. He sat up slowly to test the pain. He was amazed that it hurt dramatically less than the last time he'd sat. Brynn smiled again when he finally situated himself in a comfortable sitting position.

"I was just passing by and thought I would look in on you. What are the chances you would wake up right now? Seems God is trying to tell us something." She looked away in thought, and it appeared very adult for her childish face.

"Do other girls your age attempt to read God's signs?" Vincent's mind went wild and spat out the first question that popped into his head.

What does she mean by that? What does she know? Just how intelligent is this young girl?

He waited so long that the silence began to become stifling.

"No," she finally responded softly, still looking away. "I have only recently found the need to rely on the path he has set out before me." She paused. He took a calming breath.

"Times have been hard lately. Sometimes I feel life is just a series of chaotic events, and we deal with them as they come along the best we can. But I see things a little differently now," she told him.

He waited for her to continue, but she just smiled and stood. "I'm sorry for interrupting your recovery with my problems. It is good to see you are doing well." She finished, turning to exit.

He opened his mouth to speak, and to his disappointment, all he said was, "Thank you, Your Highness."

He was lost in thoughts of his chosen life and poor decisions; he wasn't sure for how long.

"Why do I get the feeling you have not told us everything?" He looked over, surprised to see Daryl sitting next to a young boy a few beds down the long row of injured.

The injured boy was small, probably eight or nine years old. Vincent was stunned to see that he was missing the lower half of his arm.

"Was he in the fighting?" he asked, unable to hide the complete and utter shock in his tone.

Daryl nodded gravely. "I would never have imagined such bravery out of boys. They were fearless. It was their strength and their downfall."

As if on cue, another young boy a few beds down awoke

and began writhing in pain. He groaned pitifully and gritted his teeth as Daryl rushed over to him. "Shh. Settle down, Coy. It's okay."

Daryl's hand shot out quickly with a small vial, and the boy drank and relaxed. Coy allowed Daryl to roll him over and inspect two deep gashes on the backs of his legs. As Daryl did so, Vincent met his eyes. He smiled when he saw Coy still awake.

"Hey, tough guy, how was your first battle?" he asked.

The boy gave him a shy smile through pained eyes. He hooked a thumb behind him, where Daryl worked. "Not that great."

Vincent could not help but laugh at this young man's wit.

"I am Vincent." He nodded respectfully.

"Coy," he replied, his head beginning to droop.

"Well, Mr. Coy, you are still alive to tell the tale, a tale you must share with me in the future."

Coy nodded through a yawn and laid his head down. *Now there is an interesting character,* Vincent thought as he watched the boy drift off. When his eyes found Daryl again, Daryl was looking at Vincent in a way the latter was unused to. Was there skepticism in his gaze? Or was it accusation?

The healer stood up from the young Coy and walked over to Vincent's bed, where he pulled up a chair and sat.

"I think I need to know a little more about this Jason character."

Vincent tilted his head in contemplation. "Well, let's see, he is smart and capable, some say more so than his father despite his age. He loves fighting and is pretty damn good with a blade. He and all his cronies have acquired fighting skills from Altheia, so do not underestimate them."

Daryl held up a hand. "How? The fighting skills, I mean? And which styles?"

Vincent shrugged. "From what I can tell, it's just the basics that are taught to all the boys in school here."

Daryl frowned and continued, "What is it that he wants from us?"

Vincent looked into the healer's eyes. "Isn't it obvious?" Daryl stayed silent, waiting for him to finish. "He wants Altheia."

CHAPTER 28

Lucid pounded on the thick oak door. "Father!" he yelled. No answer, not even the slightest noise. He glanced to Brynn, her panic visibly increasing by the moment. Clearly she had thought of their father as a sort of safety net. No matter what condition he may be in, the reassurance always stayed with her that if things got very bad, she could always go to him.

Lucid pounded again, this time harder, and yelled louder, "Father, open up. We just came to check on you." Nothing.

"You do not have a key?" he asked Brynn, who shook her head.

The worry on his sister's face prompted Lucid to do something he would have never even considered. He backed up a few steps, lowered his shoulder, and charged. The door buckled, and the bolt that held the lock went flying across the room. Lucid cringed and gritted his teeth, clutching at his other shoulder, the one with a somewhat fresh stab wound.

He looked around the empty room, then back to Brynn. "What the ..." was all she got out before Reginald stepped in.

"I told you not to bother him."

Lucid stormed up to the head healer, so close they almost touched noses. "And why is that? Where is he, Reggie?" he asked angrily.

The man raised his hands in defense, his eyes never leaving Lucid's. "I honestly have no idea. I would venture to guess he is camping alone in the woods, recovering. The pain of losing your mother goes deeper than you can possibly imagine. He has to come to the conclusion that life is still worth living. No one can tell him that; he will listen to no one. And that is the very reason I told you not to bother him. I understand your plight. You think you can pull him back to himself because you are his children and he loves you dearly. That is true, but remember children that your father's love for Alice goes back many years before you were born. It is rooted deep, an invincible force that is without end. He risked his very crown to be with her …" He choked up. A tear gathered in the old man's eye and fell, causing Lucid to soften dramatically. "If only the world were filled with such love," he said wistfully.

Reginald took a knee and looked into Brynn's eyes, taking her hand. "Leading is up to you now, Princess, as it has been these past weeks." Then he looked to Lucid. "As the defense of our people is up to you now. You have both done a fine job, and I am quite sure your father would be very proud." He stood and left the two of them lost in thought in their father's room.

After a moment, Lucid recovered and walked over to the little table under the window, plopping down heavily in one of the chairs. Brynn followed and took the seat opposite him.

"Now what?" he asked of her.

She looked at him a moment, then sighed, folded her hands on the table, and dropped her head. He waited while she gathered herself. She sat up and blew out a breath slowly.

"Hell if I know," she finally replied. Lucid could not help but laugh. She did not join him.

"Reggie and the council act like I am this perfect leader making all the right decisions, when really I don't have the slightest clue what I am doing."

Lucid did not laugh this time. Her lack of confidence disturbed him. "You have done very well, Brynn, better than I could have. You are too smart to be so negative. The city and its governance is still intact. Be proud of what you have accomplished."

She frowned. "Yeah, what I have accomplished? Drondos attacked us, and I froze. People died, Lucid. Boys!" Her voice rose, and her eyes were getting wetter. "I cannot do this anymore. You have to take over or find Father. Please." The pleading in her tone was new. He considered her words.

Lucid took both his sister's hands. "I am a fighter, not a leader. That is clear to me now. *You* have the head for politics. It must be you. I cannot promise I will succeed in finding Father, but I will try. I promise you that. But until then I want you to do something for me. Stop with this 'I'm not good enough' bullshit and just rule."

She rose and held her arms out. Lucid rose with her and embraced her small frame tightly.

"You are the smartest, most capable child I know." He was smiling when she pulled away. She punched him on the arm lightly.

"Shut up. I get enough shit about my age without you piling on."

He chuckled and said, "We need to talk about your language, young lady."

She smirked and, out of nowhere, said at length, "What is up with your girlfriend?"

The question caught him off guard, and he wondered what she knew. "I, uh … what is … what do you mean?" he stumbled.

She narrowed her eyes but said nothing. He waited, maybe hoping that he would not have to go over this with her. He simply did not know much about it. "Perhaps we should sit back down for this."

"I would like to initiate a series of emergency drills, sort of like a fire drill, only every man is to be armed and lined up where he is designated," she told the council as she sat among the top Altheian minds.

"Excellent idea, Your Highness," said old Master Wendell.

Her talk with Lucid had given her a much-needed confidence boost. Now, with hesitation and uncertainty shed like a snakeskin, her mind raced with preparations.

"Double the scouts on the north side of the city, specifically the beach and woods. If I were Jason, I would not attack the same place twice."

The old master smiled widely, showing missing teeth and yellow clingers that refused to fall out of his ancient head. The gruesome sight was a huge reward, however, as the old man was of few words and hardly ever of ones of praise.

"I suggest we attack Drondos now while they are not expecting it. Wipe their whole city off this island," Lucid said with anger peppering his tone.

Men, Brynn thought.

"I understand you are upset, but we cannot go charging in like that. We will lose too many fighters, and I think Drondos has done quite enough in that regard. I think it would be better to make them come at us again. This time, however, we will be prepared."

After the councillors filed out, Lucid, Brynn, and Jake sat at the large wooden table alone. Jon was standing in the corner in Jake's usual guardian position, all but invisible.

"I need to go speak with D'matrius," the head king's man began. Never one to waste words, he got right to the point. "Jon will watch over Brynn while I'm gone."

Brynn was confused. "Who is D'matrius?" she asked.

Lucid replied, "He is the leader of the gvorlocks." He met Jake's eyes. "Or so we thought."

The man stayed silent, waiting for Lucid to elaborate, but the surprise was on Jake's face. "It turns out the village where D'matrius resides is only a small fraction of their population. The few who live in the woods, they are only the diplomat clan, placed there specifically to communicate with our people and keep an eye on us, I suppose. D'matrius leads them, but there is a much larger number living in a cave south of the city."

Brynn was skeptical. "How many could possibly fit and live comfortably in a cave?"

Lucid just shrugged. "I imagine as many as they can feed. The size is not a problem; the cave goes back for miles then goes down below the surface," he said. "Where are they getting the food? Just how much can be found underground, is what I'm wondering."

Brynn waved it away. "Unimportant. What is important is that now we know. We need to use the same preparations for them as with Drondos. Double or triple the scouts, and implement drills for assembling on the beach and by the woods."

Jake spoke up, saying, "That is all well and good, but I still must speak with D'matrius. We have developed a sort of relationship over the years. Maybe I can talk him out of war."

Lucid was shaking his head. "Lya told me I killed his second-in-command. I do not know if they have the concept of friendship, but if so, those two were as close as it gets. D'matrius is probably furious. I do not think it is wise to seek him out," he said.

"It is a risk I must take. If war can be prevented, then I must try."

Brynn was not happy about his decision, but she could not argue with his point. "Fine, but do not go alone. You will take all fifty king's men with you. Hide them in the woods during the meeting if you think it best, but as your leader, I must insist. You are too valuable to me to risk on chance."

The barest hint of a smile touched the man's lips as he replied, "As you say, Your Highness."

Lya stood in front of the burned-out shell that previously housed the city's grain. Such a horrible thing that had happened to a good person. The residual energy from that terrifying night was thick in the air. She could feel it and definitely smell it. Like the scent of an old campfire, it was very familiar to her.

The roof and support pillars extending all the way up were made of wood, so nothing remained of those. The outside was stacked stone, so it survived the blaze, although it looked as if it would topple in the breeze. She closed her eyes, and clipped visions passed her eyelids in a flurry of fear and confusion. She took a deep breath and opened her eyes again.

The sun was high in the sky that day, and there was not a cloud in sight. Sweat began glistening on Lya's forehead and cheeks as she stood looking at the structure. She heard footsteps behind her and turned to see Lucid approaching. He stepped up beside her and looked up at the top of the tower.

"I have not been here yet, since ..." His words caught in his throat, and he took a breath. Lya's heart was so heavy, it felt like a boulder.

"She loved the view from the top, always had for as long as I can remember." He paused. Out of her peripheral vision, Lya saw him wipe his face. "I will kill every last one of them for this—and for the attack on my city," he said, turning to embrace her, pulling her close. "The only thing saving me from despair is you."

Her lip quivered. She looked into his eyes, and the love she saw there, even through all of the pain and loss, was so incredibly strong that she felt like the luckiest person alive. What had she done to deserve such affection?

"You are too kind, but I know the pain is there, and it is still fresh, much like soil after a rain. The dirt on top dries very fast and gets back to looking like normal, but if you dig down only slightly, you see that the soil is still wet." She brushed a lock of hair out of his face and drew her arms around him tighter. "It will dry eventually."

Lucid kissed her again, and as usual, her heart began beating much faster. He pulled back after a few moments and took her hand. "I may have lost my mother, but in the process I found you. Life's little circles," he said with a smile.

"So how was your father?" she asked, changing the subject.

He frowned and mumbled something, then turned and said, "He is missing." The prince looked up at the tower one more time, tilted his head slightly, and released Lya to walk toward the blackened building.

"Wouldn't that just be the perfect hiding spot," he said, more to himself than to Lya. She knew him well enough now to see what he intended.

He disappeared inside for some time while Lya's stomach was in knots.

Is the king really missing? she wondered. After watching Lucid risk entering an extremely unstable building, she knew the answer. Was Normin dead as well? If she knew the gvorlocks well enough, and she definitely did, then the answer was obvious.

A few moments later Lucid emerged and shook his head. He took her hand again and led her away from the tower and toward the city. "Come on. I will explain on the way."

Lya smiled and let him guide her down the stone pathway and toward the bustling city streets. He filled her in on the details, or lack thereof, of his father's grief and disappearance. He also mentioned that young Brynn had been governing the city and was doing well. No surprise there. After meeting the girl, Lya knew well how intelligent and capable she was. She liked Brynn very much and hoped the feeling was mutual.

Soon they arrived at a large shop in the middle of the busy LD. When they entered, Lya gasped as she saw dresses of every style and color imaginable. There were men's clothes as well and even interspersed pieces of armor.

A girl around Brynn's age looked up and beamed a smile when she saw Lucid.

"Hello, Catrina. Is your mother around?" he asked the girl. She nodded enthusiastically. When Catrina glanced at Lya, her smile lessened slightly. The girl ran off behind a curtain separating the work area from the customer area, and Lucid turned to Lya.

"Rebecca makes the best clothes in the city. Everyone buys her stuff." He gestured to his own clothing and smiled.

A short woman with light hair and a strong, stocky frame came out from behind the curtain with a grin. "Lucid! Hey, doll, how have you been? My deepest condolences," she said with a little bow.

He smiled. "You are too kind, thank you. Rebecca, this is Lya," he said, gesturing toward her.

The woman smiled and came over to Lya, hugging her so tight that Lya had to hold her breath. Shocked, Lya let the woman embrace her while shooting a look at Lucid, who just grinned.

Rebecca pulled back and looked her over before smiling. She let out a little whistle. "You did good with this one, honey. She is beautiful."

Lya blushed as the woman left her. Rebecca went behind

the little counter behind which the girl was sitting and retrieved a long piece of ribbon with markings all over it. She then proceeded to use the ribbon in ways that made Lya very uncomfortable. The only person who'd ever touched her in this way was Lucid, who had given the women privacy and was inspecting a piece of armor on the other side of the shop.

Rebecca took the markings with practiced efficiency and wrote them down on a tiny writing pad.

When she was finished, she stood and said, "Well, my prince, I will have something appropriate made up soon, but it might take me a couple of days. In the meantime I do have a few summer dresses that are her size." She looked to Lya. "Would you like to try one on?"

Lya was confused. Surely this woman did not intend to let her wear some of these nice clothes without buying them. She hesitated. Lucid appeared at her side, taking her hand.

"It's okay. Get whatever you want," he said with a smile.

She nodded, just to indulge the two if anything. Rebecca disappeared into the racks of dresses, her short stature making her all but invisible. When she reappeared, she held a blue dress out to Lya and nodded her head toward a small room at the edge of the large shop. Lya took the hint well enough and went to the little room. She closed the door behind her and held up the dress. Her eyes went wide.

It was amazing, beautifully decorated with a design that mimicked white flowers, and the material was softer than she thought possible. She stepped out of her old brown dress and held it up. The thing was stained, torn, and rough to the touch. She could not believe the difference between old and new. She threw down her old life and stepped into her new one with such determination that she was worried she might rip the dress.

When she exited the little room, Lucid was sitting on a

barrel of scrap cloth, inspecting a metal glove of some sort. He froze. His eyes went wild, and the look on his face was one that was beginning to become familiar. He had that same look in the ocean after the jump, as had she. She felt alive, like a real person. She actually felt pretty for the first time in her life. She smiled widely, as did Rebecca.

The stocky woman fanned herself in mock heat and said, "You are gorgeous, girl. That is perfect!" The woman came up to her holding a simple but elegant pair of sandals.

Lya slipped them on, and the former slave girl hugged Rebecca before she could escape. "Thank you so much."

Rebecca laughed and patted Lya's arm. "Thank him, girl. He's paying for it."

Lya was dimly aware of Lucid paying Rebecca some coins before the two of them left the shop. She remembered some of the heated and hurried walk to Lucid's chambers. Clearly the sight of her in that dress had ignited something in Lucid. He pulled her along quickly.

Before she knew it, he was taking the dress back off.

"Be careful with that!" she told him, stark naked with a hand on her hip. He froze before setting it down reverently, his eyes never leaving her. He all but tackled her into his bed, and she laughed.

CHAPTER 29

Normin sat in his corner, his knees pulled up to his chest and his head down. He wished people would stop offering him food. Time went by in a haze of misery and sleeplessness, and Normin found he had no reason to continue. He was lost, as were all the slaves around him.

Jason had broken him, whether it was intentional or not. There was no winning against a kid so evil.

Normin was walking back to the slave quarters again. This time it was his wife, Alice, who hung there purple-faced with that single tear of blood.

He awoke with a start, cursing. The nightmares, it seemed, would be a permanent fixture, and for that reason he slept little. He sat in his little corner day after day, mildly aware of the half-remembered training sessions and the bothersome slaves who seemed never to leave him alone. The guards would beat him for not participating properly, but he did not care. He wished they would just kill him already; then he could finally be with his Alice.

Someone was always watching him. He assumed it was to make sure he did not take his own life, but he could not have done so even if he tried. He was too weak, physically and emotionally, to do much of anything. *This world is cruel and evil. God has abandoned me. I have absolutely no reason to continue,* were the only thoughts that crossed his mind.

He had come here to save these people from a tyrant, but he saw now there was no saving them. He had been cocky, overconfident, and just plain dumb to come here. Good deeds are never rewarded, and bad ones go by all but unnoticed. God was punishing him for taking Ivan's life. It was all he could do to keep his faith.

Faith, he thought in disgust. *What has being faithful got me?*

Suddenly, he found himself at the top of the grain silo, and he was on fire. The pain washed over him. When the tower fell, he awoke, sweating and breathing hard.

It was daytime, and there was a guard saying some words at the front of the warehouse. Normin ignored it and laid his head back on his knees. After a time, the general din of conversation was much louder than usual. He kept hearing his name. He looked up to see most of the slaves grouped together in animated conversation. He ignored that as well and laid his head down once again.

When he awoke, it was Gina standing there with a smile.

"Hello, Normin," she said. He stood quickly.

"Gina! He is alive! I saw him during the battle. He fought bravely." As he spoke, her face slowly turned into a nightmarish scowl accompanied by a purple coloring, growing darker by the second.

He started awake and found he could not move his arms or legs. He looked around and noticed four large slaves holding his limbs and another standing over him with a bowl made of wood.

"This is for your own good," the man said. Before Normin knew it, they had forced almost an entire bowl of soup down his throat.

Normin had tried to fight at first; they were just prolonging the inevitable. But there were too many of them. Soon a full belly finally assisted the exhaustion and *real* sleep claimed him.

For the first time in as long as he could remember, he did not dream.

When Normin awoke, hundreds of faces stared at him. It seemed every single slave waited on him to stand and address them. It reminded him of a very long time ago when he was king of a city. One large man stepped forward. It was Trent, one of Brighton's boys.

"We know who you are … King Normin. Dan over there heard the guards talking about it," he said. Every one of the people looking on held their breath, waiting for his response.

Normin just shrugged.

"We know who you are," Trent said again, "and we know why you came. You see, we were born and raised in this shithole, made to think we are nothing, lower than the worms in the dirt. But somehow, for some reason, you saw differently. You risked everything, your kingdom, your comforts, even your life, to come here and save us. You showed us that, at the very least, we are people, too, and are worthy of saving—by the king himself of all people." Trent looked around the room at the other slave fighters, then took a knee in the customary fealty pledge. The others did the same, every man and woman kneeling for their new king. The sight was impressive. Whether from the force-feeding or the heart of these people, Normin felt a little of himself returning. Trent continued from his knee, meeting Normin's eyes.

"We accept you as our king and will follow you anywhere. We will do anything you ask of us. I do not know what you heard from the guard, but we are set to attack your city again soon. We have absolutely no desire to do that, so snap the fuck out of it and tell us what we should do!" He was yelling by the end, prompting Normin to sit up straighter.

Why are they doing this? I am nobody, just a man who inherited leadership. I failed; it's over.

Stripped of his power and his finery, of his family and friends, Normin was no different than the man who spoke. He was no different from any of them. With this thought, his brain began functioning somewhat normally.

Looking into all their faces, he finally saw what he had worked so hard for. What he saw before him was a picture of kinship, of love, of hope.

This is what he'd come for, he suddenly remembered: to earn the trust of these people and make them his own, to take them back to his city and offer them a real life. He looked around, everybody kneeling and every face staring at him. These were his people now. *Fuck Jason*, he thought. He nodded.

Jason entered the small cell below the royal manse he used as the makeshift torture chamber. The walls and floor were dirt, and it was always wet and smelled of mud and mildew. They had placed Captain Inder under the section of the room with a small drip so that every few minutes another drop of water hit his face. Jason had read in Old World books that this was effective in loosening the victim's mind.

Tim was already there, hard at work removing another of the man's fingernails. The screams that emanated from the room hit Jason as soon as he had opened the door and continued for some time. When the man finally quit screaming, Jason brought a chair over and sat in front of him. The ship captain was tied to his own chair, arms and legs bound.

Jason removed the cloth gag and asked, "Are you ready to tell me where the ship is?" The man breathed hard for a full minute, then spit a bloody gob into Jason's face.

"You fucking old prick!" he shouted and stood abruptly

while Inder chuckled. Jason wiped his face and said, "Yeah, laugh now. That little act will cost you dearly." He turned to Tim and said, "Take his hand."

The man screamed, "No! I'm sorry! I won't—gghaaa." His words were cut off by a punch from Tim that rocked his head back and sent blood spraying. Tim pulled a small hatchet from his belt and, while James was recovering from the blow, chopped down on the arm of the chair, cleaving easily through meat and bone. The small ax stopped when it hit wood with a solid *thunk*.

The hand fell free immediately, and blood flew in a spray. Inder screamed and shook with agony before passing out again. Tim cauterized the wound; they could not let him die.

Jason nodded. "Keep up the good work. Let me know when you find it." Tim nodded in return, and Jason left the man to his business. For his next stop, he sought out his captain, Frank Digner, for his daily training. When Percy defected to Drondos, the first thing Ivan did was make the man teach Frank the Altheian fighting style, and for the first and possibly only time in his life, Jason approved of his father's decision.

He hated Altheians and their unending love for the royal family, but one thing was for sure: they could fight. The skills taught in Drondos before Percy came were like toddlers playing with their first dagger when compared to the elegant and deadly moves the Altheian people studied. Jason had even heard of a higher level of learning achieved by Normin's king's men, but that knowledge was kept close by the Trigo family.

Jason found Frank training the slaves in the fenced-in yard attached to the slave quarters. He stood at the end of the dirt training yard, waiting for the captain to finish. He saw Normin out working with a small group of slaves, and he did not like that.

Should I have just killed him?

Keeping that man alive was dangerous, like having a rattlesnake for a pet. Still, Jason took comfort knowing that as long as Normin was a slave, Altheia was weakened. At one point their eyes met. Jason could not miss the hatred there. He smiled.

The session ended. As the slaves filed back into the warehouse, Jason took his turn with the captain, only with a much more intense fighting style practiced in a much nicer part of town.

The two squared off at the base of the steps to the palace. A large flat area of hard-packed dirt made for a nice training yard, and Jason, with his men included, took their training from Frank. After a lengthy lesson, Jason was drenched in sweat, so he decided he would have a bath before checking on Percy's progress. On the way to the manse, however, Randy found him and fell in, breathing hard, no doubt from the trip.

"What?" Jason asked when the scout remained silent, catching his breath.

"Something is happening with Altheia. I just saw at least fifty men, well armed and armored, go into the woods on the west side of the city."

Jason thought a moment. That seemed extremely significant. It screamed for him to take action.

"King's men?" he asked.

"You know, I had not thought of that, but yes, I believe they were."

Jason stopped walking and turned. "Fifty, you say?" he asked of his scout.

Randy nodded. "At least."

Jason began walking again. *All of the king's men just left the city. Holy shit. Now is the time.* He needed to take advantage of this opportunity. Everything was beginning to fall into place.

That city is mine.

"Stay on it. Let me know when they return."

Randy nodded and ran back the way he came. Jason had no time to waste and settled for a cold bath, not wanting to wait for the water to heat. He dressed and immediately left the palace. Going into the city, he headed for Percy's shop in the old market. As soon as he opened the door, Percy wordlessly handed him a small, thin flask.

Inside the flask was a clear liquid that Jason knew was much more volatile than it looked. A small square of cloth plugged the top. He smiled, went over to the candle burning on the little dining table, and lit the cloth. Percy's face betrayed his shock and fear. Jason did not care.

Fuck this little shop, he thought.

The flask landed against the back wall and shattered with a *whoosh.* Flames surrounded the wall and furniture instantly.

Percy said nothing but ran to his water barrel and filled his bucket. He tossed several waves onto the flames before he had the fire out.

Jason waited until the man was satisfied that his shit shack was not going to burn down, then asked, "How many did you make?"

The drink maker's face was full of anger, but he only said, "Five hundred. Delivered them to the storage house myself last night."

Jason nodded, drew his dagger, and drove it into the side of Percy's neck.

"Thanks, but I no longer have need of your services," he said, yanking the dagger out.

Percy dropped in a spreading pool of blood, gurgling his

last words for all to hear. Jason wiped his blade on Percy's shirt, sheathed it, and walked out. He went back to the torture cell; he had to. That was the last step before all of his preparations could be completed. And he *would* get that man to talk.

Upon arriving, he saw there was no need. The king walked into the little dirt cell, and the ship captain was already chest deep in his confession—and missing a foot.

Jason smiled, looking at Tim. "Get me that ship. I want it repaired and loaded with provisions immediately."

CHAPTER 30

Daryl's life had become a rhythm of bloody monotony. He slept in the infirmary most days as he had already healed the least injured and sent them on their way, so beds were easy to come by. The most severe, however, required countless hours of work and needed to be closely watched day and night.

Daryl sat next to Vincent's cot, the assassin sleeping peacefully. Daryl found he was drawn to the man for some reason. He radiated wisdom despite only being somewhere around his late forties or early fifties, the healer was not quite sure. Plus, he could only imagine what he and the other guys could learn from this man's fighting skill.

Daryl had a good view of the hallway entering the infirmary, from where he sat and watched as Alisha approached the large healing room. He noticed, not for the first time, how her ponytail swung wildly back and forth when she walked briskly. *How did I get so lucky?* he thought. Most women of nobility chose not to study the deadly arts the schooling offered, but his love was not one of those girls. She was just as good with a blade as he, maybe better. But the bow, that small invention of hers, may very well have saved the city, and it definitely saved many lives. Most women were afraid of blood or were horrified by killing, but not her. He still remembered seeing her standing there looking fierce and gorgeous, putting men down as lesser men might squash ants.

"Hey, love," she said quietly when she entered. She gave

him a kiss on his cheek and pulled a chair up next to him and Vincent.

"I love you, you know," Daryl said. She pressed her lips together, but the smile was there in her eyes.

"That was random," she told him.

Daryl was dumbfounded, like someone had awakened him from a dream. He stood.

"I honestly have no idea how I did not see it before. We have been together for over a year now. I feel so stupid for letting it go on this long."

She frowned, seeming unsure where he was going. He got down on both knees and took her hand in his. Alisha's face changed so fast that it was almost comical.

"I want to spend the rest of my life with you. Alisha Blake, will you marry me?"

She appeared stunned. Daryl had not summoned her or asked her to come at that moment; she was simply doing what she does and came to see him. Maybe this was happening because they had looked death in the face together, or he was simply maturing; he could not say. Were there any other women in the world who would come here to this bloody nightmare to do such a thing? She was it for him. He held his breath.

"Of course, you idiot," she said finally. For the first time since he had known her, a tear gathered and fell, just from the left eye, as if the other eye was still trying to act tough. He stood, and they kissed deeply, losing themselves for a minute and reveling in young love.

When they separated, he glanced down to find Vincent's eyes as wide as his smile.

"You heard that, huh?" Daryl asked. The man nodded, grinning like an idiot.

"I have to go tell my parents!" Alisha said. She grabbed

Daryl's head, violently pulled it to hers for one more passionate kiss, and left, walking much more briskly this time, her ponytail going crazy.

"How are you feeling?" Daryl asked Vincent as he sat back down.

"Don't change the subject. What a nice thing to witness. You two have a strong love. It's good to know there are still people in this world connecting in such a way. One thing I learned as a boy is that where love goes, there is also misery, but that does not seem to be the case with you two," Vincent said, looking down in thought. "Witnessing love like that makes me regret the life I chose," he said after a wistful pause.

"Why did you choose such a life? Seems lonely," Daryl said.

Vincent nodded and said, "It is, but as a child I did not look at the world the way I do now. I had lost faith in humanity, in the relationships of others. The only thing I loved in this world was the sword. I pushed away all those who sought to get close to me. I was obsessed with fighting, so much so that I used to sit under the palms on the edge of the beach and daydream about being the hero of some huge battle."

Daryl waited for Vincent to continue. The assassin said nothing. It seemed this man brooded a little more than necessary for a rich assassin. There was something else there, a sadness and regret that went beyond simply leaving his home.

"And now?" he asked.

Vincent shrugged. "Like I said, I see things differently now. If I had to do it all over again, I would probably choose a different path."

"Well, Mr. Joice." Daryl slapped his knees as he stood and said, "Today is your lucky day. Now is the pivotal moment when you get to choose. God has given you this opportunity, this second chance. Do not waste it." And he walked off to tend to other patients.

As the days passed, Vincent felt stronger and even began walking the infirmary. The conversation with Daryl had stuck with him, and he thought of the wise young man's words frequently. Vincent knew that with his skill set, if he truly applied himself, he could do very good things for this city and these people.

He noticed on his third day of walking the large room that the princess once again had come to check on Coy. Vincent did not really think it was her duty to check on a lowborn boy. He thought there might be something more between them.

When the two finished their little conversation, Brynn stood. When she spotted Vincent on his feet, she smiled widely.

She is so incredibly kind. She barely knows me, but that smile is genuine.

"The hero returns!" she said, and to Vincent's surprise, she came up and hugged him. "It is so nice to see you back on your feet," she told him when she pulled away.

He bowed as deeply as his healing wound would allow. "You are so kind, Princess. Thank you. For everything." He gestured around the room. Brynn having him brought here most likely sped his recovery dramatically. He could not have been more grateful.

She waved it away. "It's nothing. You saved my life. It's the least I can do." She smiled once more and then exited.

Vincent turned and found Coy looking at him. When their eyes met, the boy looked away quickly. He smiled and went to the boy's bed, pulled up a chair, and eased into it.

"Okay, Mr. Coy, out with it." Coy looked up, confused. "Your first battle. You are very young to be fighting. You are injured but still alive to tell the tale, a tale I must hear." He sat back, looking away at some distant point. "What I would have given to be out there fighting with you." Vincent looked back and thought he saw almost a smile on the boy's face.

Just when Vincent thought young Coy would keep his story to himself, he spoke. "I was only in town to pick up some paper," he began softly.

Vincent sat up and gave the boy his full attention. He realized at that moment just how interested he was to hear how the young hero had fought.

"Me and Jerry here." Coy gestured below himself, and only then did Vincent realize there was a beautiful golden Labrador sleeping under his cot. The dog popped its head up at the mention of his name. He sniffed at Vincent, seemed to approve, and laid his head back down. Vincent gave him a scratch as the boy continued.

"When I left the store, I heard them coming. I don't own a weapon, so I ran for the only place I knew to find one, the armory next to the training yard. When I saw Jon shouting orders, I just got in line and …" He paused and thought a moment.

Vincent stayed silent but already had questions.

"It all happened so fast, the charge, the screaming, then the battle. I did the best I could, even saved the prince's life." He looked down, embarrassed. "My victory was short-lived. I did not last long. Someone came up behind me and gave me these reminders that I am not good enough yet. Next thing I knew …" He gestured around the room.

Vincent was silent a few moments. "Coy, you aren't from Altheia, are you?" he asked. The boy shook his head.

"I was a slave in Drondos. It was Brynn who found me after I escaped and gave me a new life, a much better life. I will never be able to explain to that girl just how grateful I am," the boy said.

Vincent asked, "And this blade you got out of the armory, can I assume it was a blunted training blade?" Coy nodded.

Vincent was stunned. There was something that drew him to this boy. He seemed an unusually impressive young man from the small interactions they'd had over the past days, but it seemed Vincent had shorted him by a long shot. An escaped slave found his way here on his own, got in the good graces of the royals, and held his own against grown men by wielding what was essentially a pole with a hilt.

"Do not sell yourself short, young Coy. Even though you were injured and did not last the entire battle, that is a very impressive tale. There are grown men who could only hope to do as well."

Vincent held up a finger to the boy and stood slowly, gingerly walking over to his bed. He rummaged through his bag of belongings and withdrew a large dagger. He shuffled back to Coy, where he sat and held the blade out to him. The boy did not reach for it.

"You mentioned that you do not own a weapon. Now you do. This is a fine blade, had it made special. I have used it for years, and it has never failed me. I believe there will be a time when you will need more than a training blade, and the world needs more Coys. Take it." Coy smiled, reverently took the blade, and unsheathed it to inspect the metal.

"It's beautiful. Thank you."

The doors to the large infirmary were open wide. Down the hall, Vincent could suddenly hear the shuffling of quick steps and the shouts of panic approaching. He saw Daryl get to his feet and head for the door. After a moment, from around the corner came two men carrying a third man between them and screaming for help. The man they hauled in was screaming, eyes wide and fearful.

"Beasts, it was beasts!" he kept screaming. His body was trembling, held up only by the two men who carried him. Vincent watched as Daryl reacted quickly, laying the man down in the nearest bed to get to work. Vincent could see from his place next to Coy's bed that there was no saving the man. His lower left leg was missing, and still lodged in his stomach was half a wooden spear, his abdomen bleeding freely.

Daryl brought a small cup to the man's lips, and he drank quickly, calming slightly. "What happened?" the healer asked.

The injured man took a small choked breath and spoke: "I was hunting ... in the woods. I heard some footsteps, so I went to look and got turned around. It came out of nowhere. It ... it ..." His lip quivered, his eyes went wide, and he yelled, "Beasts! We are all going to die!" He coughed and choked. Those were the poor man's last words. Vincent glanced to Coy, who looked just as uncomfortable as he.

CHAPTER 31

What would Father do? Brynn wondered as she paced her chambers early that morning.

Normin was a bold man; he always faced his problems aggressively, head-on. Thinking about it, she knew the answer all too well and did not like it one bit. If she did it right, however, and in the right company, the young ruler was pretty sure she could at least make it out alive. She wished she had been able to witness council meetings with this sort of content so she had something to go by. But ruling a kingdom in turmoil that had never experienced such was difficult even for an experienced leader. Brynn had to come up with her own creative solutions to problems.

She exited her chambers, went down the large hall to Lucid's door, and knocked. There was scuffling. A few moments later, her brother opened the door half dressed, his hair unusually wild.

She smiled and pushed in.

"Sure, come on in," he said, closing the door behind her. Lya had a startled look on her face, but Brynn ignored it and sat next to her on the bed.

"Good morning, Lya." The girl smiled and blushed. "I think we need to go talk to this Jason guy," she told Lucid as he pulled up a chair next to the bed and sat.

"What?" he asked incredulously. "Out of the question."

"It's what Father would do or … did. I do not exactly approve of how he handled it, but what did he do when we first had a problem with Drondos? He marched right over there and did what he thought necessary. Although I wish he hadn't, because things have spiraled out of control, but you get the point. We need to march right over there and attempt to make peace. I am sure he does not want any more of his people to die. I would think a mutual agreement between cities might benefit both sides."

Lucid was shaking his head before she had finished speaking. "You don't know him. If he is willing to enslave his own people, then there is no reason to believe he cares about losing lives. If we go over there, we need to do *exactly* as Father did. Jason is an only child. We kill him; that's it."

Brynn's face felt hot. She stood abruptly and yelled, "Is that all you think about, killing? Is that how all men deal with their problems?" She closed her eyes, took a few calming breaths, and sat back down.

Lucid held his hands up defensively and said, "I am sorry. We can try it your way, but I'm telling you now, it will not work."

She frowned but nodded and said, "Just a small team, you and I, Jon, Alisha." She paused and looked to Lya, who was fumbling with her dress. "And her." Lya looked up sharply.

"No fucking way. This will be dangerous, Brynn. I will not risk …"

Brynn stood and put a hand on his shoulder, cutting him off. "You should know better than anyone that she is far from helpless."

An uncomfortable silence followed. It seemed to the princess that Lucid and Lya had not spoken much about her abilities, if at all. Lucid may not have been aware of the trick she pulled during the battle, and Brynn did not want to pry where they had clearly left dark corners.

"We will meet outside the palace tomorrow just before sunup," she said. Then she left them to their business. The last thing she wanted was to be involved in that uncomfortable conversation.

She went down a few flights of stairs and made her way to Alisha's chambers. When the girl answered the door, she looked much the same as Lucid. Behind her Brynn could see Daryl lying in bed, shirtless, with a grin painted on his face.

"Princess." She curtsied and waved her in. Once inside, Brynn sat on the bed next to Daryl, who seemed uncomfortable at her closeness for some reason.

She looked to Alisha, no preamble necessary for this woman, which was something she loved about her. "I need your help. We will be going to Drondos in the morning to attempt to meet with King Jason. I believe making peace may be the only way to prevent the loss of more lives. I saw your new bow in action during the battle, and I think it would be in everyone's best interests if you brought it along."

Alisha was nodding gravely, but before she could respond, Daryl spoke up.

"You know that by asking her you are also asking me? I cannot allow her to do something so dangerous without me. You speak of making peace, but make no mistake, Princess, we will be going into enemy territory."

Brynn frowned. "I need you here, healing. There are many still with severe wounds that require an experienced healer," she said.

"Okay, let me try a different angle. Surely you would not stop a husband from accompanying his wife on such a trip," he said. Brynn's head shot around to look at him. He was smiling widely. She looked back to Alisha, who wore a similar expression, and she squealed and rose quickly to hug Alisha.

"Congratulations!" She pulled back from her and clapped her tiny hands. "That is great news! No, Daryl, I cannot deny you that. You may come."

It was slightly unexpected, but Brynn did not think having a master healer come along was such a bad idea. After a short and excited conversation, and an entirely too long day of preparations after that, Brynn found herself lying in bed that night with sleep eluding her. She tossed and turned, falling asleep for a few minutes here and there.

Finally, tired of just lying there, she rose early and began her morning routine. Upon exiting her chambers, she found Ella on her way in with a steaming tray of eggs and sausage. She greeted her friend and politely refused the breakfast. Brynn's stomach was in knots.

When Brynn left the palace to the quiet predawn streets, her little team was already gathered. Clearly she had not been the only one stressing about this visit. At no time in the past had leaders of the two cities needed to meet, especially under these circumstances.

Without a word, Lucid and Lya began walking toward the beach. Jon and Brynn fell in behind with Daryl and Alisha bringing up the rear. It was still dark and somewhat cool. The symphony of crickets and frogs served as their marching song. No one said a word for miles as they walked along the beach, the mood among the group grave and alert. After the sun rose, they were all sweating and puffing. Still no one spoke, and no one stopped to rest. It seemed every one of them simply wanted to get this unpleasant experience over with. Hours of trekking and sweating led them to the gates of their sister city.

Brynn had never seen Drondos before and was shocked to see just how hot, dirty, and poorly maintained it was. As they approached, she could see the tops of dilapidated wooden buildings and an unnatural lack of trees for miles around the outer wall, which consisted of the large wooden corpses stripped from the land. The main gate was closed when the party arrived, guards posted on the twin parapets attached to either side of the gate. One spotted them and shouted down.

"That's far enough. Who are you, and what do you want?"

Brynn stepped forward and craned her neck upward to yell at the man. "I am Brynn Altheia, daughter of King Normin and acting ruler of Altheia. This"—she gestured to Lucid—"is Prince Lucid, and the others are my guards. We come in peace. I simply wish to speak with King Jason," she finished.

Silence.

The man stared down for a few moments then looked over each person in her entourage. The guard disappeared without a word, leaving the group to wait uncertainly in the hot sun. As the minutes ticked by, Brynn glanced to each of the others and tried to pass out hopeful and reassuring smiles. She had no clue what to expect here. It was not as if they had a protocol in place. Would Brynn and her group be allowed to enter? Or would Jason and his soldiers simply march out and attack?

Just as panic began to set it, Brynn imagining the army massing just on the other side of the gate, she heard a large bar being cranked up, and the doors to the city slowly opened. Inside it looked abandoned other than the twenty or so guards standing ready to escort them.

No citizens walked the market district, and there were no smells of food or sounds of crafting, just dry dirt paths snaking through a mess of buildings in different stages of collapse. A large man dressed sharply in his armor stepped forward and said, "Please follow me." Then he turned and walked away, the sea of men forming a hole for the Altheians to pass through.

They followed the man through the space allotted, and

the mass of men fell in behind the group. Brynn could feel the tension radiating off every man, strong as the midafternoon sun. Blood had been spilled between their people, and Daryl's words flashed back to her: "Make no mistake, we are heading into enemy territory."

She cursed herself for not bringing more guards as she realized just how vulnerable they were at that moment. The fact that she was trusting their lives to this horrible king was a slap in the face.

This was a bad idea, Brynn thought as she glanced to Lucid. He seemed to have the opposite mind-set. His back was straight, his chin was high, his hand was on his pommel, and his predatory eyes scanned constantly. The vicious look he wore on his face was new to her, as if he were looking, with a challenge and a threat, into the eyes of any man daring to get too close. He was calm, confident. She loved her brother at that very moment more than she ever had. She took a deep breath, relaxing her tense muscles.

They finally reached what looked to be the edge of the city. Two large buildings stood out, one on her right, because it was the nicest and best-maintained building she had seen yet, and one on her left, because she was curious how the thing still stood. The guard turned right and the group followed, trailed by the small army of men.

Soon they were led into the wooden palace and down a long hallway. The smell was the first thing Brynn noticed, mold with a hint of chamber pot. A large meeting room became visible on her right, its doors standing wide to reveal several young men sitting around a large round wooden table. The tall guard stopped at the door and gestured for them to enter.

Brynn strode forward, meaning to show bravery where they might see her weak because of her age. She glanced to Alisha, who looked scary with that weapon on her hip and a huge bag of arrows on her back.

As Brynn approached the king of Drondos, his eyes unnerved her. He was smiling a humorless grin that made her feel like she was meeting with a madman. He was not particularly tall or large and not quite ugly but not exactly handsome. He was young, younger than she would have expected, maybe fourteen or fifteen. Short dark hair cropped very close allowed the scars on his head to show through the stubble. That and his fit build led her to believe he was a fighter unlike his father. She had known the previous king only by reputation, and from what the councillors had said in meetings, his son was something entirely different.

Again she chided herself for having underestimated the danger here. To Jason's left was a large young man with red hair and a cool confidence about him. Next to him was a taller youth, thinner and tenser. He fidgeted with a small curved dagger. To Jason's right was another thin youth, younger than any of the others, who sat quietly with his head down. Once everyone was fully inside the meeting hall, the tall guard closed the door behind them and took a seat at the table next to the quiet kid.

"King Jason." Brynn nodded slightly. "I am Bry—"

"I know who you are." He cut her off and glanced around the group. "All of you, what are you doing in my city? I should have the lot of you executed."

Lucid adjusted the grip on his pommel and stepped forward slightly, the anger in his tone barely contained as he said, "Then why don't you give it a try?"

The big youth stood abruptly and slammed his big ham hands on the table. "Is that a threat? How dare ..."

Jason put a hand on his arm, silencing him. He sat back

down but glared daggers at Lucid. Brynn shot Lucid a look, and he eased back, letting Brynn take the floor.

"We came here to make peace. I want no more blood spilled on this island. No more of either of our people need suffer. I am convinced we can come up with a system to share this place evenly, fairly. Maybe we could even set up some kind of trading sys—"

"Let me just stop you right there," Jason said with more volume than before. "You come here to my home asking for me to share the island that has been my ancestors' place just as long as yours, *Princess*." He spat the last word like a curse. "We are both descendants of the original settlers. You Altheians have just forgotten what it's like to be hungry."

His disrespectful tone and casual anger had put her off guard. This young man had been angry at Altheia his entire life. Something else stood out as well: he seemed way too confident for someone with so few troops in the face of thousands, almost as if he had a card yet to play and perhaps more than one. He was hiding something, Brynn was sure of that, and she, for the first time in her life, did not want to know.

The great eleven-year-old ruler of Altheia, the youngest in history, felt an idiot for coming to this place, the very center of the people who had attacked hers. She underestimated Jason's callousness and intelligence, and suddenly the sensation of being greatly outnumbered in enemy territory scared her to death. She bit her tongue hard to keep from shaking with fear. She felt extremely uneasy and simply wanted to get home and away from this man.

After attempting to swallow the lump in her throat, she said, "Clearly there is nothing we can do to change your mind, so with that, we will just go. Thank you, King Jason, and your councillors, for receiving us." She nodded once and spun, trying her hardest to keep a steady pace and not sprint to her city.

They silently marched down the hall and soon exited the ugly, smelly royal manse for even worse dirt streets. The sun was high and the afternoon hot, so the hard-packed dirt seemed to bake in the sun, and the heat drilled her from above and below. Once clear of the group of soldiers who'd escorted them in, she began walking faster. The guards did not move and just looked at the group numbly. It seemed they were not so quick to escort them back to the gate.

Something caught Brynn's attention, however. As she was about to turn onto the main road, she heard the now familiar sounds of fighting close by. At a glance she saw that the warehouse leaning heavily was not abandoned at all. Hundreds of men, boys, and even young women sparred in a makeshift yard adjacent to the drunk warehouse.

Slaves, she thought, and this time holding back the tears was neither possible nor necessary. They fell freely as she stared at what that pig of a man called his property.

People, more real than ever before, began looking back at her. These were not numbers or tallies on a sheet of paper. These were not rumors or unconfirmed reports. These were people, held against their will and forced to do Jason's bidding.

The rest of the group surrounded Brynn. Lucid swooped in, taking her by the shoulders and gently guiding her away, back toward the main gate. She glanced over her shoulder for one last look and gasped.

There in the back of the crowd of slaves, almost invisible behind another man, stood her father. She cried out and yanked away from Lucid so fast that her knees buckled as she spun, kicking up a cloud of dust when she fell. She looked up again quickly, desperate to see his face.

Nothing.

Through a fogged brain and teary eyes, she imagined it could have been anyone. Lucid knelt and took her hands, looking into her eyes with such concern that her mind began to clear. Lucid was her rock.

"Are you okay? What happened?" he asked. He looked over his shoulder, following her line of sight, but clearly saw nothing. She looked over one more time; she had to be certain. She was, and she nodded at her brother.

"I'm okay. It's just … hearing it is one thing. Seeing with my own eyes is another. He is so cruel, Lucid, and much smarter than I gave him credit for."

He pulled Brynn to her feet and kept one hand in hers as he walked her away, toward home.

"I agree, but there is no reason to lament. For now we will use our heads and come up with a plan to free them in the future. Let's take this information and use it. It went much better than I thought."

She laughed at the absurd statement. "I completely failed at making peace, and he threatened to execute us."

Her brother simply shrugged. "Just once, but we are still alive. Plus we got to learn about our enemy. Call it a win."

From the windows of the third-floor gallery, Jason watched the former royal family retreat. He smiled. The king's men were gone from the city, five of the most important people on a long trek back home in the sun. "Have we retrieved our ship?" he asked the room.

"Yes, Your Grace. The repairs have been finished, and it is loaded and ready to make an escape. But if I may ask, escape from what?" Captain Digner questioned.

"If all goes well, nothing. It is officially no longer any of your business, Captain. However, this next bit is very much your business. Now is the time to attack," Jason said to his councillors, who were gathered around the windows.

"Are you sure?" asked Frank. "After that little show of yours, they will know we are coming. They will be expecting us."

Jason turned and placed his hand on the oversized blade strapped to his belt. "First of all, old man, watch your disrespectful tongue around your king. Second, I do not mean soon or tomorrow. I mean right fucking now," he said, his voice rising to almost a screech. "Get your fucking asses moving and muster. *Now!* We march in one hour!"

CHAPTER 32

Normin struggled through the rest of training. His mind kept flashing back to his children, his beautiful daughter dressed in finery, acting leader of thousands of lives, and Lucid finally back where he belonged, clearly taking her lead and guarding her closely. It seemed Normin had severely underestimated his brilliant daughter and overestimated his battle-hungry son.

Lucid had always been more interested in fighting than learning anything about ruling. Brynn, however, had attended every council meeting since she'd wandered in after learning to walk. She knew every citizen's name, even upcoming births and their estimated days. She probably could even tell you the names of the unborn Altheians.

Normin's heart surged with pride and broke all at once. He had seen both his children thousands of times, every day for seventeen years now, as he was a very active father, believing it important to instill the traits and characteristics of his parents and their parents before them. This time was unlike any before as he had not seen his children in weeks, maybe months—he could not say for sure. He ached to run to them and embrace them both.

He was leaning out from behind Henton to get a better look, when he thought he saw Brynn looking right at him. He watched as she fell in the dirt. His eyes felt much hotter than usual, and against his better judgment, he stepped back out of sight. At that moment, it had never been more clear just how trapped he was here.

Normin Altheia, descendant of the founder of Blysse, had come to Drondos a king. Now he was a prisoner of his own making.

When the party was out of sight, he took a breath and looked around. He was shocked that he could have forgotten for even a second that he was not the only one trapped in the hell of Drondos. All these people—his people, who were also sons and daughters of the original families that settled here—deserved better. Each and every one of them had the same rights to live their lives as he, the king. With this conclusion he made the decision to abolish the kingship upon returning to power and maybe begin some sort of citizen-based ruling system.

A shout pulled him from his thoughts, and he turned to see Captain Digner striding toward the training yard at a speed that seemed unnecessary. Normin was nearer to the center of the yard, so he could not hear what the captain was yelling, but the volume and urgency heard from this distance was cause for concern. Soon the order filtered through the ranks as the men began scrambling and yelling.

"Muster."

The single word and the weight of what was to come sent a chill down Normin's spine. Before he knew what was happening, a small crowd was gathering around him. They strapped on swords and armor, checked the balance on blades, prepared water, and kept a watchful eye on him.

More and more faces appeared, not grouping around him so as not to arouse suspicion from the watchful guards. They all seemed to be going about their business, but Normin knew better. He could feel their eyes shifting to him every few seconds. Trent was the first to ask what seemed to be on everyone's mind.

"We are attacking Altheia. What do we do?" he said quietly.

Still more nearby faces turned to meet Normin's, waiting on his reply. The volume of armor and sword noise died shockingly quickly.

In the silence he said, "Nothing."

If the silence was shocking before, it was deafening now as the people closest to him digested his short answer.

"Nothing?" Dan asked.

Trent looked confused as well. "What do you mean, nothing?"

Normin put a hand on each of their large shoulders, looking into the men's eyes in turn. "I want you, all of you, to do absolutely nothing. We will march to my city, but after that, you will follow no order but my own if one is given. If not, do nothing."

Neither man looked to be satisfied by that answer, but they seemed to have put their trust in Normin, so they moved off to pass the order around the army quietly. Normin assumed most would share the two men's confusion, but that did not matter. As long as they stopped following Jason's or the captain's orders, Normin could handle the rest alone.

Digner set a brutal pace as he marched the army double time out of the front gate and wheeled them toward the beach. It seemed they would take a different route this time and attack from another angle. All Normin could do was pray that Brynn had prepared some sort of early warning system. Already they were speeding down the very same path his children had chosen. He was positive of that fact as, being on the front line, he spotted their trail in the sand.

Walk faster, he willed his kids.

Hours passed as the army moved closer to Altheia, the sun beginning its descent toward the sea. The pace was a very fast walk, almost a slow jog, and the captain allowed for no rests. Normin hardly noticed. With all the time spent with light food and heavy training, he was in the best shape of his life. Terrified the army might catch up with his children, he wished he could stop time and tell the sun to pause just for a bit. But as with a lot of other things in this world, he simply had no control. He looked around nervously as the army moved closer and closer.

Before he knew it, they were close. He could not see his city yet, but he knew the beaches on the island especially well and began to recognize certain trees and the curve of the water's edge. Just as he was watching the tops of the trees for a view of the palace, he could hear something over the thunder of a thousand feet, something so familiar and so close to his heart that he almost stumbled at the sound.

The bells of the cathedral were ringing. He thought it the most beautiful thing he had ever heard. This was not the daily chime or the tolling of bells to announce an event or a royal birth. This was a constant, nonstop ring that echoed throughout the whole of Altheia. Normin could picture Ryan at the top, yanking that rope for all his life was worth and sending out a call that would be impossible to ignore.

An alarm, Normin thought and smiled. *They will at least be prepared.*

Everything was playing out so perfectly that he feared he had missed something in his meticulously thought-out plan.

God be with me.

No sooner had Lucid and the rest of the party crossed the threshold into the palace than the bells began ringing a steady back and forth, *ding, ding, ding, ding.* Lucid looked quickly to his young sister, whose eyes had gone wide.

"He sent his army right behind us!" Brynn said, shock

turning quickly to anger. She balled her tiny fists, her face turning red.

Lucid gave her a second while she clenched her jaw, took a breath, then approached him and took his hands with both of hers. She looked into his eyes then, not as the child he had seen about the palace his whole life. Those cute, innocent brown eyes he had seen laughing and joking with friends, the eyes of his little sister, were gone and had been replaced by those of a woman, an angry woman. The two words that came out of her mouth next shocked Lucid to his core.

"Kill him."

He would have thought her joking, but the look in those intense brown eyes showed the sincerity behind her statement. She, the one who had revoked the king's power for murder, was asking Lucid to kill. She had seen something when they met with Jason, something dark, something evil. Maybe it was seeing slavery firsthand, or maybe she just did not want any more of their people to die. The reason did not matter. He had wanted this all along and only kept it in check by the distraction of love and the respect for his young sister's ruling decisions. He was a rabid dog on a leash, and Brynn had just cut that leash.

Lucid nodded and turned to go, but he grabbed Lya first and pulled her close, kissing her deeply.

"In case I don't see you again, I love you."

The admission caused her lower lip to quiver. Tears gathered in her eyes.

"I won't leave you. I'm coming," she said.

He shook his head. "There is no one left to guard Brynn. I need you to protect my sister as you would me." Tears fell. Lucid wiped them away with his thumbs. Lya looked into his eyes and nodded, visibly uncomfortable at the thought of losing him. She smiled. He kissed her one more time and nodded to Jon, Daryl, and Alisha.

"Wait," Lya said as Lucid was just about to exit the large doors to the palace. "I love you too."

Lucid smiled widely and left the two in the safety of the palace. *God be with them,* he thought.

Lucid, Jon, Daryl, and Alisha walked down the stairs and into the bright evening sun, the streets a chaotic mess. Men and boys were running to and fro, strapping on swords and armor, lining up in crooked and broken formations.

Jon went to work once again, shouting orders and straightening the lines. In a very short time, men were armed and ready. Columns ten wide and ten deep formed, beginning at the base of the palace steps and extending all the way to the edge of the lower dwellings. Lucid marveled at his best friend's knowledge of battle tactics. Where Jon had found the time to learn all of that, Lucid might never know, but he was exceedingly grateful to have such a man on his side.

After what Lucid thought was only a handful minutes, his people prepared to take the charge. Once again he and Jon stood at the head of their army on the edge of the city just in front of a large grassy field. The only sounds were small shifts of footing and taps of metal against armor. A man coughed, and Lucid could hear the crickets chirping from the woods on his left.

A wave crashed on the shore in the distance, and in the silence that followed, Lucid could hear the next wave gathering—or was that footfalls? His question was answered almost instantly as the army of Drondos cleared the trees on the beach side of the city and came into view. The front line stopped short, forming up and waiting for the troops in the back to get into position. The Drondos army did not have a formation of any sort, more like one long line of ragged troops followed by the next line and so on. It lacked any sort of organization and just seemed to Lucid as one large mob.

Lucid looked across the field on the northern edge of Altheia that separated them and waited, meaning to let Drondos charge as he stood his ground. He could see Jason and his men on the left side of the formation. One of them shouted a command. At this, a single man began moving forward slowly.

The king could see through the edge of the tree line. The sight was so familiar to Normin that he felt he might be in a dream: Lucid and Jon standing at the head of their people, more than willing to risk their young lives to protect them.

"Forward!" Digner shouted.

Normin began walking, followed hesitantly by everyone else. They moved through the woods on the northern edge of Altheia. Jason and his little group of goons marched alongside. *Please let this work,* Normin prayed as he moved closer and breached the tree line, giving the massed Altheians a view of the slave army. He stopped along with the rest of the front line, allowing those in back to get into position.

"Charge!" came the shout.

Normin's heart was beating very hard and his were palms sweating as he reached for his sword. He did not unsheathe it right away. Instead he looked to his left and right, making sure not a soul carried out the command.

"I said attack!" Digner shouted again.

Normin put one hand out to stay his new army from attacking his old army. He drew his sword slowly, took a breath, and walked several paces so he was between both armies. For the number of people gathered around that field, the wind was the only noise. Still, Normin yelled with a loud and commanding voice: "I am King Normin Altheia, and I command all of you"—he paused for emphasis and looked at both sides—"to drop your weapons and stand down!"

Normin saw absolute shock ripple along the Altheian side, countered by sheer anger on the faces of Jason and his men. The slaves reacted instantly, no hesitation, without a word. Every man dropped his weapon in the grass.

"Dad?" Normin heard Lucid and a more distant shout that made his heart beat a little faster. He then glanced to the Altheians and noticed all of his people were dropping their weapons as well. He smiled.

"What the fuck are you all doing? I am the king. I command you to attack!" Jason was shouting and shoving his councillors toward the army of slaves, thinking to muscle the former into making the slaves listen to his commands.

Lucid sheathed his sword and began moving toward Normin, slowly at first. As he got closer, their eyes met, and he broke into a run.

It had worked. Normin had achieved what he thought impossible.

Jason was outnumbered and surrounded, and he looked extremely angry. He had lost control of his army. With every soldier on the field at Normin's command and his children running to embrace him, that may very well have been the best moment of his life. He had done it; he had sacrificed much and risked everything to save these people. He almost laughed at the joy of how it all had come together.

Lucid reached him first. The young man almost crushed Normin in a bear hug, followed shortly by Brynn, who was weeping openly and looked ready to throttle him. She shoved Lucid aside to bury her face in her father's chest as she hugged him.

"Where the hell have you been?" she yelled, her words muffled by his chest. He held her then, and just for a moment he forgot about everything he had gone through to get there.

"Questions later. Right now I ..." He stopped short at a glance over their shoulders, his eyes squinting to see in the shadows of the trees.

Shit! he thought. *Jason sent men around the flank!*

But as he watched the figures emerge from the woods on the western edge of town, he saw that they were not men of Jason's. They were not men at all. *Holy shit. I had no idea there were so many,* he thought. As far as his eyes could see in both directions, gvorlocks emerged from the woods, silent as death. They charged instantly upon leaving the tree line. It was everything Normin could do to hold his bladder at the sight of innumerable giant killers running at them with stone spears and axes.

Lucid turned and looked, and then his head snapped back to Normin. He shamefully admitted, "I killed one. The treaty is broken."

Normin's mouth dropped open in shock. He felt betrayed, even hurt, as he asked, "Why?"

Lucid looked his father in the eyes, and with as much conviction as was possible at that moment, he replied, "For love."

Normin was very confused at that. He opened his mouth then closed it again. The king drew his sword and began sprinting back toward the slave army. Brynn seemed to panic and took off running back to the safety of the palace.

Over his shoulder, Normin shouted at Lucid, "Keep the men lined up. Wheel them around. Prepare for battle."

Normin ran as fast as his aging legs could carry him, which was actually faster than he'd ever thought possible. Fear pushed him harder. The army, just a dozen yards away a moment ago, now seemed on the other side of the world. He could see signs of a struggle toward the right side where Jason and his men had been positioned. He did not see the group, but he did see bodies lying bloody on the ground. Several slaves had Jason and the youngest one pinned down.

"Get them up!" Normin shouted when he got within earshot, running right for Jason.

Normin grabbed the kid by the gaps in his chest plate and forced him to turn and look at the emerging gvorlocks. "Do you see that?"

He did see them, and the fight went out of him instantly. Normin could hear piss hitting the ground as the color drained from the boy's face.

"They will kill every last one of us if we do not fight. They do not care what city we are from, and they do not give a shit about your crown or mine. Now is decision time, son. You fight with us"—Normin glanced at the now free men around him, who were all watching, waiting on him to give a command—"or run home like a coward and wait to die in your bed."

Jason actually looked his age at that moment, just a scared child. No doubt he had never seen anything like the gvorlocks. The kid swallowed hard then glanced to the slaves. Seeing their sheer bravery in the face of death and such undying commitment to Normin, Jason wiped away tears and straightened up a little.

Normin released him and nodded, turning to yell at the former slaves. "Form up with the others! Now!"

He began sprinting back, followed closely by his new people. Normin did not see Jason keeping pace, but it mattered little. Either the kid would fight and die or go home and die. As soon as Normin began to move back toward the Altheian side, however, he saw the next line of gvorlocks emerging from the trees. These held long spears straight toward the sky, as if to show the whole world the gruesome sight of severed heads mounted on the points, many still dripping blood.

That can't be good, Normin thought as he sprinted.

As he got closer, however, he saw the faces. His king's men, every one of his fifty, were dead. His heart felt so heavy all of a sudden that he had trouble communicating with his feet and almost tripped.

Maybe Jake was not with them. Surely he was guarding Brynn, he thought hopefully.

As he got closer, he saw his friend's face mounted and was thankful that, at a full run, in the heat of battle, no one would see him weep.

Brynn's relief and utter happiness upon seeing her father alive and well was short-lived. When she caught sight of the gvorlock army, she ran. Terrified of their size and numbers, she could think only about getting back to the safety of the palace walls.

Lya had attempted to follow when Brynn ran for her father but was not fast enough. They met halfway between the palace and the place where the army had massed.

"We need to get inside now!" she told the former slave girl, slowing her stride only slightly to grab Lya's hand and drag her toward the palace.

The two sprinted up the steps and were startled when they reached the huge palace doors, which opened to reveal Vincent, Coy, and a few of the others with wounds that clearly did not stop them from fighting. Vincent walked stiffly. Coy limped heavily, still wearing bandages around his thighs.

"You cannot fight in that condition," Brynn told Coy sternly. She would not let him get himself killed. She had become attached to this shy boy. No, it was more than that: she liked him. Looking at him now with fierce determination in his eyes, Brynn wondered how she had missed the connection before. Something drew her to him, but until that moment, she did not know what that meant.

"I can fight," he said stubbornly.

Brynn smiled and released Lya's hand to take his. He tensed and looked much the same as he had the first time she had seen him, minus the dirt and with the addition of some pounds. She turned him around, and they walked back into the palace together.

The small group of injured men had made their way down the palace steps and were joining the rest of the army, all except one. The lone man's gaze had followed the princess and her little friend inside, and when he turned back to look at Lya, he had a smile painted on his face. Lya, terrified at the invasion and the possibility of losing Lucid, had twisted her face into an expression that was the exact opposite of the man's. His smile died as he spotted the gvorlocks over her shoulder. His mouth dropped open.

"What the fuck is that?" he mumbled to himself.

She looked at his face then and, to her surprise, saw extremely subtle hints of familiarity there, as if she knew this man.

He bowed slightly and ran for the battle before she could say a word. Lya turned then, alone on the palace steps, watching the man she loved take the initial clash.

Screams erupted as the battle began. She glanced back at the palace doors one more time before descending the steps and heading for the battle.

Lucid adjusted his grip, cocked his sword back, chose a gvorlock target, charging directly at him, and began tracking his footfalls. When the gvorlock got close enough, Lucid struck, but so did the huge beast. Lucid achieved the killing blow, driving his sword into the gvorlocks chest, but the creature's momentum carried and Lucid found himself flying backward. It was all he could do to pull his sword out and keep his grip as he slammed into the front of his army.

The adversaries managed not to stab the prince. The men directly behind helped him get his feet planted once more. He glanced about at his people, who were dying savagely to gvorlock spears instantly as they clashed. The size of the gvorlocks and their number made this battle impossible to win. That much had become clear after the first swing of a blade.

We are all going to die because of me. The thought made Lucid so angry with himself that he growled and began cutting down the large green-eyed monsters in a flurry of swings and jabs, meaning to protect as many of his people as possible from the consequences of his actions.

After a series of bodies fell, he spotted his father close by, holding his own against three of them. Lucid had never seen his father *really* fight; no one had. Until recently, they had never needed to. Watching him now, Lucid found it distractingly beautiful and was hard-pressed to look away. It was as if Normin had eyes in the back of his head and four arms. And he was fast, incredibly fast, for a man who had seen over forty years.

Two of the three gvorlocks Normin was fighting fell simultaneously, Lucid had no idea how, and the third thought it best to run off and pick a new, easier target. A few yards away, the retreating gvorlock charged at Bruce Mathis. Lucid could only watch as it impaled the man on its spear at a full run. A man nearby with a patch over one eye shouted and dispatched the gvorlock quickly, going down to kneel next to the old farmer.

"Eyes front, boy!" Lucid heard his father yell at him.

Lucid turned just in time to catch another beast charging at him, spear leveled. He crouched and prepared himself to spring. He waited. At the last second before impact, he ducked the spear and, with his left hand, grabbed at the gvorlock's shoulder as it went by, swinging up to the creature's back. Lucid quickly pierced its skull with a solid downward thrust and rode it as it dropped to its knees and then fell dead. As Lucid rolled with the impact and jumped to his feet, he looked back at the charging enemy, still pouring out of the woods. He scanned around for Jon and was shocked to see him standing at the top of a tall mound of dead gvorlock corpses, whipping his sword around in a frenzy with deadly efficiency. He looked like a demon, covered head to toe in the dark liquid that he spilled with each swing, standing tall over the battlefield.

Heavy footsteps were approaching quickly. Lucid spun to see another gvorlock charging at him. It was close this time, too close, so all he could do was drop to the ground and ball up like a coward. It worked much better than he expected as the thing tripped over his fetal form and toppled like a boulder behind him, where Normin skewered it.

Lucid shot back to his feet to take the next charge, but there was no need. A short arrow shaft struck the next gvorlock in the center of its huge forehead in a burst of gore and it hit the ground face-first, unmoving.

More men were joining the fight every minute, Lucid knew, but was it enough? On the front lines, out of his peripheral vision, he saw fewer and fewer men fighting while more gvorlocks continued to pour out of the woods.

"We can't hold!" he shouted at his father. "There are too many of them."

Normin did not answer. When Lucid looked at the king,

he was standing wide-eyed, staring at Vincent. The assassin was fighting with a style that seemed to be of his own making, using backflips and spins with a level of efficiency that made his father's skill look meek.

"Don?" Normin said. Vincent's head shot around to look at the king. He finished the gvorlock he was battling and approached slowly, almost cautiously.

"Hello, Normin," Vincent said.

Lucid glanced to his left then and saw the front lines had made a hard push, Altheians gaining a little ground, leaving Lucid and Normin near the rear of the fighting. He took a moment to catch his breath. He was confused but kept his mouth shut and simply watched with interest. He looked to his father, who was attempting to speak, but not words came out as he stared at Vincent.

When Normin finally collected himself, his muffled question was all he uttered: "How is this possible?"

Vincent gave a half smile and replied simply, "You look good." Then he added, "I have missed you."

Lucid could take no more, unable to follow what was happening. He asked, "Father, who is this man?" He glanced at Normin and froze. Behind his father, entirely too close for anyone to react, a gvorlock was bent over, sneaking up behind him. Before Lucid could even take a breath to scream, the thing lunged.

Two feet of wooden shaft protruded from the front of Normin's chest. It seemed the world froze and everything around them fell away. The king gasped and looked down at the bloody weapon.

"Oh shit," he said, and collapsed.

"*No!*" Lucid screamed as he went after the gvorlock.

Lucid stepped up and, with all his strength, drove his blade into the creature's neck. He twisted the blade back and forth, opening up a huge hole in the thing's throat. The blood poured out in a wave down its massive chest, and the gurgling sound that followed was sickening. The prince yanked his sword out and knelt by his father. Vincent was already there, holding Normin's hand and speaking to him.

"I am so sorry, Normin. I should have never left. I should have been here. I am sorry I left you to deal with the Crown alone. I am sorry I abandoned our family and our people. I am sorry for everything."

Lucid glanced at the man, still unsure what he was babbling about. The king's breath was hitching; he seemed to be choking on his own blood as he coughed, causing it to spray.

"Oh, no, no, no. *Daryl!*" Lucid shouted. He looked around. Jon's column was doing well, and it seemed the front lines had gained another few feet. He looked left and right and saw that his people were holding strong for now. A moment later the healer appeared at his side, covered in both blood and the dark liquid that coursed through the gvorlocks.

One look at Normin, and Daryl's face changed, his sense of urgency fleeting. He simply put a hand on Lucid's shoulder and looked into his eyes.

"I am sorry, Lucid."

The prince shook his head violently and stood to confront his friend. He yelled, "Help him now! Or so help me God, I will kill you too."

Lucid took an offensive stance, but Daryl only held up his hands.

"You know there is nothing I can do, Lucid. You know this." The healer did not move and did not say anything else. He just stood there with his arms raised and with the most hurt expression painted on his face. Lucid let himself fall next to his father. He cradled his head.

"This … is … my brother," Normin managed to choke out through agonized coughs. "Take care … of … Bry——" Another cough and a spray of blood. "*Hope*," he whispered as his eyes closed slowly. Those were King Normin Altheia's last words. Lucid wailed.

CHAPTER 33

The sounds of battle began getting louder as Lucid wept over his father, still holding his head. It almost felt as if he were just sleeping. Then Normin's last words finally struck him as his own sobbing eased and he looked at Vincent. The man was looking at him through his own tears.

"His brother?" was all he said to the man whom he knew as Vincent.

The man nodded and wiped his face with his palms. "My real name is Don Altheia, but I have not used that name in over thirty years."

"Altheia?" Lucid asked. The man nodded again. Lucid was skeptical, then looked down at his father's face, the face of a man who had never once in his life lied to anyone, not that Lucid knew of anyway. Lucid realized then just how close the clash of weapons and screams of men was. He laid his father's head down carefully and stood.

He wanted vengeance on a scale he'd never imagined possible. He wanted to stand there over his father's body until every last gvorlock was dead at his feet. It would not be possible, although he would make a solid attempt.

Many minutes, possibly hours, went by, he could not say, but eventually the tide of gvorlocks became overwhelming. Even the Altheians' superior fighting skill was no match for the endless enemy numbers.

"We have to get inside the palace! It is our only hope!" someone shouted. Just then a lightning bolt struck Lucid.

Hope! The ship!

It seemed that even though his father lay dead on the ground, he was still saving Lucid's life. Lucid eventually received a break from the endless tide, the gvorlocks thinking it best to pick easier targets, and in the clearing of bodies, he spotted Lya a dozen yards away, looking like an angel.

It was shocking to see her out at all. Her clean dress and light hair stood out strongly against all the blood and mud. She waded through the carnage unafraid and knelt next to Lucid's father.

With tear-filled eyes, she looked up at him and asked, "Is this him?"

Lucid's face twisted; he could not hold back the tears as he nodded. She kissed Normin lightly on the forehead then rose and embraced Lucid. He held her tightly and inhaled her scent. She was just about all he had left, and he never wanted to let her go. He raised his eyes and shouted.

Four gvorlocks had snuck away from the main battle and were breaking into the palace.

Brynn led Coy to the top floor, to her father's room. With its being the highest level, she felt they would be safest there. He said nothing as she helped him limp along, but she could sense his unease at being forced inside while people fought for him.

As the pair walked by the council chamber, Brynn noticed that some of the councillors were there, seeking the same safety of rock walls as she. She stopped and went inside, thinking safety in numbers might be better than just her and Coy alone. Old Master Wendell, Reggie, and Mr. Redkey were sitting at the large table, unable to hide their fear. These men were not fighters.

"What are those things?" Reggie asked of Brynn as soon as she and Coy entered.

Brynn released Coy's hand and gestured for him to sit in the chair next to the one she had chosen. "They are called gvorlocks, and apparently we had a peace treaty with them that has been compromised."

She sat and glanced at Coy, who looked uncomfortable.

"Why were we not made aware of all this? These are things the high council should be privy to," said Master Wendell.

"That is a question you must ask Father when you see him next," she replied.

Mr. Redkey asked hopefully, "You saw him? He has returned?"

Brynn smiled and nodded. "I saw him just before that fighting started. He is fine and fighting for us as we speak."

The men around her visibly relaxed, until they heard the crash against the palace doors. Sounds of battle had become much too loud for Brynn's liking, and now it seemed the gvorlocks had made it up the palace steps and were trying to break in. The room was silent as death. She felt as if this were a nightmarish game of hide-and-seek, only instead of simply being *it*, they would be dead.

Despite the fear written all over their faces, Reggie stood, followed by Master Wendell and Ryan. They drew their weapons and approached the door, which they closed, standing guard. Brynn's amazement at their bravery was shattered almost instantly as the doors burst open, taking old Master Wendell out of the fight before it even began.

The huge door had swung inward and knocked him back against the wall with a horrifying thud. He did not rise again.

Four of the beasts charged in. The fear was so intense that Brynn felt light-headed, as if she might pass out. Through hazy eyes, she watched in shock as Reginald and Ryan fought hard to protect their princess. It was an amazing sight, especially considering their advanced age. One gvorlock fell, then another, then a third. Just as Brynn was beginning to think her side might win, Reggie took a spear in the chest and fell. Ryan lasted a little longer, but the result was the same.

Brynn screamed as she watched them die. The men fought well, but inevitably they died, having been outmatched. She stood with her back against the far wall, Coy next to her in a similar position. The last of the beasts approached, like a jaguar stalking its prey. He took its time, smiling and whipping its spear around. Clearly it was enjoying this.

A growl erupted from the young boy next to Brynn. She glanced to Coy and watched as he drew a large dagger and stepped in front of her. She tried to stop him—she wanted to, but her body would no longer respond to her thoughts. Helpless, she stared as the gvorlock laughed and approached the former slave.

The beast took a quick jab with its spear toward Coy's chest. To Brynn's surprise, the boy knocked away the blow with his dagger easily. The gvorlock spread its stance and made a more solid attempt, leaning into the jab and extending its tree-trunk arms. Coy spun like a dancer around the blow and punched down with his dagger through the beast's extended arm. It wailed. All of the playfulness left the fight at that moment.

A flurry of swings and spins followed, Brynn barely able to follow the wooden spear attacking. Coy held his own, but seeing as he was injured, small, and outmatched by ten men in strength, the result only seemed to hinder the gvorlock slightly.

The creature growled in frustration, grabbed Coy with one hand, and threw him across the room like a scrap chicken bone. He screamed as he flew, and when he hit the ground, he struggled to rise. The gvorlock approached Brynn slowly, spear cocked and ready. Shaking with fear, she closed her eyes.

This is how I die. At least I will see Mother again.

She cringed, waiting for the pain. She heard a disgusting sound, and the creature wailed, a huge, deep boom that echoed and caused Brynn's eyes to shoot open. What she saw could not have been more shocking than if it had been her mother standing there. She watched as the gvorlock fell face-first into the stone floor of the council chamber. Attached to its back, stabbing forcefully over and over, was the boy she had rescued.

Brynn had brought Coy back from the dead that day when they met, and looking at him now, drenched in gvorlock blood and with a fierce look on his face, she could see that this was not the same boy. Then she sank to her knees and cried.

No, no, no, no. Not Brynn too, was all Lucid could think as he sprinted up the palace steps and into the main foyer just few dozen paces behind the gvorlocks.

He could not fault Lya for failing to protect her; things were happening so fast and were so chaotic that it was difficult to be upset about anything. Fear for his sister pushed him harder as he flew through the halls and up the stairs to the top floor.

The doors to the council chamber were flung wide, and it was quiet, too quiet. As he got closer, his footsteps slowed. He could hear his sister weeping.

When he rounded the corner, what he saw was something he could not quite comprehend. Bodies, both gvorlock and human, littered the room, and among the carnage and blood, against the back wall of the chamber, sat his sister and the young slave boy she had rescued. They held each other as he spoke comforting words to her. Still clutched in his small hand was a long dagger drenched in gvorlock blood.

"Are you all right?" he asked the pair as he approached. They looked up, and both nodded slowly. After taking in the room, Lucid finally pieced together exactly what had just happened. He knelt in front of Coy, grabbed him by the shoulders, said, "Thank you," and hugged him.

Lucid pulled away and looked over his sister. "Are you sure you are okay?" he asked, looking into her eyes. She gave him a forced smile and a nod. "Good. Then we need to get the fuck out of here."

He helped her to her feet, and as he did so, she asked, "Where is Father?" the question posed in passing, almost nonchalantly. But Lucid felt as if she already knew. His lip quivered as he looked into her eyes, taking a shaking breath. That was all the answer her simultaneously tiny and huge mind needed in answer. She shrieked.

CHAPTER 34

Lucid, Brynn, and Coy exited the palace to a world unknown to them. The battle still raged heavily all around them. The gvorlocks had begun to take a heavy toll and seemed to be winning. Bodies of Lucid's beloved citizens littered the ground, bloody and broken, in all directions. It took everything the prince had inside to ignore it and move on.

Lucid spotted a line of survivors including Jon, Vincent, Daryl, Alisha, and other faces he was glad to see still alive. They fought at the edge the clearing. It was not going well.

Despite this, flames danced in the air all around the group. It took Lucid a moment to realize the flames were projectiles flying toward the crowd of gvorlocks at terrifying speed. When they landed, flames exploded across the large beasts in an uproar of burning flesh and screams. Lucid looked to where they were coming from and spotted Jason and little Bryan Inder working to load and fire a small sling of some kind.

Did he mean to use that against us? Lucid thought, but he shook it off quickly as there was just too much happening to be upset.

I will not let those gvorlocks kill all of my people, he thought. Lya had followed him quietly into the palace and stayed by his side as they exited. She saw the despair that surrounded them. He turned and took both her hands in his, looking into her eyes.

"I would never ask you to do something that you are not comfortable with, but now is not the time to be scared or modest." She looked confused at first.

"I need you to buy our people some time to escape."

He waited, watching her face change.

She glanced at the huge number of gvorlocks and replied, "I don't know what you want me to do. I don't know what I *can* do."

He smiled and reached up to brush a lock of golden hair away from her face. He had no idea what she was or why she was capable of such things, but looking at her at that very moment, sunset illuminating her beautiful face, he did not care. Only two things were important to him: one, he loved her deeply regardless of what she was, and two, he absolutely knew she could be the savior they needed at this moment. It was an odd feeling having such strong faith in someone after such a short time. "You can do this," he told her confidently. "I believe in you."

This time, it was she who kissed him deeply. Lucid noticed when they parted that her face changed from something like uncertainty to hard determination. She nodded, closed her eyes, and held her breath.

Lucid ran toward the cluster of men, trusting in his love to do what was needed.

"Fall back!" he yelled when he got within earshot. "Get to the ship! Everyone run for the west cliffs now."

He reached the fighting lines. Jason set down his sling and approached slowly with his hands raised. It was confusing to Lucid—until Jason spoke.

"It is not there. The ship, I mean. It is in Drondos, along with your captain."

It took Lucid a moment to process what Jason had done.

He punched the little brat, connecting solidly with Jason's jaw. The kid went down like a felled tree.

"You son of a bitch!" Lucid screamed at him while Jason clutched his face, spitting blood. "You mark my fucking words, you little prick. If Inder is dead, I will kill you myself." It was then that the ground began to shake.

Lya watched as Lucid ran to the crowd of fighting survivors. No, not watched, as her eyes were closed. She felt him. So prominent in her mind was he and so strong was her love for him, as her power crept in, that Lya thought she might be able to feel him this way from miles away.

She would do anything for him, and that very much extended to his people, the people who had taken her in without even a question or argument. She received odd looks at times, but for the most part these people had embraced her so wholeheartedly that she yearned to save them—what was left of them.

As her anger rose, the power was building to something she was unsure she could handle. It felt as if her head was going to explode. When she took a small breath, the world spun, and she hit the ground on her knees.

There it is! she thought, realization dawning on her: the earth.

Why she had not attempted to reach for that power before was unclear until that moment. It was too vast, too powerful for her. It was like attempting to palm a boulder the size of the statue of Jerald. It just was not possible. She had to try though. Everything was at stake: her love, her new life, her new people.

Lya let herself go, lost in the power and pain of it all, and grabbed at it. As soon as she did this, the ground began shaking. As if the earth itself were itching to avenge the dead scattered around her, it responded. Just as she had once imagined the chasm between a slave girl and a prince, she imagined another larger and more real chasm between the lines of gvorlocks and the retreating humans. The ground shook more and more violently, and before her closed eyes, a crack formed. Screaming with agony, she pried it open. Then, nothing.

Lucid stared in disbelief as the ground opened up between him and the gvorlocks.

"Everyone head for Drondos!" he yelled, but the sounds of rock on rock drowned out his words. The earthquake made moving at any pace very difficult. Lucid struggled to keep his feet under him.

Screams erupted from enemies falling to their deaths into the maw of the crevice that began to open. It seemed the very ground itself was trying to eat them.

Instantly, every gvorlock eye snapped to Lya.

They know! Lucid thought. He shot around to look for her.

When he saw her lying on the ground unconscious, his heart dropped, and he screamed to the survivors, "Get to the ship now!" in a tone that sent them all running without argument.

He sprinted along the crack she had made for them, ground still shaking, with gvorlocks staring as he ran. When he approached, he noticed her chest rising and falling. *Thank God,* he thought, gathering her up carefully. For the second time with Lya unconscious in his arms, he ran. Only this time he had no clue where he was running to.

Brynn fell to her knees as the ground shook and opened up. Coy was there to carefully pull her to her feet. After that they held onto each other for balance, staring open-mouthed. When the world leveled off, Brynn barely heard Lucid scream something violently as he ran back toward Lya. It was Jon who responded:

"Jason! Lead the way. Everyone follow him. We march to Drondos."

And the long trek to their sister city began once again.

Jason led them away from the war zone and out of sight of the gvorlocks before turning north toward his city. They were a poor lot, all limping and breathing heavily. Blood streamed from unchecked wounds, and the sound of moaning and grunting in exertion was all that reached Brynn's ears.

They followed Jason, Brynn feeling numb both physically and mentally. The very ground shaking and splitting apart, all the bodies and blood, all the death—it was difficult for her to grasp that all this was real. She felt like a ghost just floating along.

Am I dead? she thought.

The princess was amazed at the pace they set, Lucid pushing Jason hard with Lya slung over his shoulder. The run was brutal on Brynn. She found it hard to even keep on her feet. She fell multiple times, but Coy was always there to pull her to her feet and get her moving again. She glanced around and noticed an uncomfortably small number of citizens running with them. Still, it all went by in a haze of exhaustion and grief. Next thing she knew, they entered the main gate and were walking the streets of Drondos. After walking through the empty streets, they arrived at the edge of town, where two men entered the royal manse to retrieve Captain Inder, who apparently had been kidnapped.

When the man, or what was left of him, exited, a fight erupted. The Inder twins were screaming. Jon, a picture of barely contained rage, was holding them back, and Jason was on the ground, holding his nose with a hand that quickly filled up with blood.

Brynn barely noticed. It was all just too much. She felt like the world was slipping away from her. Her parents were dead, along with most of her people. Her home was broken and abandoned. She was unsure if she had the strength to continue.

"Are you okay, Princess?" she heard. She looked over.

Coy was there, looking at her with much concern, but she could muster no half smile or courageous words. She looked away without a reply, dazed.

Daryl was tending to Captain Inder but did not look satisfied after patching him up. Jason was lifted to his feet and shoved forward.

"Lead us to the boat," Lucid said angrily, Lya now cradled in his shaky arms like a child.

The group shuffled toward the west side of town then down a winding trail that hugged the cliffs. They exited through a small gate and went down to the beach where the ship floated. Once the group crossed the little bridge and walked onto the boat, Derek and Jon lifted the gangway while little Bryan Inder took a post at the helm at the top of the aft castle.

No one argued.

"Raise the sail," his small, unsure voice shouted. Everyone just stared or shifted their footing uncomfortably. No one knew what to do. Miraculously, Brynn noticed Billy Aimes approach some of the ropes and begin working, followed hesitantly by some of the others. Once the sail was raised, the wind caught it and the ship lurched forward.

As the princess of Altheia stood at the back of the ship and watched the shoreline of her family's lifelong home of generations recede, she wept.

Once on board, Lucid had Lya in a cabin sleeping comfortably. He was finally able to take stock of everyone who had survived and who had not. Lucid did not have the head for numbers as his sister did, but he estimated around four thousand Altheians had lost their lives. Sixty-seven people out of thousands remained, and the boys were broken to find that Russell was not one of them.

Lucid, Jon, and Daryl mourned their friend with heavy hearts, along with Reginald and the council, Rusty, Normin, and so many others. A lot of people had died because of Lucid's decision to take Lya, he did not fail to notice. He was so lost in grief and guilt that he avoided most everyone and spoke to no one for weeks as the ship rocked endlessly through a sea of blue. It had been fully stocked with provisions, but according to a starving city, "fully stocked" was not as abundant as one may think.

More time went by without a word to anyone, not even Lya. Lucid could see the emotional toll that this alone was taking on her, but deeply drowning in despair himself, he had nothing to say to her.

Then, about two months into their journey, the food ran out. Still they sailed through the nothingness of the ocean. One day, about a week after running out of food, Mr. Baker jumped over the edge, preferring drowning to starvation.

Despite all of this, Lya's belly did not shrink. When she told Lucid that she was carrying his child, he wept. Not because he was happy—under normal circumstances he would have been ecstatic seeing his child in her growing belly. But there was no hope, there was no food to help the child grow strong, and they were trapped on a piece of floating wood. He was not even close to being a father yet, and already he was failing the life within her.

If we were not dying, she would be showing by now, he thought as he watched her blankly stare out at the ocean one afternoon. Stuck in the middle of absolute nothingness, unable to feed his love and his child, he could take it no longer and considered following Mr. Baker.

That night, Lucid walked to the bow of the rocking ship and looked out at the blackness of the dark ocean. *How easy it would be to disappear into that blackness, to become it.* Then he dropped to his knees and looked up to the stars.

"Dear God, I have never attempted to speak with you so intimately before. I did my duty by going to cathedral like everyone else and saying the words, but we both know there was never any sincerity behind them. This feels so selfish because everything that has happened is my fault. But if you are listening, if you are up there, I need you now as I never have before. I am Lucid Altheia. Hear me now, Father of the world. Please save us. Not for me—I would trade my life for theirs if needed. For my people, the people who have followed mine for generations, for Lya, for my unborn son. Please, God ... save us."

Just then, there was a shout from the crow's nest. With that one word, and the timing behind it, Lucid's entire way of looking at the world changed.

"Land!"

Printed in the United States
By Bookmasters